MERCENARIES

JACK LUDLOW

Allison & Busby Limited
13 Charlotte Mews
London W1T 4EJ
www.allisonandbusby.com

Hardcover published in Great Britain in 2009.
This paperback edition published in 2009.

A CIP catalogue record for this book is available from
the British Library.

10 9 8 7 6 5 4 3 2

ISBN 978-0-7490-0785-0

Typeset in 11/17 pt Century Schoolbook by
Allison & Busby Ltd.

The paper used for this Allison & Busby publication
has been produced from trees that have been legally sourced
from well-managed and credibly certified forests.

PEFC
PEFC16-33-111
CATG-PEFC-052
www.pefc.org

Printed and bound in the UK by
CPI Bookmarque, Croydon, CR0 4TD

JACK LUDLOW is the pen name of writer David Donachie, who was born in Edinburgh in 1944. He has had a variety of jobs, selling everything from business machines to soap. He has always had an abiding interest in the naval history of the eighteenth and nineteenth centuries, which he drew on for the many novels he has set in that period. Rome, in the days of the Republic, is another area of special interest. The author of a number of best-selling books, he now lives in Deal with his partner, the author Sarah Grazebrook.

Available from
ALLISON & BUSBY

In the Conquest series

In the Republic series

In the John Pearce series

To Donald Grazebrook

Not least for being the only person, when I mentioned the subject of this book, who knew what I was talking about.

Italy in the 11th Century

PROLOGUE

For the funeral rites of a man once so powerful, this interment was a muted affair. The monks of the monastery chanted their plainsong while the Archbishop of Salerno read the service in a tone close to a whisper. The mourners were few, the two most important being the dead man's son and daughter. In the belfry, where no bell could be tolled for fear of disclosure, a servant, mallet in hand, stood guard to watch the road to the city, hidden behind the hills to the north.

His task was to warn of the approach of danger, given this was no ordinary service, but one fraught with risk both for those attending and those performing the rites. The horses on which the archbishop and his retinue had arrived were out of sight at the rear of the buildings and to a passing eye nothing unusual was taking place in the abbey church.

Guaimar, once the powerful Lombard, Duke of Salerno, was being buried in the Latin rite with the simplicity which had come to be the measure of his reign, and those who knew him well in life were aware that in part he had died of a fractured heart, deposed from his lands and titles by an act of the most diabolical treachery. The monks with whom he had shared his final years were burying a brother – no greater nor lesser a man in the sight of God than they themselves. To the archbishop the service was that which he owed to a one-time generous benefactor, who had given much to the diocese and protected church property from despoliation by such endemic raiders of the shores of Italy as the Saracens of North Africa and Sicily.

The young man bearing the same name, Guaimar – just turned sixteen – and his sister, Berengara, two years his junior, were performing a duty they owed to a loving and revered parent, a man of reasonable disposition in a world that had required steely resolve. Raised in the ducal palace, the towering fortress of the Castello de Arechi, they too had found themselves torn from all that had been present in their lives. Yet if they had lost a home and a way of life, their father had lost a fiefdom his family had held, not without difficulty, but continuously, for three hundred years. Now he was to be laid to rest, not with his ancestors in the family vault, but close to that of his eldest daughter, whom he had loved greatly while she lived.

The single soft hammer blow on a resonant bell was enough of an alert: there were horsemen on the road, armed and coming at speed. The sound made the bishop turn as white as the plain surplice he wore; to avoid raising suspicions he had left his mitre and his glittering episcopal garments in the vestry of Salerno Cathedral. Suddenly he was gabbling the service, for he wished to be away from this place. Pandulf, Prince of Capua, called the Wolf of the Abruzzi, who had usurped the dukedom from the man he was burying, professed to be a Christian, but he was a man who never feared the wrath of God when it came to laying hands on his vicars on Earth. The Archbishop of Capua languished in Pandulf's own dungeons and his counterpart of Salerno had no desire to share his fate.

'Normans.'

That one word was enough to send the bishop and his attendants scurrying away to find their hidden mounts. In the belfry the sentinel watched the approach of the horsemen, mailed knights bearing lances from which fluttered the red and black colours of their leader, Rainulf Drengot, the man who had broken the heart of the deceased. Once the duke's son-in-law and his military support, Rainulf had married his late daughter, gaining as her dowry the valuable Lordship of Aversa. Upon her death, and purely out of naked greed, he had transferred his allegiance from Salerno to Capua, and it was a measure of how powerful this Norman mercenary had become in Campania that one such act of treachery had been enough to alter completely the balance of forces in the region.

'Now we'll see who truly believes in an afterlife,' said young Guaimar, his eyes fixed on the departing archbishop. That cleric was not alone: the elderly abbot, too, saw good reason to absent himself and so did some of his monks. Yet there were others whose belief in Christ, or their love of their late brother, was proof against fear and one monk stepped forward to finish the liturgy as the body was lowered, while others stood by to slide the covering stone over the grave which had been dug, as a mark of respect, before the altar of the church.

That flat block of marble, already with the name and titles of the deceased carved upon it, was pushed into place as the banging commenced on the church door: the hilt, no doubt, of a Norman sword. The dead man's son, as chief mourner, pressed into the hands of one monk a contribution to the funds of the establishment, a small purse of gold, for he was no longer wealthy; none of what their father had once owned – land, castles, coffers full of coins from the dues of the trading port, jewels and family heirlooms – would come to him. They were now the property of the Wolf.

'Let them enter,' Guaimar said.

'Your safety, my Lord, and that of your sister.'

'Do they make war on children?'

'The Normans, my Lord, make war as they please.'

'Yet they are Christians. I cannot believe they would despoil the sanctity of the church.'

The look on the face of the monk was one of doubt; in his cloistered life he had never met one of these devils from the far north, now banging furiously on the great double doors, but what he had heard left him in no doubt that they were as bloody and profane as the Saracens who had, many times, defiled this very building. Guaimar indicated with a nod that the monk should proceed, then he took station behind the grave of his father, Berengara holding his hand.

'Do not worry, sister. If Prince Pandulf had wanted us dead, we would have been in the grave before our father.'

Looking at her with a forced, confident smile, hoping he had the right of it, he took in the pale, long face, the dark almond eyes in flawless skin and a figure, though yet to be fully formed, which promised much. She was set to be a beauty, and for that she might have more to fear from these barbarian Normans than she did from her bloodline.

They came in with arrogant purpose, half a dozen big men in hauberks and conical helmets, while outside, through the now open doors, Guaimar could see a whole troop of mounted support, couched lances proud. The leader of the band, taller than Guaimar, had his sword unsheathed, a heavy weapon that the more willowy youngster thought he himself might struggle to wield. His boots, studded with metal, sent up sparks from the flagstones as he approached.

Guaimar knew this man just by his build and his walk; he had been at one time captain of the men who served closely his father, his personal guards, always present at his side. There was little to see of the face, no hope of reading the expression, though below the nose guard and the eyes at either side the lips were turned down in disapproval. He marched up to the opposite side of the gravestone and looked down, then used the tip of his weapon to trace the Latin inscription on the tomb. The snort he emitted had in it a fair measure of derision.

'He was too soft, this man.'

'He was too good, Osmond,' replied Guaimar, 'too trusting. He did not know that loyalty was, in you people, only the higher price any prince was prepared to pay.'

'Did your father not once pay Rainulf to turn against Pandulf?'

'He did, but he did not just pay him in money. He believed that he had formed a bond of family, only to see that crumble when my sister died. How does your treacherous Lord, Rainulf, like his new bride? If she is anything like her uncle, Pandulf, I would scarce feel safe to sleep at night.'

The tip of Osmond de Vertin's sword was suddenly pointed at Guaimar but, young as he was, he did not flinch, and his eyes held those of the Norman mercenary. Unable to stare the boy down, that tip moved to point at Berengara, and her brother squeezed hard on her hand to make sure she did not react. It came forward, as if to touch her chin and lift it. Guaimar, with his free hand, pushed it away, gently to be sure, but firmly.

'You have grown, young lady,' said the Norman. 'I used to bear you on my shoulders.'

'I have grown to hate,' she replied, in a firm voice.

'This milksop you have just interred has sired perhaps a brood made of sterner material than he.'

'We will not bow to you, Osmond.'

'No.'

The great broadsword was suddenly above Osmond de Vertin's head, and Guaimar wondered if, even in a place of such inviolability, he was going to die for his defiance. The only act he could think of was to pull his sister to stand behind him. But the Norman was not even looking at him. The sword swept down on the slab covering their father, to slice at the words inscribed there, words that named his line and inherited titles. They may have been taken away from him in life; they should surely be his in death.

The one-time captain of the ducal guard reversed the sword for greater effect, holding it in two hands and stabbing downwards. Chips of marble began to fly from the slab, as Osmond de Vertin hacked away, breaking up the newly engraved inscription, turning it into meaningless gibberish. All the titles the family had ever held were there, like a roll call of the duplicitous cauldron that was South Italian politics.

Principalities, duchies and counties won and lost, but never surrendered, for no claim to a fief once held by these Lombard magnates had ever been relinquished: Prince of Benevento, Duke of Salerno, Amalfi and Sorrento, Count of Puglia, Calabria and even, at one time, long ago, of Capua itself, all were destroyed by a man who lacked the knowledge to read them. After dozens of strokes, the sounds of which were amplified by the bare stone walls of the church into something more baleful than the act, a heavily breathing Osmond stopped and looked at Guaimar once more. Behind her brother, Berengara was weeping.

'There. He is no more, not in life, nor in posterity.' Guaimar said nothing; he merely laid his hand on his heart, itself an eloquent enough message, which Osmond understood. 'I should let that sentiment rest, boy, or you may find yourself with a slab of marble over your own head.'

'I do not fear to die.'

'I will remember that, should I ever receive orders to kill you.'

Osmond de Vertin was unaware of how those words impacted on the youngster, for his brave face had concealed one thing: he doubted the Norman would commit sacrilege by killing him here in the church, but that did not mean his life was not to be forfeit once he stepped outside. Osmond had just told him he would survive this visitation, and if he could do that he could begin to work towards the day when all the lands and property of his family would be restored and these barbarian Normans could either be evicted from Italy, or brought under some kind of control.

Fifteen years had passed since the first Normans had arrived in Salerno, a band of warriors returning from a pilgrimage seventeen years into the new millennium who, merely because they were present and possessed of both swords and bottomless courage, had taken up arms to repel a Saracen raid on the city, an enterprise so successful that it had seemed natural to beg them to remain.

That they had not done, but they had gone north and spread the word, in a land awash with fighting men of their kind, who had, if you excluded internal squabbling, too little warfare to occupy them. South they came as mercenaries, welcome for their military prowess, eager to aid the Lombards in throwing off the yoke of Byzantium, a dream as yet unrealised. But their presence had turned into a curse, then grew into a plague, until no Lombard lord south of the Papal

States could hope to safely hold his fief against his neighbours without their paid help.

Osmond de Vertin, typical of the breed, spun on his heel and departed the abbey church with the same air of arrogance as he had when he entered, leaving behind a youth and a young girl to wonder not only if they would ever come into their inheritance, but if they would ever see the back of these damned Normans.

CHAPTER ONE

The Norman/French Border 1033

William de Hauteville could smell their destination a long time before it came into view, though he was at a loss to fully explain it. He pushed himself up on his stirrups to better test the air, away from the odour of his own sweating mount. The familiar stink of dung and horse piss was there, that mingled with woodsmoke and the strong odour of roasting meat, yet paramount was a powerful latrine smell that was damned unpleasant.

'That, boy,' growled his father, when he called ahead to ask for explanation, 'is the smell of an army too long in one place.'

Tancred de Hauteville had taken part in many a campaign in his forty years, so it was, to him, familiar

– the stench of too many fighting men and their animals in too confined a space. It would be strange to all his sons and the companions of like age who rode with them – they had never seen or been part of a host of the size gathering in the Norman borderlands of the Vexin, a ducal army gathered in one place, preparing for battle. Suddenly Tancred pulled up his mount, hauling the head round to face those following.

'Remember what I have said,' he barked. 'Behave yourselves.'

Forced to halt their own horses, the half of the party not of his blood nodded attentively, for he was their lord and master. His sons, a half-dozen in number, regardless of age, adopted the blank expression of those hearing a familiar parental admonishment, delivered too often.

'None of your pranks and japes,' their father continued; he knew his sons to be much given to mischief. 'You will be among grown men, fighting men, quick to the knife and careful of their honour, who will not take kindly to your stupid jests. Do you heed what I say?' The last words being shouted demanded an eager response, albeit a false one in the family members. 'William, I look to you in this.'

'Yes, Father,' William replied, with the weary sigh of an elder brother often employed as a surrogate parent.

'Now hold your heads up high,' Tancred concluded,

as he turned his horse again and kicked it into a trot. 'Let them know you are of the house of de Hauteville.'

That did produce a common response, for if these young men were proud of anything, it was their bloodline.

Having passed the picket set to ensure the encampment was not pilfered, the band stopped at the top of the rise overlooking the assembled force. The River Seine, a supply lifeline their duke would hug as long as possible, ran twisted and silver along the floor of the valley to where it was joined by the tributary of the Epte, hard by the hamlet of Giverny; here the land of the Normans bordered that of the Capetian Franks.

The north bank was now bare of the trees that had been cut down for firewood, which also allowed clear passage for the hundreds of horses to be brought, in turns, to drink their fill. Boats, some empty, others still laden with wheat, meat, hay and oats, were drawn up on another stretch of cleared riverbank with labouring serfs toiling to unload them. On the mound that overlooked the encampment stood the large double pavilion of their liege lord, the commander of this force, Robert, Duke of Normandy, armorial pennants fluttering from each corner, knights of his familia, in full mail and helmets, in plain view standing guard at the entrance where hung the tasselled gonfalon denoting the ducal title.

'Christ in heaven!' cried William as he took in the size of what lay before them.

Tancred looked askance at that exclamation, which bordered on blasphemy, not something of which he was tolerant. His children transgressed in that area often – as they did in many other ways – and just as often he was obliged to box their ears. Yet he let it pass this once; had he not himself felt much the same when he first became part of such a multitude and very much around the same age serving the present duke's father? Then he had fought against the Capetian Franks, the very people to whom the Norman host was about to be allied.

In a blink, Tancred was back in his own youth, stirrup to stirrup with his own father, his uncle of Montbray on his other side, part of a line of Norman cavalry, ahead of them a Frankish host, their shields and fighting metal glinting in a low dawn sun. He could recall clearly the mixture of thrill and fear, the need to avoid the kind of fidget that would alert his elders to his anxieties, the snorts and tossing heads of the horses, the pennants on the lances of those leading the attack fluttering in a zephyr of a breeze.

The shouted command came eventually to have the horses move forward, slowly, holding their line, the point at which the command came to break into a trot that signified the commitment to the attack, followed by the sense of the world narrowing down to that which lay right before you and immediately to left and right, his father raising his lance for jabbing or throwing and he doing likewise, the line of shields which looked like an unbreakable wall coming closer and closer. But break it did, faced with the charging horses of the finest mounted warriors in the known world.

'I have never seen such a sight, Father!'

Those words brought Tancred back to the present, and to the knowledge that, with God's Good Grace, his sons would ride with him in a like contest and win their spurs, as would his vassals, who included his fiery Montbray nephew, a doughty and eager fighter, even if the lad was an ordained priest.

'None of you have, but perhaps if chance favours you, you will see it often.'

Serlo and Robert, mere boys, along as squires to their elder siblings, had kicked their donkeys to get alongside him, eager for explanation. Their brothers shared the curiosity, but affected an air of indifference, which they thought befitted their greater age, causing their father to smile at their posturing, given they were just either side of eighteen. With pointed finger, and in a voice that was inclusive to all, he identified the ducal pavilion, as well as the lesser posts of the Constable and the Master Marshall, set slightly lower on the slope.

From there to near the riverbank stood the various

contingents who had set out their fire pits and cloak-covered bedding around the small round tents of the lords to whom they were vassals. Close to the water's edge and in the shade of some still-standing oaks, the blacksmith had set up a temporary forge, fire aglow, his hammer already employed. Likewise the armourer was at work with his vice and stone wheel, sparks flying as swords were sharpened, pommels roped with twine and hand guards bent in sword practice made square. Next to him the saddler toiled on the stout, newly constructed, rough wood bench, on which he would carry out repairs to harness and saddles.

'The de Montfort pennant, Father,' exclaimed Drogo, son number two, pointing to a far-off flag close to the river.

'I see it, boy, but I think as cousins and relations to our Lord Duke we can present ourselves there first.'

'Which will not please the Sire de Montfort,' Drogo responded, with the kind of smirk that indicated the certainty that the response would be angry; he was not disappointed.

'No, it will not,' Tancred snapped, adding a touch of hypocrisy in the blasphemy line, 'but he can go to the Devil.'

Unseen by his father, Drogo exchanged an amused glance with William who, too close to the parental temper, could not respond. Count Evro de Montfort, richer by far in both land and goods, and their nearest powerful neighbour, claimed that the de Hautevilles were vassals to him. Tancred was adamant that he held his demesne and title direct from the duke; mention of the de Montfort claim was one sure way for his sons to rile him, though not the only one, given he had a touchy nature.

Spurring his mount, Tancred led his party along the ridge, turning inwards when they were abreast of the ducal pavilion to ride between squatting groups of the duke's own knights, few of whom spared them a glance. He dismounted by the large open flap at the front, followed by his sons. The other six lances did likewise, but they knew their duty: they would stay with the animals until their master had completed his business.

'Tancred, Lord of Hauteville, with his sons, to see his cousin, Duke Robert.'

One of the familia knights standing guard turned a head to look at him, eyes at either side of his nose guard showing no sign of welcome. The man before him had shouted that request, clearly desiring to be heard inside the canvas, in the forepart of the double pavilion, where the scribes laboured and the servants toiled. One of them would certainly scurry through to the duke's quarters to tell him who sought audience, and if this grizzled fellow was a relative it was unlikely he could be denied.

Habit dictates that no fighting man can be in

proximity to another without assessment. Before Tancred stood a fellow of a height not much less than his own, in mailed hauberk and a helmet bearing the colours of his duke, hands resting on the long sword centred before him, the point in the ground. As a familia knight he was part of the personal contingent of warriors who would fight alongside their Lord and, if necessary, die to protect him. From what could be seen of his face it was lean and hard, his body too, as befitted his station and duty.

The summing up of the supplicant Lord of Hauteville started with the grey hair, tinged at the tip with a residue of the golden colour it had once been. The ruddy, weather-beaten face, much lined, showed numerous scars that looked as though they might come from hard warfare, wounds to cheek as well as one dent to skin and bone that had been inflicted under the line where a helmet would be worn. The blue eyes were as hard as the jaw was firm, and as if to add to the feeling of hazard that emanated from this old man, two of those sons who stood immediately behind him helped form a trinity of impressive size and girth, for both exceeded him in height.

The hurrying figure that emerged from the gloom of the tent had the hunched body, tonsured head and ink-stained fingers of a monkish scribe, and his voice, when he spoke, was silky enough to match his appearance. 'His Grace, the noble Duke Robert, will receive you.'

'Good.' Tancred turned to his two eldest sons and said softly, 'He knows I would wait till Doomsday if he refused.'

'But he bids your sons wait outside,' the monk added.

'Nonsense,' Tancred snarled, 'they are his blood relations.'

As Tancred moved forward, indicating that his offspring should follow, there was a visible twitch in the shoulders of the guard, as if he was about to intervene, but the older man had already passed by and, faced with William and Drogo de Hauteville, that gave him pause. The two that followed were younger but well on the way to sharing the looks as well as the imposing build: even the boys that brought up the rear, hands firmly grasping the knives at their waist to go with an arrogant stare, had a lot of height for what looked like tender years. Their father led the way past the open mouth of the silently protesting monk and made straight for the inner sanctum that lay through a second open flap.

The voice, strong and irritated, spoke before the eyes of any of those just entered had adjusted enough to identify this liege lord or any of the numerous folk attending upon him, all stood in silhouette against the strong sunlight shining through the rolled-up rear canvas of the pavilion.

'I said your sons were to stay outside.'

'You would not slight your nephews, cousin?'

Tall enough to look over his father's head, as his eyes adjusted, William saw the speaker was a man of decent height, though less than his own, fair of hair and beard, and richly clad in bright mail covered by a fine red surcoat bearing the ducal device of his two golden and recumbent lions.

Those attending him varied from a hunchbacked fellow who looked like a jester, a clutch of richly clad knights in fine garb, to a stout man in the clothing of a high-ranking prelate. But they all shared one thing, a look of plain distaste at this intrusion by a bunch of sweat-stained, leather jerkin-wearing ruffians. To each and every one, as he took up station alongside his father, William gave an engaging smile.

'Cousin?' the duke replied, in a piqued voice, looking Tancred up and down, taking in that he alone was wearing mail and a surcoat, albeit a threadbare overgarment that had seen many better days. 'Do you not find that to be an outmoded form of address with which to approach your liege lord?'

'We share a great ancestor in Count Rollo, sire, do we not?'

'Of such long standing that it is no longer appropriate. The consanguinity has lapsed, Tancred. Count Rollo has been dead near a hundred years.'

'But he is well remembered in my humble demesne, as are his deeds. I tell my sons of them often. However, if it displeases you I shall be content to address you as brother-in-law.'

'To a half-sister fourteen years deceased?'

The tone of Tancred's voice, which had been playful, hardened immediately, and William, the only one who could observe any part of his features, saw his jaw tense. 'She lives on in her sons. To slight them is to slight her memory.'

Duke Robert's face showed the frustration such a reminder had engendered, which clearly pleased Tancred, who had regaled his offspring more than they cared to hear of how he had known this man since he was a mewling child, had even held him as a baby, chucked his cheeks as a boy and playfully fought with him as he grew up. He had related to the youthful Robert and his elder brother Richard the great Norse sagas that he had learnt at his own grandfather's knee. There had been a time, Tancred informed them all, when what shone from those deep-set green eyes was respect for a noted warrior. It was plain to William – if that esteem had ever existed – it was now no more.

His father saw the same lack: Robert, Duke of Normandy, who these days liked to be called the Magnificent, was probably unaccustomed now to anything other than flattery and agreement, so malleable, so Frankish, to Tancred's way of thinking, had his court become. The older man came from a generation that did not fear to tell a liege lord to his face that he was in error. His own father had spoken to the late Count Richard, even after he had elevated himself into a duke, as an equal, never forgetting their shared heritage as Viking warriors and the rights that went with it; there could be no vassalage that did not rest on respect.

The duke was now looking beyond Tancred at this troop of sons: he would be aware there were even more of this tribe back in the Contentin, another five boys and a trio of daughters. Truly their father had the loins of a goat, and had found both in his late half-sister and his second wife a fecundity to match his carnal exertions: the only years in which his wives had not been brought to bed with child had been those when he was away fighting.

The one standing next to Tancred, who would be the eldest, was damned impressive, taller by half a hand than his father and his other brothers, with a look in his eye and a lazy smile that was not one that could be associated with respect. If anything he looked amused, as if what was happening bordered on an absurdity that might at any moment cause him to laugh out loud.

'Name them to me,' he said, relenting.

Tancred named William as his heir, then brought the others forward one by one and by age, each to execute an awkward bow that would not be seen as too obsequious. 'Drogo, Humphrey, Geoffrey, your sister's youngest Serlo and, though not a true nephew, my first born by my second wife, whom I named after you.'

That obliged the duke to fix his namesake, and call the thirteen-year-old Robert de Hauteville forward. What he saw was as affecting to the eye as the sight of his brothers, for his namesake was big for his age, even bigger than the year-older Serlo, and that boy was no dwarf: Tancred bred sturdy sons.

'It is a good name, Robert; wear it well, boy, in respect for me.'

The voice that responded was newly broken and slightly rasping. 'I shall endeavour to do so, sire, upon my honour.'

'Now that I have named my sons,' said Tancred, 'and they have seen the duke they are eager to serve, I would ask to speak with you in private.'

'On the matter of?'

'That which I have sent word to you before, the obligations of family.'

The pause was long, the silence of it oppressive, as the two men, liege lord and vassal, locked eyes, both seeking to hide a deep and mutual repugnance. To the duke, who clearly now forgot how he had enjoyed listening to those tales of heroism and fickle Norse gods, Tancred, with his nostalgic adherence to the old ways, represented a relic of a bygone age and was given to haughtiness with it. The Normans were no more Viking now than those indigenes of the Neustrian March whom they had conquered, intermingled with and married, no more Norsemen than the Angevins, Carolingian Franks or Bretons whose lands neighboured his. The older man lived in a dead past and had no gaze for a different future.

'Your late brother was aware of such an obligation, my Lord.'

The sudden rigidity of the duke's bearing was evidence enough of the way he took that last remark; his dead brother was a subject no one in his entourage dared to mention, and few outside that circle, even his most powerful vassals, would do so either, likely as it was to produce a towering rage. The accusation was that Robert had murdered, in fact poisoned, his elder brother Richard, to gain the dukedom, hence the other name by which he was called, albeit out of his hearing: not Robert the Magnificent, but Robert the Devil.

The men around him, courtiers all, waited for the eruption, but they waited in vain, though a sharp eye would have detected the effort involved in containing it.

'Leave us,' Robert commanded, standing stock-still until the pavilion had emptied of courtiers. 'Your brood too, Tancred.'

Tancred laid a hand on William's arm. 'I ask that my heir be allowed to stay.'

'He may if he undertakes to remain silent. I am not given to discoursing with boys.'

William knew those words were meant to anger and diminish him; he had in his own mind long ceased to be a boy by many years, so the amused expression he wore broke immediately into a full smile which, gratifyingly, seemed to nonplus the speaker.

'The rest of you, leave us,' said Tancred.

They obeyed, but the last sound Tancred heard was of Serlo de Hauteville mimicking his younger half-brother, his voice high and mocking. 'I'll endeavour to do so, sire, upon my honour. Shall I lick your arse, sire?' That was followed by the sound of a scuffle, then the bellowing voice of Drogo.

'Stop scrapping, you two, or I'll sling you both in the river.'

'An unruly lot, your sons,' the duke said softly. Then he wrinkled his nose, for they had left behind them a strong odour of unwashed travel. 'Rustic too.'

'They are fighters, sire, as I have raised them to be and they have proved their worth many times against any who would trouble my lands. They ride well, handle both sword and lance as they should. Manners, if you think it something they lack, can be acquired.'

Duke Robert was looking at William as he replied. 'And what is it that you want for them?'

'If I mention your late brother, sire, I do so out of the respect I had for him.'

The response came as a hiss. 'My relationship was more of the kind we have just overheard outside this tent.'

'It was always understood that when my boys came of age, they would become part of his familia and serve him as knights of his body. That he died before that came to pass...'

The interruption was sharp. 'I know from your repeated correspondence you would like me to do the same!'

'They are your blood relatives and would serve you well.'

'You have great faith, Tancred, in the connection wished upon us by blood.'

'To me it is a sacred bond which surpasses all others, outside the grace of God.'

'Not a view with which I agree. Why are we here gathered on this riverbank, if not to support one brother, the King of the Franks, against another, not to mention the King's own mother who sees the wrong one of her sons as the ruler of Paris?'

There was bitterness in that last part: Robert's own mother was not fond of him.

'The Franks do not share our ways,' protested Tancred.

The reply was almost weary. 'Your ways, Tancred, and long gone they are. I doubt even your own sons share them.'

'They would never fight each other!'

'Are my ears mistaken? Did I not just hear that very thing.'

'I mean with weapons. William here would tell you no different. Certainly they come to blows and will wrestle, what brood does not, but no son of mine will ever raise a sword against his own brother. To do so is to invite the mark of Cain.'

The duke looked as if he had been slapped, but William also detected his determination to avoid a loss of control. 'On pain of your wrath?'

'Yes.'

'You will die one day, Tancred, and then maybe your wrath will be meaningless.'

'God's forgiveness will still be necessary.'

'God,' Duke Robert said, almost sighing. 'There are ways to gain his forgiveness.'

William felt his father's hand on his shoulder. 'I wish you to take them into your familia. Let them serve close to you and prove their worth. I count each one of my children as a blessing, but my patrimony is too small to support them all. Let them win both their spurs and some reward in your service, let them earn their own demesne from you.'

William de Hauteville knew that the duke was going to refuse, even though he did not speak: it was in his eyes and the ghost of a smirk that made the corners of his lips twitch.

'Perhaps they may come into more than that,' the older man said, which made his son suspect he had come to the same conclusion.

'More?'

'William, leave us,' Tancred said. 'What I have to say now is not for your ears.'

'Father,' William replied, executing a slight bow. Once he had gone Tancred spoke softly. 'You are unwed and childless, sire...'

For the first time Robert of Normandy really raised his voice. 'I have a son and a daughter.'

'Born out of wedlock.'

'As was your late wife,' the duke snapped.

'Your brother died without issue, which places my eldest son, William, your nephew, as one of your near blood relatives.'

'There are others, not least the child of my father's sister.'

'Edward of England, that milksop! He is a man who fights on his knees. I fought on behalf of his father and he was a dolt. If you have family around you, at least have those with warrior blood, men who do not fear to lay down their lives.'

'Do you think me a fool, Tancred?' Robert asked softly.

The negative shake of the head he got in reply lacked conviction.

'My own William, not yours, is my nearest blood

relative, and given the love I have for him, I would not surround him with a tribe who might see, as blood relations, advantage in doing him harm. Do you really think I am mad enough to invite into my household your brood, all of whom, no doubt, thanks to your prattling, think they have some right to my title?'

'Marry, have sons. Mine do not seek your title, they seek your respect.'

'Even if I do marry, I would name William as my heir.'

'Then stay alive, Robert,' Tancred growled, 'for there will be men in the hundreds who seek to do him harm, men to whom your dukedom is a glittering prize, though I swear on the grave of your sister not one of them will bear my name. I see the men you consort with and I can smell their measure. You surround yourself with silken tongues and see loyalty where there is only self-interest. The men you asked to leave our presence will not dare dispute with you, as I will and as they should, but this I will tell you straight. They are not going to respect a bastard boy regardless of how much you love him.'

'Dispute with me! What has a bare-arsed baron from the Contentin got to tell me that I should take heed of?'

'This bare-arsed baron has fought the Franks, the English and the Moors and he would tell you this campaign on which you are engaged is folly. A new

Capetian King mounts his throne in Paris and his brother disputes his right? He calls on you to aid him and you oblige, and that is an error. We should let these Frankish brothers fight each other as much as they wish, for there is more advantage in that than there is in aiding one against the other.'

'You know nothing, old man.'

'I know your father would have stood aside. No doubt you have received promises of reward, of land and castles, but they are only as good as the strength you can put in the field in the years to come. Let your Frankish King Henry become powerful enough, which he will surely do with no one to contain him, and he will take them back and more besides.'

'Yet you came to fight?'

'It is moneyed service. The King of the Franks will pay for every lance you put in the field and I have mouths to feed, but I would gladly forgo it to let the Capets stew in their own fratricidal juice.'

Like a bursting damn the fury of the Duke spilt over, and he shouted in a voice that no canvas would contain, so loud that it was very likely audible on the bank of the Seine.

'I think you came to beard me, Tancred, not for the silver you will be paid. You ask that I respect your sons? Well I will do so by not having you and them slung into the pit of the nearest donjon. I will do so by letting you join the battaile of the Sire de Montfort, as I say you are obliged to do, even if you dispute it. But when we fight, if we fight, make sure you are not in my sight when it is over, for I may forget that you married my sister, forget that you loyally served my father, and have that head of yours off your shoulders and, to protect myself and mine own from vengeance, take those of your sons as well down to the youngest babe in arms, as well as rip out anything carried in the womb of your wife. Now get out.'

'Sire.'

CHAPTER TWO

CHAPTER TWO

It was a chastened Tancred de Hauteville who emerged from the ducal pavilion, and there was no need for him to tell anyone, sons or supporters, that he had failed in the task he had set himself. His grim visage was evidence enough, even if they had not heard the shouts emanating through the canvas. It fell to William to ask the obvious question.

'Do we stay?'

'What choice do we have?' Tancred replied. 'By the time we got back home we would be paupers with barely a fit horse left to ride.'

'Then let us hope there is a battle,' Drogo said. 'It would be shameful to have ridden all this way just for some pieces of silver.'

'Don't go despising silver, my lad, it helps you eat when times are lean.'

'When are they ever anything else, Father?'

'Come, while I bend the knee to a swine so that you may fill your bellies, and on the direct command of our noble duke.'

Tancred was careful to call upon the Master Marshall before he approached the tent of his designated leader, first to register his arrival and second to indent for sustenance as well as monies owed to twelve lances in travelling from their home of Hauteville-le-Guichard to the River Epte. It was another monk who entered the details on a scroll, a clever sod who disputed the distance Tancred claimed to have travelled and thus the amount of time he had been en route, calculated at seven leagues a day plus fodder for mounts. After a long and acrimonious dispute, the Lord of Hauteville was forced to accept the clerical reckoning or risk being denied any payment at all.

'Make your mark,' the monk said, proffering an inked quill and a small piece of linen. When Tancred had done so, he added, 'You may collect your payment when this has been passed by my master.'

'The Devil awaits these scribblers,' he swore as he emerged, which earned him a frown from his priestly nephew, who was holding the reins of his horse, though he refused to be cowed. 'How can a man who swears to love God enough to renounce the common life treat a simple soul as if every word he utters is a lie?'

'Would it be too much to say, uncle, that it might be

based on a familiarity with simple souls?'

There was really no response Tancred could make to that, given that Geoffrey was his confessor and, though he would never breach the sanctity of the booth, he knew only too well that he had been obliged to request from his uncle much penitence for that particular transgression. Tancred was not more dishonest than the average, just human, and Geoffrey represented a deity who knew the need to forgive that failing.

The old knight threw several shaped pieces of wood to his eldest sons. 'Tokens to draw supplies for our animals and us. We shall have meat to roast and bread to eat it off. Serlo, Robert, get some wood and a fire started, the rest of you see to the horses while I beard our pouter pigeon of a leader.'

'Perhaps,' said Geoffrey, 'you had best give me safekeeping of your weapons.'

Tancred smiled at that. 'No, it is my fist you must worry for. I long to box Evro de Montfort's ears. He is not worth the price drawing blood would carry.'

'Might I suggest, uncle, that I accompany you anyway. De Montfort may produce edicts and the like with which you will not be familiar.'

Which was a tactful way of saying that, unlike his sons, tutored by Geoffrey in the basics of education, Tancred could not read. 'You will also restrain me from violence, will you not?'

Geoffrey grinned. 'That too, my lord.'

The party split up, Tancred and his nephew to go to the de Montfort pavilion, while the others led their horses through the lanes of tethered mounts, makeshift tents and fires that filled the air with woodsmoke, each with its band of lances sat around, strangers until they came close to the men from their own part of Normandy, fellows they had met at local assemblies, or at the main religious festivals in the half-built cathedral in Coutances. Many a call came from recumbent figures, some asking for news of home, even if they had only left it days before the de Hautevilles.

There was still clear space next to the river, the least desirable part of the meadowland, being plagued as it was by biting insects. Soon axes were being employed to lop off tree branches of the right sort to serve as sharpened stakes that, driven into the ground and strung with a rope, served as a line to which the animals could be tethered, the horses hobbled for extra security. Before that saddles and harness had been removed, and once the mounts were watered, fed the last of the oats and linseed they had brought with them, and given a pile of hay on which to munch, they needed to be groomed: coats brushed, hooves picked clean and oiled, noses cleared, tails and manes untangled, genitalia swabbed on stallion and mare and their arses washed clean of any left-over dung.

The youngsters, having dug a shallow pit and got a main blaze started, lit smaller fires in a circle round the area in which they would eat and sleep, covering them with dampened grass once they were well alight to create a curtain of smoke that would deter the flying pests that infested the riverbank. From the bundles carried by the packhorses came the means, in the form of two metal triangles and a spit, to roast the cuts of pig as well as a hanging griddle on which bread could be baked, the whole to be washed down by skins of apple wine.

Robert was left to look after the fires while everyone else cleaned harness as well as their own equipment and Serlo went off down the riverbank in search of figs, pears and herbs. When he came back with a couple of fowl birds, necks wrung, and a sizeable marrow, none of his seniors asked from where he had acquired them: the youngster was known as an accomplished pilferer.

While all this was taking place, Tancred, or to be more accurate, Geoffrey, was in dispute with a man who claimed, with written texts he was inclined to wave with gusto, that he had rights of vassalage over the Hauteville demesne, an obligation the owner of the land hotly disputed. The whole of the Contentin, the most western part of Normandy, bordering the great ocean, was in a state of flux when it came to land tenure and an increasing attempt by the greater lords, not least the duke himself, to impose feudal obligations. Much ink and more blood had been spilt in claim and counterclaim.

Count Rollo of blessed memory, more of a convert to Christianity for convenience than belief, had gleefully acted like the Viking he was, suppressing and robbing the ancient monasteries and churches, stripping them of their plate and jewels. He had taken their land as well, which had been parcelled out to his fighting supporters, men like Tancred's grandfather. His great-grandson Robert, a more committed believer, was attempting to put right what he saw as the sins of the past as well as impose feudal obligations on a warrior race that felt them alien and Frankish. Naturally, avaricious sods like de Montfort had weighed in with claims that, if accepted, would further increase their wealth and power, while turning most of the local lords into mere vassals.

'If my Lord owes fealty to anyone it is to the Bishopric of Coutances,' Geoffrey insisted, in a voice as calm as his interlocutor's was agitated. 'They owned the land before it was appropriated by Count Rollo.'

'Of which there is no bishop,' spluttered de Montfort.

Nor will there be, Tancred thought, while my like and I draw breath. The families who had profited from Rollo's seizures knew very well that a bishop in situ in Coutances could bring matters to a head and not to their advantage if bribed by the likes of de Montfort, men who had the means to get their way. They had therefore chased out of Western Normandy any cleric who attempted to take up the post, and no bishop had any power who could not occupy his see.

'But that surely underlines the point, my Lord,' Geoffrey continued, 'that this case cannot be progressed until the matter is decided upon in a consistory court, and that court has to be convened in Coutances and overseen by the holder of the office of bishop. The edict you have presented to my Lord of Hauteville has no validity until that court has pronounced upon it.'

Realising the cleverness of his nephew's ploy, Tancred was content just to glare at Evro de Montfort, a man he hated with a passion. More than once he and his sons had sent packing lances sent by this man to impose his will, many with blood still dripping from de Hauteville wounds when they made their return; others had been less ambulant, and had obliged Tancred to employ a horse and cart.

It was not just the fellow's attempts to increase his power locally; he was richer than all of his neighbours, with larger lands and holdings amassed not through military service, but by the slippery route of marriage. He also hated him because he had one possession for which Tancred longed, a proper stone donjon from which he could dominate the locality; this while his neighbours, the de Hautevilles included, still occupied simple stone manor houses adjoining a motte-and-bailey castle constructed of mud and wood.

De Montfort looked up at Tancred, being a good deal shorter and overfed with it. 'Then I am forced to ask my Lord of Hauteville why he is prepared to fight under my banner. If that does not imply vassalage, what does?'

'I am here at the express command of my liege lord, who no doubt fears that the men you command require stiffening with a better class of knight.'

'What my Lord of Hauteville means...' said Geoffrey de Montbray.

'I know what he means, priest, and to show I am given to believing what I hear, maybe I will put the de Hauteville knights in the forefront of the battle.'

'If you will promise me a battle,' growled Tancred, 'I accept the station.'

'We move to La Roche-Guyon in the morning, to rendezvous with the King of the Franks.'

The way de Montfort said that, puffed as he was with his own conceit, created the impression that the King of the Franks would be attending upon him.

Darkness was upon them by the time they had eaten, and they bedded down on palliasses stuffed with fresh straw, covered by cloaks stretched between upended lances to ward off the chill of the night, and chill it would be with a clear, star-filled sky and a bright moon. Tancred was first to slumber, assuring, by his stentorian snoring, that everyone else took longer to achieve the same. The two who could not sleep, being too excited, were the boys Serlo and Robert; indeed their endless whispering to each other had been another bar to rest amongst their elders and they had been told more than once to shut up.

Sick of tossing and turning, they were soon up and wandering about among the sleeping soldiers and the dying embers of their fires. There were men guarding the rim of the encampment, for the locals would look to pilfer or, indeed, recover things that had been taken from them to feed this host, but within the perimeter there was no movement save the odd fellow stumbling to the riverbank to relieve himself. The horses and donkeys were asleep on three legs, only moving when changing from one to another.

'I found an anthill earlier,' hissed Serlo.

'Where?'

'Along the riverbank and up a track that led to a hamlet where I stole the fowl and the marrow. Big ants too, who looked to have a good bite on them when I poked the mound. What do you say, Robert?'

No explanation was required for the kind of mischief Serlo had in mind, for his half-brother had a quick brain. 'Can we do it in the dark?'

'It's on the edge of a clearing. Fetch your palliasse and let's go and see.'

'Why mine?'

'My idea,' Serlo insisted, 'so your bed.'

Accepting that was fair, Robert took the bed he no longer occupied and, having emptied it of straw, followed Serlo down to and along the riverbank until they came to the track he had found previously, well worn and obviously one the locals used to fetch water. Moving cautiously, in case this was one of the points with a guard, they crept into the darkness afforded by the trees and, once their eyes had adjusted, made their way inland. The clearing, judging by the smell, was some kind of midden and the boys could see the pile of waste in the centre. With Serlo pulling his arm, Robert was directed to the mound, which lay between two rotten tree trunks and was surrounded by leaf mould.

'Find something to poke it with.' There was always a hesitation when Serlo issued any command; with only a year between them, Robert was never willing to acknowledge the rights his elder half-sibling assumed. 'Come on, brother, we don't have all night.'

A stick was found, a broken branch of which in summertime, when kindling was less required, there was ample choice. Serlo took the stick and poked hard at the mound, the result being immediate. Even in the gloom they could see the mass of glistening black ants emerge to defend their hill, rushing around, looking for something to bite. Serlo threw down Robert's open palliasse and began to poke furiously, bringing out even more defenders, who, apart from those few who stuck to the stick, started milling around and disappearing in what was effectively a sack.

'Here, you have a go,' said Serlo, and a willing brother took the stick, not realising that it had been passed to him just as a couple of ants reached the point at which he was holding it; the first bite made him drop it quickly. He issued a muffled cry and swore at the nip, not mollified by the assurance that came from Serlo.

'At least we know they do bite.'

Picking up the stick, Serlo brushed off the ants and used it to corral those racing around on the canvas palliasse which being strange to them they had congregated in, then he grabbed the edge and closed it, trapping those inside, while a good shake dislodged those on the outside, the top being spun to ensure they stayed trapped. Back in the camp the boys crept by their slumbering companions – this jape would not be visited upon their own and, well aware of their family antipathy to Evro de Montfort, they picked the last fire glow nearest his tent, moved round to the far side, and tipped out the contents right by the sleeping soldiers.

They were lying down when the commotion started, shouts and cries, and in the moonlight dark figures of men furiously brushing themselves. The noise was excuse enough to stand and get a better look, as other groups around the one they had attacked were awoken by the commotion, and that included the Lord de Montfort, who could be heard querulously demanding quiet. It took an age for things to die down, for men to be sure that the nipping ants were either all dead or gone. By that time two very contented youths were sound asleep.

They were all up with the grey dawn light, the fire relit to bake breakfast oatcakes, the watering and feeding of the horses seen to while the cooking was taking place, the seniors washing in the river once their equine chores were completed, hundreds of men whose feet churned up the muddy bottom to turn the Seine downstream brown. The packhorses were reloaded in advance of the blowing trumpets, which came from the top of the hill. A messenger came from de Montfort to tell Tancred to bring up the rear of the battaile, the place of least honour, which he knew to be a response to his jibe of the previous night.

'Cover the horses' nostrils,' he commanded, 'and your own. We will be eating dust this day.'

Trumpets blew again, and the de Hautevilles saw the duke, at the head of his familia knights, lead the way east, each battaile mounting to follow in the order laid down by the Constable, leaving behind them a sloping field of flattened grass covered with dead fire pits, the bones of their food, piles of used straw, as well as heaps of dung that, along with the contents of the latrine, the locals would soon gather to use on their crops.

The move was necessary: no army of any size could stay in one place for long – they ate up the countryside regardless of how well they were supplied by river. As well as the horses of knights and squires, the duke had along the contents of his stud. These were replacement animals for any losses those fighting in his cause might sustain, part of the bond a liege lord made with his vassals regardless of the terms of service. If a knight lost his fighting horse in battle or in any event on the march, the duke provided a substitute. William had estimated the size of the force at some five hundred lances, which meant at least fifteen hundred mounts as personal possessions; add the duke's horses and that rose to over two thousand.

It had been drummed into him since he first mounted a pony as a child that his horse was a paramount possession, as important as a mailed hauberk and gloves, a sword and shield, as well as the helmet that protected his head. A Norman might fight on foot and often did so, but he would still need a trio of horses to transport him to the battle: a destrier to fight on if it was a mounted assault, a lighter cavalry horse as the means of getting from one place to another – also essential for foraging and reconnaissance – and at least one sturdy packhorse to carry his equipment.

All needed to be fed, watered and rested for part of the day; drive them too hard and they became useless. Given his guess at the numbers, he was trying to work out the quantity of supply and as usual, when faced with a difficult calculation, he turned to his cousin Geoffrey, his tutor in all things, for an answer.

'William, I have taught you this, I am sure.'

'I have a figure in my mind for hay,' William lied, 'but I wish to see if I have counted right.'

'How can you be wrong, it is so simple? If there are two thousand horses and each requires thirteen librae of hay per day, you need some four hundred bushels, always assuming that there will be a certain amount of pasturage and that oats are provided by the Master Marshall on the route of march.'

'Libra? You use the Roman measure?'

'What else would I use?'

'I was thinking of Charlemagne's livres.'

'So what is it in Charlemagne livres?' Geoffrey asked.

'Different,' William replied, hastily, 'very different. Take care as we cross the river.'

Fording the Epte for those towards the rear of

the column was more taxing than for the men who had gone earlier: not the entry, but most certainly the churned up exit, as the faggots laid on the bank originally had long come apart, leaving a widening sea of earth turned to sludge by hundreds of hooves, mixed with liberal quantities of dung from horses nervous on the slippery ground.

The de Hautevilles were forced to dismount and lead their animals up the slimy bank, becoming covered from head to foot in what they were wading through as they dragged reluctant mounts though the muddy ground, not least from what was kicked up by hooves. Tancred's mood was not improved when his two younger boys decided the destroyed riverbank provided an excellent mud slide, albeit one which washed them clean when they ended up in the dirty brown water, that parental ire made worse when he tried to kick them for a second attempt and ended up in an undignified heap.

'Welcome, Father,' called William, 'to the land of the Franks.'

Picking himself up, a figure now a uniform brown from head to toe, and slithering to where William stood, he nodded and patted his son on the back. 'It's enough to make a man curse his neighbour, which is expressly forbidden in Scripture.'

A swiftly swinging foot took William's legs and, landing on the muddy ground, he could not avoid

slithering down into the river to where Robert
and Serlo were now engaged in a bout of water-
fighting, his journey accompanied by the bellow of
his mollified father, as well as the laughter of his
brothers.

'Or to put in his place a disrespectful son, which is
not. Now get up here the three of you and let us be on
our way.'

Given the water that had dripped off those ahead,
it was a good distance till the footing under their
animals was dry, by which time they had dismounted
again to walk, giving their horses some necessary
relief and, once the mud had dried, for it was a warm
summer day, trying to brush themselves clean. The
army halted at noon and, after taking on food and
drink, men who had travelled in their own lands
in leather jerkins now donned their hauberks and
helmets; they were no longer in Normandy, with no
precise knowledge of where their enemy lay – it was
time to be ready to fight.

Their route was still dictated by the River Seine,
running between bluff white cliffs topped by dense
forests on one bank, and rolling open country to the
south, their aim to reach the great fortress of La Roche-
Guyon, which for two hundred years had defended the
Frankish border. The castle was invisible from the
approach, being, as it was, built into the chalk cliffs,
a bastion any invading army bypassed at its peril,

given that the strong garrison of mounted knights would emerge from unseen openings at the bottom of the cliff face to fall upon the rear and engage in bloody execution, before disappearing back into their impregnable warren.

La Roche-Guyon also guarded a spot at which the Seine could be crossed and there were few of those between Rouen and Paris, which rendered the fortress doubly valuable. By now the whole host knew that the Duke of Normandy had pledged his men to the Frankish King on condition that the castle, as well as the rest of the French part of the Vexin, be surrendered to his control. It was a measure of how desperate the Capetian monarch was that he was prepared to give up such an asset, one that protected his capital from a potential enemy who would now be only three days' forced march away.

Henry Capet, King of the Franks, had set up, beneath the hidden fortress, a great round pavilion of his own, there to await his ally. His army was encamped elsewhere, for there was precious little open ground between the cliffs and the river. By the time the host passed the pavilion the duke and his senior commanders were inside to hear the whereabouts of the King's rebellious brother and to agree how he was to be met and where.

The Normans did not join with the levies of the King for three days, two of which were spent setting up and breaking camp, travelling short distances to new pastures and integrating themselves into a truly disciplined force. The de Hautevilles had much to occupy them apart from that: they needed to get to know the men alongside whom they would fight, riding with them in conjoined lines under the direction of the Sire de Montfort, ensuring that they had clear knowledge of the commands he would issue.

Tancred might loathe the man as well as his pretensions, and dispute whether he had the right to lord it over him in his home region, but he was, to his mailed glove, a soldier, and one who knew that to allow a dispute of that nature to interfere with their common purpose in battle was to invite disaster.

Battle was imminent but few knew when, though rumours abounded, while sorting those from fact was a daunting task: there were many who would believe and disseminate any tale, however stupid it might be. But the day came when all doubt was gone: the enemy was at hand and tomorrow they should clash. The sudden increase in the attention paid to the condition of mounts and weapons, the depth of prayer that came from constricted throats at the mass held in the dying light, was evidence of that, for those in entreaty knew that, on the morrow, some of them would die.

Geoffrey confessed Tancred, his sons and followers,

as well as the two boys, who would stay with the horses and the duke's baggage train. It was not unknown for that to be a prime object of an enemy assault. It was evidence of their youthful foolishness that they hoped such a thing would happen, for in their minds they were certain that they alone could repulse it.

CHAPTER III

CHAPTER THREE

The summons for Guaimar and Berengara to attend upon the Prince of Capua was delivered at dawn and without much in the way of grace. Osmond de Vertin had turned up outside the small gatehouse lodge they now occupied in the heart of Salerno, banging on the door with the same impatience he had shown at the abbey church. He had brought along two spare horses, one with a saddle suitable for a young woman, and he was in no mood to wait for their – particularly her – need to properly prepare themselves.

It was a measure of how unthreatened these Normans felt that, on this undertaking, not one was wearing mail, a helmet or carrying a lance. They were dressed in soft hats and surcoats over leather jerkins, slashed on the sleeve to allow the breeze to cool their bodies. Both the youngsters, with the prospect of facing the Wolf in his own lair, had donned elegant court clothes and covered them with cloaks, guaranteeing a warm and uncomfortable journey.

So hurried was the rousing out and departure that it took time for Guaimar to realise the different colours these men wore, no longer the red and black of Rainulf Drengot, but the yellow and green of the Prince of Capua, an indication that Osmond and this band of Normans who garrisoned Salerno must have changed their allegiance. What this portended he could not tell.

It was a journey undertaken at speed, a steady canter, with frequent changes of mounts every two leagues and a strong party sent ahead to clear the road, and God assist any peasant who got in the way. Those walking were forced into the storm ditches while anyone driving a cart was as likely to find it tipped on its side, and fear made sure they hid well their deep resentment, some even bowing to the passing horsemen. Nothing was allowed to interfere with the passage of this band, with the chief escort proud of the way his power was so decidedly demonstrated. Many a glance was directed at Berengara, in the hope of observing she was impressed.

A journey of twenty leagues took all day, even across a flat, featureless plain on a well-maintained Roman road, and they had little chance to snatch food and drink at the infrequent stops. It was telling that Osmond bypassed the home and camp of Rainulf Drengot near Aversa, which was on the direct route to Capua, underlining that he no longer served the mercenary leader.

It was a weary and dust-covered party that, in the gathering evening gloom, rode through the Norman guarded gates and into the courtyard of Pandulf's palace-cum-fortress, tucked in a bend of the River Volturno inside the walled city. As soon as they were dismounted, before even they had a chance to ease their aching limbs, Guaimar and Berengara were ordered into the great hall in which Pandulf was wont to receive visitors.

'Bring them forward.'

The voice called from the end of the hall, which, though lit, was too dim to distinguish the speaker at such a distance, but it was one known to them. Guaimar felt himself pushed in the back and as he advanced his sister did likewise. Closer to the raised dais at the end of the great hall, Pandulf was sitting in a throne-like chair, with one leg casually thrown across the arm.

Dark of colour, and with swarthy skin – which hinted at Saracen blood – Pandulf was a handsome man who prided himself on those looks. Guaimar had only met him on two occasions prior to the day he usurped his father's place, but he could clearly recall the easy charm, the deep and attractive voice, as well as the ready smile and the twinkle in the eyes that engendered trust in those who had not before dealt with him. Anyone who had experience of his true nature did not trust Pandulf at all.

Yet no one could deny that he had luck, or was it that easy manner, smile and magnetism which so blinded people to his true character. The citizens of Capua were not fooled: the whole of Campania knew how much they hated him, knew how they had rejoiced when he had been deposed himself for earlier acts of chicanery as he played Byzantium off against the power of the Western Emperor, always for his own gain.

Yet somehow, having been taken to Germany as a prisoner by the previous emperor, he had thrown himself on the mercy of Conrad Augustus upon his election and had succeeded in convincing that newly crowned overlord of his good intentions. Conrad had set him loose and he had returned to claim his fief. The same citizens who had rejoiced to see him go had paid a heavy price for their hate: many had died, burnt at stakes or strung on ropes hanging from the walls of this very castle. So had Guaimar's father!

'You've grown, you pups of Salerno,' he called, as though he was greeting old friends. 'Pray take off those cloaks so I can get a good look at you.'

He sounds just like a benign and favourite uncle, Guaimar thought, as he undid his clasp, the cloak being taken from him by a silent retainer who appeared from the gloom at his side. That's the way he talks: jocular and friendly. It made him think of the Garden of Eden snake.

Pandulf was on his feet, and coming down to meet them, his smile wide, his eyes fixed more on Berengara than her brother. 'Grown did I say? Blossomed more like.'

Berengara had dropped her head, but close to, Pandulf lifted her chin. Then he took her hand and led her to a pool of stronger light, forcing Guaimar to follow. 'You have turned into a beauty.'

'We came as quick as was possible, sire.'

The hard voice of Osmond de Vertin, seeking praise for the speed with which he had carried out his orders, changed Pandulf's face, making the eyes less twinkling and the mouth harder, but that slight change of expression was reversed as he faced his new Norman recruit.

'You have done well, Osmond. You and your men must be weary. Take them to the guard quarters and give instructions that, while we dine, you too are to be fed.'

Guaimar was looking at Osmond as Pandulf spoke, and he sensed the man's disappointment, not hard given it was written on his features. Did he feel he was elevated enough, now he served Pandulf directly, to remain in their company? Had he expected to dine at the princely table? Osmond stiffened in a sort of salutation, then spun on his heel and stalked off, his boots stamping hard to demonstrate his displeasure. It was doubtful if Pandulf noticed; he was back staring into Berengara's upheld face.

'We too must dine, but first I think you, young lady, should be granted some attention from the maidservants of my wife, to ease the strains of the journey. I have words to say to your brother.'

'I have no objection to Berengara hearing anything you have to say.'

'But I have, Guaimar,' Pandulf replied in a sharp aside, before making a gesture with his hand that summoned one of his retainers. 'Take the young lady to my wife's private chambers. Ask that she be looked after and made more becoming, if that is possible.'

Berengara looked at Guaimar, who nodded. If he intended them harm, there was nothing he or she could do about it. If he did not, it would make no difference. As soon as she was gone, Pandulf returned to his chair, and, throwing himself into it once more, looked at Guaimar with an amused expression.

'You too have grown, boy.'

'It is, I believe, normal to do so.'

'The question is, having done so, what have you grown into? A paragon or a nuisance?'

'It might be possible to be both.'

Pandulf laughed. 'Take the word of one who knows, Guaimar: it is not.'

'Your superior knowledge, so painfully gained, humbles me.'

'Are you clever, Guaimar?'

'Modesty forbids an answer.'

'Then you think you are, and your modesty is false. If you were truly self-effacing you would have given a different response. So let us assume you are clever and you are aware of that gift. What do you think opposing me will gain you?'

'Have I opposed you?'

'I do not know and for me that is not comfortable.'

The desire to tell this man how much he hated him was strong, but it had to be kept in check. Pandulf was not a person to challenge when you were entirely in his power, he being famously capricious, and all this polite banter could be a blind: the dungeon might be waiting, indeed his sister might have already been taken there. If the Wolf saw him as a threat, he would not hesitate to take steps to neutralise him. Guaimar thought he only had one asset: his own youth and lack of experience.

'You do not answer?'

'In truth, Prince Pandulf, I do not know what to answer. I am but a boy, in the presence of a man too well versed in the byways of discourse to challenge.'

He knew Pandulf was vain, just as he knew, with

his dark and handsome looks, added to that insincere, friendly manner, he had the right to be. Right now, that insincerity had him adopting a look of confusion.

'I wonder, Guaimar, if you understand me, or my purpose?'

'As to the first, I would not presume. To the second, I plead ignorance.'

Pandulf was on his feet again, and coming close. 'You bear yourself well, boy. No doubt you think I have brought you to Capua to harm you.' The dark brown eyes, big pools of deep enquiry, bored into those of Guaimar. 'Again you do not answer.'

Suddenly Pandulf was pacing up and down in front of him, speaking in a rapid voice. 'I prayed for the soul of your father as you did, and I beg you to believe that I intended him no harm. Things were done that had to be done!'

That produced a pause in both talk and walk, accompanied by a hard look, a challenge to call him a liar. The response being a bland expression he was off again. 'People talk ill of me, I know that, but in my heart I alone know that what I have done has been for the greater good of the Lombard cause. I do not act to benefit Pandulf, but to benefit the whole of the region of Campania and, after that, all of Southern Italy.'

Staying silent and controlled at that piece of mendacity tested Guaimar's self-control to the limit.

'What have we Lombards tried to do these last

hundred years?' It was not a question that sought an answer. 'We have tried to rid ourselves of the yoke of Byzantium. And have we succeeded?' Pandulf bellowed, before again answering his own question. 'No!'

Guaimar could feel his nails digging into his palms; how could this walking paradigm of treachery talk so when he had aided Byzantium in the crushing of the last Lombard revolt. That was what had cost him Capua and made him a prisoner in Germany!

'We have not succeeded,' Pandulf continued, 'because we have not been united under the right leader.'

The boy could see where this was going and decided he had to cut off the flow of lies and self-justification to which he knew he was about to be exposed.

'And you wish to unite us?'

Pandulf was clearly animated, as he rattled off an incoherent plan to bring together all the Lombard magnates of South Italy, into a great confederation; of course, under his banner. He would unite all the Normans as well: he had the means to buy the service of every band in the region and that would deprive the enemy of their prowess. With a mighty host he would throw Constantinople out of the whole of their Italian fiefs.

'And then, Guaimar, we can tell Conrad Augustus to go hang as well, to stay in Germany and out of our affairs. Finally, we will be free.'

'Do you not owe Conrad a great deal? Did he not free you?'

That earned Guaimar a pout. 'I, boy, owe nothing to anyone.'

Guaimar was no stranger to the notion of Lombard independence, of a great kingdom that would embrace the southern half of Italy; he had heard it from his father all his growing years. It was a dream constantly alluded to and never realised because unity amongst the various rulers was impossible. Even with his stiffening of the Normans he had engaged as mercenaries, Melus, the last leader to try had been badly defeated, as much by internal squabbling and treachery as the army sent by the Eastern Emperor. Even the Normans had been chastened by that lost battle.

'And Guaimar,' Pandulf continued, in a silky voice, 'do not doubt there will be rewards for those who aid me, great rewards. Pandulf knows how to be a prince, and one day, we must hope, a king.'

Was it possible? Guaimar did not know, though on balance he saw it as doubtful. There was only one thing of which he was sure: he would not ever follow this man, who now held him with both hands on his shoulders, beaming into his face. Then one arm was thrown round his waist and he felt himself propelled forward.

'Come, let us eat. Your sister and my wife will be waiting.'

* * *

The dinner had been a trial. Both youngsters were exhausted by the travel, and even more so by the endless stream of Pandulf's grand designs, the flow of which was as ceaseless as the rich food and fine wines. Eventually even a man as insensitive as their host realised they were falling asleep at his board, and he called for candle bearers to light them to their chambers.

Guaimar, tired as he was, still felt it necessary to ensure his sister was safe and comfortable, and so went to her chamber. About to gently knock, he saw that the door was very slightly ajar, and he pushed with outstretched fingers, swinging it open silently. Berengara was standing with her back to the far wall, her hair loose and in a shift, her hands pressed against the stones and clearly, by her expression, deeply distressed. He knew it was Pandulf, with his back to him, even although he was partly disrobed. Seeing her saviour, his sister's eye swung to meet his, and that forced Pandulf to turn round at speed.

His shirt was open, and so were his breeches; the man was obviously aroused, it was in his eyes as well, and it took him a moment to come out of that state and realise that whatever he had intended was not now possible. Caught in the act of seeking to deflower Berengara he yet had about him the wits, or was it the ready ability to tell a barefaced lie, which had served him so well.

'I came to bid your sister a good night's sleep before going to my wife.'

'As did I,' Guaimar snapped.

There was a moment when the youngster wondered what Pandulf would do. He had the power to call armed men to remove Guaimar, the power to do with Berengara this night as he pleased. The youngster never knew what it was that persuaded him to snatch up his jacket from the floor and leave. Was it that he needed the boy as an ally? Was it the proximity of his wife; she would be disturbed by any commotion? The one thing it would not be was remorse at having been discovered, of that he was sure.

'Then that is a duty I leave to you,' Pandulf said.

'I would like that we return to Salerno tomorrow,' Guaimar said as Pandulf came abreast of him. The Wolf paused for a moment, flashed that engaging smile as though nothing suspect was happening, and nodded.

As soon as he was gone he had Berengara weeping in his arms. Having got her into the large bed, settled her down and waited till she went to sleep, he spent an uncomfortable night lying across the now closed door.

Guaimar was once more in the company of the Archbishop of Salerno, this time in his episcopal palace, set in the hills above and away from the filth and stink of the city. From the balcony, across his manicured gardens, they could see the wide sweep of the Bay of Salerno shimmering in the summer heat, set off by the sparkling blue of the Tyrrhenian Sea. In the harbour lay the ships that brought so much wealth from the Levant to Italy; to the boy it was like looking at a constant stream of gold, the river of wealth that had, over five centuries of Lombard rule, raised his family to magnificence. He was not here for the view, but for enough of that commodity to make a journey, from one of the few sources of funds he could, with some safety, tap.

Not utterly disposed to refuse to part with money, this high cleric had to go through the ritual insistence on poverty, the diocese being much put upon by those seeking charity. 'The church of Salerno is not wealthy, my son. Our new overlord has set a high tariff on our coffers.'

'I doubt you gifted Pandulf all the plate my father gave you.'

There was hesitation before the truthful reply. 'We preserved some, with difficulty.'

The archbishop, as he said those words, could not help but look like a thief and it was an unchristian thought in the boy to think him that. The man was bent in the back from age and some affliction of the bones, while his head was permanently tilted to one side, the whole subject to some slight palsy. That did not explain a certain shiftiness in his eyes, which with his broad nose, flabby cheeks and loose lips created an impression of a man naturally given to larceny.

'It is the use of that which I seek from you.'

'The gifts your father gave to us were made to Holy Church, my son. They are not my personal possessions of which to dispose.'

'I must ask you, Your Eminence, how you think the church of Salerno will fare under the thumb of Prince Pandulf, especially if he discovers what you have withheld from him?'

That got Guaimar a sharp look; was this boy threatening to reveal what had been withheld? 'I fear we will not prosper. He is rapacious, as you know, and we have our garrison of Normans in your old home to enforce that which he wishes. They too prey on the tithes we receive, money which should be transmitted to Rome.'

'And how would that same church, as well as Rome, fare under my family restored?'

The head, already wobbly, shook with firm resolve. 'A speculation, my son, for which I might pray, but I dare not hope.'

'A speculation that might be worth investment.' The old man did not reply. 'There are powers greater than those of Pandulf.'

'You refer to Bamberg and Constantinople?' Guaimar nodded. 'They are distant, my son.'

'If they could be persuaded to take up our cause...'

The interjection was quite sharp. 'Our cause, Guaimar? I cannot see the Emperor Michael or his wrinkled harlot, Zöe, taking up our cause.'

The nuances of that remark were profound: Michael was Byzantine Emperor by marriage, a young husband, risen from the position of secret lover to an empress in her sixth decade who had already exhausted one spouse. It was a liaison seen as typical of the corrupt court over which they held sway. Yet it was the other point that was significant to this cleric: Constantinople was the seat of the Orthodox Church.

To seek redress there for the depredations of Pandulf of Capua would not sit well with a representative of the Vicar of Rome. The two versions of the faith might coexist and espouse harmony a thousand years after the Crucifixion, but neither welcomed encroachment. With troops from the east would come their faith, and this priest had enough trouble with the Orthodox religion as it was; a great number of the citizens of Salerno still practised in that discipline, a hangover from direct Byzantine rule.

'I would, of course, prefer to seek help from the Western Emperor.'

'Conrad Augustus is a good son of the Church.'

A good son of the right church, Guaimar thought. Personally he did not care from where help came. Even as a Lombard, and the scion of a line that had tried to rid themselves of Byzantium for a century, he would accept armed assistance from there if it could be had. Any eastern emperor might be seen as anathema to the Church of Rome, but he was less of a Satan than Pandulf. Yet what the archbishop was saying seemed plain: funds for a trip to Bamberg and the Emperor Conrad might be possible; money to seek aid in Constantinople was out of the question.

Time was also of the essence; as children he and his sister, if they had been left in straightened circumstances, had also been left in peace. That could not last; being dragged to Capua proved that and Berengara was clearly at risk from Pandulf's unbridled lust, which could descend upon her at any time. As Guaimar grew to full manhood Pandulf, who would see the youth was popular while he was not, would also see him increasingly as a threat. The archbishop must act, he must do so now, and the youngster could think of only one lever he could apply.

'I would, of course, should I make my way north, pass through Rome to seek the blessing of Pope Benedict.'

That made the old cleric look even more devious; the boy had named possibly the most tumultuous city in the whole of Christendom, east and west, yet it was a place where intercession could be sought. Not much in the way of armed help, but spiritual assistance. If this boy could get the Pope's blessing on his endeavour, that would weigh heavily with the Emperor Conrad. It would also be possible to send to Rome with Guaimar news of how difficult life had become in Salerno, which might still the constant demand from the Pontiff for tithe money.

Moving indoors, the archbishop sat down, and put his conjoined hands before his face, as if in prayer; in truth he was examining Guaimar. Could this slip of a boy, with no experience, achieve that which he sought? Certainly he was a comely youth, with dark straight hair, even features in a sallow complexion and a pleasant disposition, so like his late father in his lack of martial bearing. Yet he also seemed to have on his shoulders a head older than his years, and in those almond eyes a hint of intelligence, so he might impress the Pontiff with his air of guileless simplicity.

'You would travel alone?'

'No, Your Eminence, I would ask my sister to accompany me.' The raised eyebrow was question enough. 'I would not expect her presence to aid me much in Rome, but should I be able to continue to Bamberg I have heard that beauty can melt hearts in a secular court. Perhaps, even if she is not yet mature, she can do that to a Holy Roman Emperor.'

'And you will ask for?'

'My title to be confirmed and for an imperial host to come south so Conrad can enforce his rights as the heir to Charlemagne.'

The cleric was a Lombard, as was this boy; the notion of seeking aid from any imperial court was not natural to a race that hankered after independence. That they should invite into their region either power showed just how much Pandulf had set matters on edge. The Dukedom of Naples, sandwiched between Salerno and Capua, would be next if the Wolf was not checked, the Lord of that valuable fief being fearful enough to seek to appease the Wolf, rather than antagonise him, with constant gifts of gold. He too, in such times, would accept help from wherever it could be found.

'The Charlemagne claim is one that Constantinople has never accepted,' intoned the archbishop, leaving Guaimar to wonder if a reprise of the obvious was a clerical trait. 'They insist they have the rights of a suzerain in South Italy.'

Faced with that evident truth, the young man could only reply in kind. 'They have not sought rights on the western side of the Apennines for a hundred years.'

'But they respect no other claim. It would not do us good to have both emperors fighting over us, as they have in the past, like a dog bone.'

'Would Byzantium send a host to contest that claim if Conrad was beyond Rome with an army?'

'Unlikely, I grant you. But could even Conrad defeat Rainulf Drengot and his Normans? No one here has done so.'

'I do not wish to defeat the Normans.'

'Forgive me...' the Archbishop protested.

Guaimar was fired up with the idea he had, and that made him cut across a man unused to such behaviour from a greybeard parishioner, let alone a callow youth. 'They are mercenaries. We must find the means to purchase their support.'

'Your father...'

The old man was interrupted once more.

'Is dead! I am his heir, and it is my right to decide policy and it cannot be the same as that which brought him to an early grave.'

The priest was quite sharp; not even in rule did dukes talk over him. 'You are heir to a patrimony in which you have no power, my son. You lack warlike qualities, so I do not see you as some great military captain scattering your enemies before you. Need I remind you that your father trusted Rainulf Drengot only to be betrayed? He gifted him a great deal for his loyalty, but that was not enough.'

'I shall have to find something to give Rainulf which will bind him to my cause.'

'And what could that possibly be?'

'The answer to that lies elsewhere.'

'Why do I have the impression that you are keeping something back?'

Guaimar was being evasive; he had an idea but it was one he did not want to openly espouse. He also knew he was in danger of alienating this man, and that he could not afford. 'I am, but I do so in concern for you.'

'Explain.'

'What if you were to share the fate of Pandulf's own archbishop?'

Even sitting, such a notion made the bent old man shiver, for it was the stuff of his nightmares. He had heard of the treatment meted out to those in the Wolf's dungeons, the priestly eminence and the bishop's mitre no protection, and was aware that the Prince of Capua was as arbitrary as he was cruel. No crime need be perceived or committed to render him that fate; he could be taken to the oubliette at any moment for merely holding his office.

'What if you had all the aims of my mission and Pandulf sought them from you? He would apply hot irons to your body and rack you to get them, would he not?' That got a slow nod. 'So I will keep to myself what I plan, then you cannot be tortured to reveal it.'

That sent the archbishop back into a reverie behind his seemingly praying hands. There he was weighing up doing what had been asked or doing nothing. Both were fraught with risk, but this boy surely proposed the lesser of two evils, the possibility of a return to the peace and prosperity he had once enjoyed under his father. Imperial armies had come before, but always they had gone home again having ensured their rights.

'Very well, my son, I see it is the duty of the church to support you in this.'

'Your Grace will not regret it.'

'There is a Jew just off the marketplace who will advance sums against plate I have hidden in his vaults. I cannot give you enough to have you journey as you should, like a prince, but journey you must. Only I beg of you, even if you plan to do so in disguise, do not pass through Capua.'

'The Volturno near the sea is low at this time of year. We do not need the bridge in Capua to follow the road to Rome. We and our animals can wade the river.'

'Then I ask you to pray with me, my son, for the success of your endeavour. May God protect you and keep you safe on your journey.'

The archbishop, with some difficulty, dipped to kneel on a hassock by his feet and began to murmur a prayer, one in which Guaimar joined him. He thought this young man without guile, but it was he who was the fool. Guaimar had not pointed out to him that if Pandulf found out about his mission and guessed how it had been funded, he would rack and sear this priest regardless of ignorance or knowledge.

CHAPTER FOUR

A week of manoeuvre had come to an end; the field of battle had been set. The Norman host rose stiff from their slumbers to a damp, grey dawn mist, and before they fed themselves, on a morning of expected conflict, more prayers were said, each fighting man using his sword to represent the Cross on which their Lord Jesus had died so that they may be saved. Murmuring the Stations of that Cross they entreated the Almighty that their sins might be forgiven, their fears evaporate, their deeds be courageous and if they should fall that their souls be granted entry into paradise.

Prayers done, their fast could be broken; some, as they ate, made loud jokes to hide their concerns, others laughed at those sallies with too much mirth, but most were silent, concentrating on being sure that everything about their equipment was in perfect order: that their sword could not be sharper, nor less so the blades of their knives and the points of their lance. Many spoke to their horses as if they were still speaking to God, for in battle, their mounts would be as great an aid to survival as their faith.

The destriers they would ride – tough horses bred not for speed but for steadiness and fearlessness – picked up the mood and those inclined to be restless anyway became hard to control as they were saddled and caparisoned, with many a knight or squire required to be swift on his feet to avoid a flashing hoof or a quick nervous bite.

For the first time, the de Hautevilles unpacked their surcoats, new and bright, woven, sown and dyed especially for this day, bearing the same blue and white chequer as their painted shields. Each knight attended upon another, making sure that belts and straps on waist, knee and forehead were tight, that the girths on the horses were not frayed or loose, that the stirrups were of the right length to bear easily the weight of a standing rider.

If Tancred de Hauteville was fussier than most, intent on ensuring that his whole convoy was in perfect condition, that was part habit, but more that he was leading his sons into battle for the first time. It never occurred to him that they would disgrace him, or fail to fight as hard as any man in the duke's army, but over and over again he repeated the mantras that they had heard from his lips all their lives about how to handle their mounts, how to pay attention to commands, which way to hold and use their lance while ensuring that their shields protected them from the counter-thrusts of those they would be attacking. If he noticed that the murmured agreement from the lips of his sons and their like-age companions sounded bored, it did nothing to dent his insistence.

William was doing much the same as an elder brother, acting as if he had battle experience when he had only participated in local skirmishes, and annoying his siblings mightily. But they no more rejected advice from him than they did from their father, for in truth they knew the elder brother to be using his concern to allay his own nervous anticipation. And all were prey to the same thought: they had sought this day since they were children contesting with wooden swords, dreamt of it when as youths they first rode and sought to control, with nothing but their knees, a fighting horse. Now it was upon them, it did not seem so splendid as it had in anticipation.

The anxious tics evaporated when the horns blew to assemble. It was like a signal, for the mist lifted as the rising sun began to burn it off, and the men of the Norman cavalry were greeted with the first sight of the Franks they would fight alongside, a footborne host marching in its own cloud of dust, heading in straggling columns towards the nearby field of combat, men whose heads seemed to be bowed already with weariness. The sound of a beating drum drifted on the air, the steady beat in time with those hundreds of silent feet.

'They look sapped already,' said William.

'Beaten,' Drogo added, 'though they're not yet running.'

'Then be glad you have a horse to carry you,' growled Tancred. 'Now get your helmets on and mount up.'

The move to do so was carried out with a degree of inflexibility, for even young and strong as his boys were they were hampered in their movement by the weight of their mail hauberks, indeed Geoffrey de Montbray, a small cross of the crucified Christ swinging on his chest, had to have a leg-up to mount, which earned him a few remarks about the diminishing power of the deity he represented.

'As long as I feel his power in my sword arm, cousins, that will suffice, though I will pray for the souls of those I smite.'

They were horsed by the time the duke rode round the camp to take a salute from his troops. Mounted on a magnificent grey animal and wearing mail finer than those of his vassals, he exuded confidence and

William de Hauteville, for one, wondered if he felt as he did: that whatever rank they held, whatever other matters impinged on their lives, this was the high point of their existence. Nothing mattered more to a Norman of noble birth than the ability and willingness to engage in battle; nothing had greater importance in their society than the ability to wield a sword and win a fight. Let others till the soil and harvest the crops, let others tend the sheep, the cattle, the chickens and the goats. A knight had but one true purpose.

Behind Robert rode the Constable of the host and the Master Marshall, as well as that high-ranking prelate William had seen in the ducal pavilion. He was not in clerical garb now: like cousin Geoffrey he was equipped for battle, albeit his mail was covered by a more priestly surplice, for he alone had the right to wear proud on his breast the sign of the Cross. Before each assembled battaile he stopped, bowed his head, uttered a short prayer, then blessed them with two swift strokes of his right hand.

Inspection complete, Robert, Duke of Normandy, stood in his stirrups and addressed his knights, his voice strong and carrying. 'This day, we must help the Lord to whom I am a vassal, the King of the Franks, assert his right. Base is the brother that seeks to usurp the power of a rightful king.'

The slight ripple of noise that ran through the army was quickly suppressed; how many listening wondered at their duke's use of those words?

'My Lord of France has an army, but he does not have what I can bring to him, which is the best and most puissant mounted host in Christendom. You are Normans!' They jabbed their lances and cheered, which Duke Robert killed off with a raised hand. 'I have no doubt today will bring victory to our arms, and I have sworn before my Lord Bishop of Fécamp that in thanks for this I will undertake a pilgrimage to the Holy Land. My life and soul I commend to God this day, as I commend yours, and since my being is in his hands, I will not shrink from the loss of it, if the Almighty so wills it.'

That brought forth a cry of emotion, a denial of the obvious fact that no man in a fight could say what his fate would be.

'I ask only the same of you all. Should I fall…'

That needed another ducal hand to silence disagreement. As that was imposed, a gap opened behind Duke Robert, to admit a small boy, perhaps no more than five years old, sat on a white palfrey; dark haired, pale of complexion and slight of build he came to take station beside the duke, significantly by his right hand.

'Should I fall, I commend to you my son, William of Falaise, may God preserve and keep him. He is my true heir, and you, my vassals, must serve him as you would serve me.'

With that Robert bent from his mount, low, to kiss his son. He indicated that his ducal gonfalon was to be brought forward, and the boy was obliged to kiss that, and loud was the subsequent cheer for the universal sign of inheritance. It would have taken a keen eye and ear to note that not all were joining in the acclaim, to note that in some quarters there was not only silence, but a look of doubt, if not anger. If they had been close enough to Tancred de Hauteville, as his eldest son was, they would have heard him grinding his teeth.

The horns blew on the Constable's signal and Robert swung his horse to lead his men to the field of battle under the fluttering banner of those two recumbent golden lions on a bright-red background that was the standard of his house.

Naturally, being cavalry the duke sought the high ground, an aid to any mounted attack. On this elevated position the sun-dappled battlefield lay before the men in the front rank, which included the de Hautevilles, like some kind of yet-to-be-sewn tapestry. The king's rebellious brother had drawn up his army with its left fixed on a river, with a force of cavalry on a mound to his right, protecting the mass of his infantry and ensuring they could not be outflanked there. The ground, from the river, rose to where the cavalry sat, not much, but it indicated to at least one keen eye that the line of attack for the king's infantry was on the flatter ground, where the river would offer protection to their right as well.

'I wonder if that river is fordable?' William asked.

'You think to surprise them, brother?' asked Drogo, sat on William's right.

'I fear more they may surprise us. Those horsemen on the right might not be the whole force pitted against us. What if they have pushed another battaile to cross further downstream and come upon us behind this position?'

'We would see them.'

William pointed to the rolling hills on the opposite bank. 'Not if they are in the folds of those.'

'The duke would turn and destroy them,' insisted Tancred. 'Man for man we are ten times any Frank, be he horsed or not.'

'Which would,' William responded, 'draw us off and if that happened at the right time...'

'You're imagining things,' his brother insisted.

'Probably, but they hold the ground, Drogo, forcing us to come to them and our friend yonder is definitely intent on a defensive battle...'

'How can you know that?'

'He is standing his ground, which means he is waiting to be attacked.'

'Though you forget to add it matters not what he does,' his father said.

'I'm just speculating.'

'Anyone would think you were in command.'

There was no rancour in that remark, more a touch of humour.

'I'm just thinking what I would do if I was, or even more, what I would do if I was the enemy, which I cannot but believe is a good notion.'

'Can't you see it?' Tancred interrupted. 'The King of the Franks hopes to do this without help. The last thing he wants is for Duke Robert to win his battle. If he did he would have used us first to seek to break the enemy line. But he has not, and I can tell you if he can win on his own, with just his milites, he will do so, which might just allow him to repudiate whatever promises he had made for our support.'

'So we could have come all this way for no purpose, money service aside.'

The eyes on either side of his father's nose guard were not pleased at that reference, so William decided on silence, but he could not help but let his mind speculate on all the possible ways in which this battle could be played out. The king's foot soldiers would, even if they tried to attack across the whole front of the enemy line, naturally trend towards the flat ground and once they were engaged the enemy cavalry, using the slope before them, might try to drive them towards the river.

It was not necessary to beat them, merely to crowd them into a smaller frontage and so reduce the power of the assault. Draw off the Normans then, and their allies would be in trouble, but such a tactic only worked if the rebellious brother had enough mounted men to split his force, and Drogo was right; there was no evidence of that.

Henry Capet had started his attack. Pikemen at the front, they were moving forward in a line getting more ragged as the uneven ground broke the cohesion of their formation. William could see his notion had been right; the men on the far left were veering right towards the river, they could not help it: the slope dictated they do so. Whoever led them had seen the problem and called a halt to redress the line.

'Crossbowmen,' said Drogo.

'He is using them to keep his enemy in place,' said Tancred.

'His enemy, Father, is happy to stay where he is. Those bolts are doing little damage at the range they're firing. They would be better kept until the range is right.'

'God in heaven, I have bred a Caesar?'

William threw back his head and laughed, loud enough to make his horse skittish. 'You might have, Father, but it is as likely to be a Nero as a Julius.'

Silence descended, apart from the snorting of

the horses, a thudding hoof and the occasional loud fart before they voided their bowels. Redressed, the attacking line began to move again, but the one thing the commanders had not done was to rectify the way the force was still compacting. There was an ethereal quality to what they were observing. Barring the occasional trumpet, no sound could be heard, though there must have been a mass of shouting as the leaders exhorted their men and those men yelled to give themselves courage.

The two lines converged until they were only twenty paces apart and suddenly that silence was ruptured, as the attackers broke into a charge, the yelling that came in one bellow from several thousand throats rolling up the hill, the clash of metal on metal added to that as the armies clashed. To William what happened next was like watching the tide, a gentle one that lapped the sandy beaches not far from home. The join where men were fighting, being pressed to stay engaged by the masses behind them, wavered this way and that, like wavelets running up and receding on a beach, and for an age it seemed there was no advantage either way. Then the defenders slowly but surely seemed to give, and William noticed the enemy cavalry stirring.

'Do you think we are close enough?' he asked.

'How would I know?' his father responded.

'Well I just thought…'

'Don't think, William,' Tancred replied sharply. 'Take the word of one who has been in this before. Thinking in a battle will drive you to forget what you should be doing, which is what others have decided. You're here to fight, let others do the calculating.'

William de Hauteville was not about to say so, but such a notion induced a feeling of deep disquiet. He wanted to say the time had come for them to attack. The enemy cavalry would fall upon the disorganised flank of the King's foot soldiers and if there was no one there to rally them to face the onslaught that part of the host could be rolled up and thrown back on the centre, which might panic and crumble.

Asked how he knew this, he would have been unable to say, but he felt sure of his conclusion. He had been raised in a warrior household, had heard his father describe every battle he had been engaged in, and not just him but every fellow knight who was a visiting friend. There was, in each contest, they had said, a moment of decision, and for William, that moment was right now.

'Why is the duke waiting?' he demanded, unable to stay silent.

Tancred de Hauteville sighed. 'For the same reason as his ally hesitated to let us open the fight. He wants the King of the Franks deeply troubled before we intervene. For our liege lord, this has to be his victory.'

'So when?'

'Soon.'

The enemy cavalry had moved, though they had no discipline, but little was needed for what they were obviously trying to do and they charged off their raised ground, using the slope to gain momentum. As soon as the cavalry charged, the enemy front solidified, no longer being pressed back but instead holding and in some places pressing forward. Frustrated at what he was witnessing, William was suddenly aware that the duke was to the fore, a convoy of his familia knights bearing his banner and ducal gonfalon, raised high, alongside him.

'I told you,' he heard his father say.

Then the arm dropped and the gonfalon dipped, and as one, the whole Norman front line, a hundred lances, moved forward. When their horses had gone ten paces, the second line began to move. Though none of the de Hautevilles could see it, their eyes being fixed on the task ahead, the rest followed in unison, five lines of warriors. Humphrey's horse, always more excitable than those of the rest of his family, wanted to do what all horses do, race his fellows; it took a strong hand on the reins to bring his head in and slow him down.

'Hold your line,' Tancred ordered, long after it was necessary.

All eyes were on Evro de Montfort's banner, for that

set the pace, which increased to a canter as the slope before them increased. Each man's world had narrowed to those on either side and what he saw before him. The commander of the enemy cavalry had slipped half his force sideways – clearly he had anticipated the Norman move – while the others were still engaged in pressing back the now disordered infantry. They had turned to face and charge the oncoming Normans. Unbeknown to the men in the front line, those to the rear had, under their own commanders, slowed their pace back to a trot.

For the front line, a horn blew three high notes, and the Normans stood in their stirrups, shortened and looped their reins, to be gripped by the hand below their forearm shield straps. They then dropped their lances to couch them, a solid line of points facing the oncoming enemy, who by now, in their wild charge, were a disordered, galloping throng. The Normans did not gallop; they held their pace and their cohesion, though the speed increased to meet the oncoming threat. Beside him, William could hear his father calling on every saint in the canon, but he could not look at him; like every knight in the line he had picked the man with whom he was about to collide and all his concentration was on ensuring that the fellow would take the point of his lance.

What told, as it always did, was that Norman

discipline. Their line was solid, so that each charging enemy, seeking to avoid an oncoming lance, might pull his horse to right or left, only to find himself faced with exactly the same danger from another. It takes, not a brave man, but a fool to maintain his charge in the face of near certain death, so it was no surprise that the enemy cavalry sought to slow their mounts and to seek a chance to defend themselves. Their swords and axes swung at the lance points, but for every one that was fractured or sliced off, another took the rider or his horse.

Men went down on both sides; it could not be otherwise, but the Norman lances pressed forward still with great solidity, men and horses falling before them. Those like William whose lances were lost had out their broadswords and were hacking away at the enemy, still stood in their stirrups, swinging their shields to deflect return blows. One swipe of William's sword took an opponent at the join of neck and shoulder with such force that it split him to the lower chest, covering his attacker in a fount of bright, warm blood.

As soon as discipline became fractured, the second telling feature of Norman warfare was exercised: the quality of their battlefield leadership. Evro de Montfort might be a tubby and self-important little pouter pigeon, but he was a proper commander and his yelling voice was calling for his battaile to disengage. This they did and followed him to the left, beating off those of their opponents still fighting. If the enemy cavalry thought they had scored a victory they were soon disabused, for the lances of the next battaile, led by an on-fire Bishop of Fécamp, were on them before they could spur their mounts into motion.

Hit by repeated waves of Norman lances the number of bodies on the ground rose as they took the now stationary or retreating enemy. They were a beaten foe, looking for a way to flee and in doing so they would leave their footbound brothers to face certain defeat. De Montfort had led his men to take station behind the as yet unengaged Duke, yelling that they should reform. Only then did Tancred realise two of his convoy were missing.

'Drogo, Montbray.'

'Will have to rely on God,' William shouted back, wondering why his mouth was so dry.

Suddenly, with the enemy cavalry in flight, there before the Norman host lay the exposed mass of the still-fighting rebel milites, and it was clear that the Norman horse had the power of decision over men on foot, which they moved to execute. Behind the front line panic took over as, pressed on the flank by slashing horsemen and to their front by jabbing pikemen, the rebel force broke as each man sought to save himself.

They found Drogo standing over a recumbent enemy, who by his attire was a wealthy individual, to be informed the fellow had sought mercy for ransom. Montbray was on his knees, the cross he wore in his hand, his surcoat bloody, praying for the souls of those deceased who had fallen to his own lance and sword. There were dead horses too, and many more wounded, some with injuries that would mean they would need to be quickly despatched. Better that than a lingering death.

On the mound once occupied by the enemy cavalry, Duke Robert met the King of the Franks and they embraced with the kind of ceremony of two men whose trust for each other is limited. All over the field of battle below them and their colourful retinues the dead were being stripped of their arms and what they wore, while some of those too wounded to survive were being despatched by the foot soldiers of the Frankish King. The rebellious brother had fled the field as soon as he saw that his cause was doomed, not pursued for there was no need. Where would he go? Few would offer him sanctuary.

'It's the oubliette for him,' said Tancred, to his men, all of whom had taken possession of enemy horses and weapons. The old man had hoped to get to the baggage train of their foes but it was clear that had been plundered by the household knights of the

Capetian King, none of whom had deigned to take part in the fighting, leaving that to the Normans.

They were on their way back to the encampment, surrounded by equally weary fellow confrères, when they came across Serlo and Robert, leading half a dozen heavily laden packhorses. The boys grinned at their sire, only to cease to do so when his voice thundered out to ask them what they were about.

'Can you not see, Father?' said William. 'Our two little robber barons have beaten the Franks to some booty.'

'They were supposed to stay out of harm's way.'

William laughed. 'They are your sons, sir. They do not know how.'

'I'll tan their hides.'

'Only after we tot up what they have managed to steal.'

The de Hautevilles did not linger, not from fear of Duke Robert's anger, but because, once they had been paid for their service, the cost of maintenance fell on them and that was cheaper at home than loitering here. They sold or traded what they had taken from the field of battle, as well as most of the contents of Serlo and Robert's enterprise. Drogo even sold his ransom at a heavy discount to the Constable, given it would be easier for a high official to collect on a prisoner housed in Duke Robert's castle of Moulineux.

On the first night they camped back on Norman soil, and after all had been seen to with horses and food, Tancred sat down his boys round a fire to tell them what they already knew: there would be no service in the ducal household, no chance to raise themselves in that service. There were other things of which they were aware, whatever their age: that this had dashed their father's long-held hopes and the reason – the property on which they had been raised was too small to support them all.

'I had hoped, as you know, that you would win your own advancement. We fought today, and fought well, but who can say what the future will hold?'

It was William who underlined what his father was driving at. 'With Duke Robert allied to the King of the Franks, there is little prospect of war service…'

'I have no desire to arm myself with a plough,' Drogo insisted.

There was a weariness in Tancred's voice as he responded to that. 'I raised you to do what I did, and that is fight. That you can do, but William has the right of it.'

'The duke might fall out with the Franks,' said Geoffrey de Hauteville. 'They are not natural bedfellows.'

'How long will that be?' Tancred replied. 'One year, two years, ten? The Bretons were our allies today, as well. As for the Angevins, they too are supine. For the first time in my life the borderlands are at peace.'

'Which is why our Duke Robert can go on pilgrimage.'

That opinion came from his namesake, really too immature to be taking part. It was a measure of Tancred's gloom that he did not remind the youngest son present of the fact. 'Jerusalem? He will be gone a year at least, possibly two.'

'He may well come back a monk,' Drogo scoffed.

'Would that be so bad?' asked Montbray.

A period of silent reflection followed, as each son contemplated a life of peaceful husbandry, albeit such an existence would be punctuated by the kind of local conflicts endemic to the Contentin, not one of which would ever advance them in any way. They were no more farmers than their sire, and so it seemed to the eldest they must do what he had done when a young man.

'We too should seek the solution elsewhere,' said William.

'A pilgrimage?' Drogo demanded, in a voice that showed what he thought of that idea.

'Your soul is beyond redemption, brother,' William replied, grinning, 'and you know that is not what I meant.'

'The work of God is being pressed east of the Elbe, converting the Slav barbarians.'

William looked at Montbray. 'That is your work,

cousin, not ours. We need to fight for recompense, not to spread the faith.'

'Which means Spain to fight the Moors, or Italy?' Tancred said, without enthusiasm.

William nodded. 'Those who have returned from Italy seem to have done well.'

'Which is a tenth of the number whose bones are still there.'

'Show me an alternative.'

'I could try to speak with Duke Robert again,' his father responded, but in a voice that held out little hope.

'Beg!' William exclaimed. 'Not even to a duke would I have you do that and I cannot ever see myself bending my knee to a man who denies consideration to a blood relation in the way he has so clearly done.'

'Let me think on it.'

William de Hauteville was quite brusque with a parent to whom he normally showed great respect. 'It is not yours to decide, Father, it is up to each one of us who is of age to make that choice for ourselves.'

In the firelight, all of Tancred's sons could see the disappointment in his face, looking more lined in the flickering fire than it truly was. From oldest to youngest, they all knew the hopes he had entertained for his house, hopes that through his sons the name of de Hauteville would stand high in the annals of

Normandy, hopes held over many years that had been dashed in the last week.

He had said many times how they would rise in the service of their liege, had said the death of Duke Richard made no difference, his brother would inherit the title and the obligation to the sons of his sister, and that, given the way he had raised and trained them to be warriors, they could be so assured of advancement. Their half-siblings too would prosper in the same way, on the backs of their established brothers.

He had put aside their doubts when his repeated requests to the court, written for him by his nephew of Montbray, received no reply. He had kept them training, and saw them use their skills in various local quarrels. His boys were not just good: they were, as fighters, exceptional, so much so that in the part of the Contentin in which they lived few dared to dispute with the family now so many were grown to a good age. A de Montfort would because he commanded enough lances; no one of the same rank as Tancred dared.

On the journey home to the demesne, in which every avenue was discussed, what was a notion became a decision. Money constrained them, even with what they had just acquired; only two could make the journey, but they, if they were successful, could send for the others. William claimed the right to be first, which naturally meant Drogo asserted that he should be the other. Humphrey and fourth son Geoffrey would follow, while their cousin of the same name declined to even consider a move to Italy. His ambitions lay in the Church and Normandy.

No one even mentioned Serlo or Robert, which had no effect on the first and genuinely annoyed his half-brother, who saw it as a slight for his not sharing the same mother.

CHAPTER FIVE

The Jew was not one to open his door to a stranger, but in a place like Salerno, bustling but not large, everyone knew the features of the old Duke's heir, for they had seen him paraded alongside his father at every religious festival, Roman or Orthodox, held in the city since he was a babe in arms. He recognised the boy as soon as he threw back the cowl on his head. He was also a man from a race that had learnt to be cautious: he knew that any gentile could represent danger to an Israelite, and the boy standing close to the doorway lantern more than most.

So, through a hatch in his heavily barred door, he bade the youth re-cover his head and walk off into the gathering gloom of the evening, bidding him come back in another two chimes of the cathedral bell, time in which he made sure his premises were not being observed by agents of Pandulf or his Norman hirelings and, by use of his contacts with the less salubrious orders of the city, that his cloaked visitor was not being followed.

When Guaimar returned he had no need to use the knocker: the door was opened as he lifted his hand and he was swiftly drawn inside. From his doublet, Guaimar produced a wax tablet bearing an imprint of the archbishop's seal, which the Jew, a tall man dressed in good woollen garments, took close to a wad of flickering tallow, then held the object in even closer proximity to his nose.

'You recognise the seal?'

'I do, honourable one.'

'I am scarce honourable now, sir.'

'You are your father's son, that is honour enough.'

There was something in the way the fellow said that which made Guaimar ask a question, his brow furrowed with doubt. 'You knew my father?'

'It is not an association he would have been keen to let all Salerno know about, but I was often of use to him.'

'In what way?'

The Jew chuckled. 'Let us say that rich men, powerful men and others sometimes need to transact business that must be kept from prying eyes.'

'What kind of business did my father have that required your services?'

'Secrecy was our bond. I would not tell even you, honourable one.'

'Then how can I know to believe you?'

'You bear the seal of the most saintly Archbishop of Salerno, but I do not ask how you came by it. Nor will I tell anyone who enquires that you came here or what it is you wish for. That will be our bond, the same secrecy as I kept for your father so that his subjects were not troubled in their respect for him.'

Those words implied something underhand, even perhaps double-dealing, transactions kept hidden from those who trusted him. Was the father he so revered not as upright as he thought?

'I need money.'

'Many people who come here have that need.'

'You hold in trust certain items for the Archbishop.'

'He fears the clutches of the Wolf.'

'He asks that you advance me sums of coin, with them as surety.'

'How much?'

'How much is there?'

The Jew laughed, a low and growling affair that shook his shoulders, but attractive. 'I have a bond with the archbishop too. You must tell me what it is you require and let me decide if what I hold will meet your needs. I see you hesitate.' Guaimar nodded. 'If you do not tell me I cannot help you.'

'I do not wish to disclose too much.'

'Do you plan a bribe?'

'No.'

'A purchase?'

'Perhaps that,' Guaimar replied eagerly, too eagerly for a man as wise as the fellow he was talking to.

'A journey then?'

The way Guaimar looked then produced from the Jew a hearty guffaw. Then he came forward, took the youngster by the arm, and said, 'You would grace my house if you would make use of my private chamber.' The boy found himself led through a door into a sumptuously furnished room and invited to remove his cloak. 'Pray be seated, honourable one.'

'I do not know your name.'

'Kasa Ephraim, ho…'

'I am Guaimar,' the boy said, quickly, cutting off the honorific. 'To say more is excessive.'

'This I know, and I do not seek to flatter you by addressing you so. I think it is no more than you deserve.'

'I am without titles which go with the tribute.'

'You have nobility in your blood, and I think very likely in your person. You will take some wine?' Guaimar nodded and picking up a ruby-coloured glass jug, chased at the tip with silver, Ephraim began to pour a deep-red wine into a golden goblet. Having passed the goblet to Guaimar, he settled himself in another chair. 'I am bound to ask after your sister. She is well?'

'She is well, but given to anxiety.'

'With the Wolf of Capua on the prowl, that is not a surprise.'

'Do you have a bond with him?'

'No, but he may have a bond elsewhere, and if he has it will probably be with one of my race.' The Jew raised a flat hand, palm upwards. 'Please, drink. And so, Guaimar of Salerno, of what service can I be to you?'

'I have told you.'

'Forgive that I dare to disagree. You have yet to tell me what journey it is you wish to make, and how you plan to make it.'

'I have not said I am going on a journey.'

'You are young, honourable one, and I think clever, but I am a man who deals with men of all kinds, some of them best off in the shadows. I have learnt much in my time, and...' He indicated his surroundings. '...I humbly say that I have made a fine return on the occupation I follow.'

Guaimar suspected he traded with the local merchants and smugglers, who worked hard to avoid the customs dues of the port. If he did, had his father known, and if he had, why did he not put a stop to it? It could only be to do with money, secret money, for that was clearly this man's business.

'Your father understood that for certain matters to be controlled they must in some way be allowed. Yet that did not mean that all revenues should be lost.'

Or openly declared, Guaimar thought, before he spoke. 'Can you read my mind?'

'No, but I can see that I would have sent your thinking in certain directions. Now enough, tell me of your journey, so that I may help you, and be assured, honourable one, you do not just have to depend on the items left in my care. I would see it as a privilege to help the son of a man for whom I had so much respect.'

'I want to go to Bamberg, with my sister, passing through Rome, my aim...'

The Jew held up a hand. 'I do not think you need tell me that. How will you travel?'

Having lied to the archbishop about heading north, avoiding Naples, to cross the nearly dry summer riverbed of the Volturno between Capua and the sea, Guaimar had no idea why he told this Jew of his true intention.

'We shall go due east through the mountains, seemingly heading first for Mount Gargano, ostensibly on a pilgrimage to the shrine of Saint Michael. Then, once clear of observation, we will head north. A monk who knew my father says he will guide us to monasteries in the Apennines where we may take shelter.'

'Such a journey requires preparation, the use of horses and mules, as well as the purchase of supplies. You would be stopped from going, and even if you were allowed, Pandulf would attach to you an escort. He is no fool.'

'I have been assured the monks of my father's late order will gather what I need with discretion.'

'Better you go secretly by boat to Ostia.'

'With whom?' Guaimar asked, and when he got in reply a shrug, he added, 'Smugglers?'

'They are people who are accustomed to evasion. That you need very much to do.'

'But they are not to be trusted?'

'Trust is a word much abused. Your father trusted the Normans, did he not, and they broke their word and his spirit. You suspect I deal with these people and you are correct, but with them too, I have a bond. These monks of which you speak, good Christians they may be, but even if you could get away from Salerno, undetected, one of their number could betray you, on what is a long journey, for what Pandulf would pay them as reward.'

'Our identity would be kept secret once we were clear of the city.'

'No!' Ephraim insisted. 'I think you must go by the route I suggest. You can be aboard a boat and out at sea before anyone has an inkling you are gone, and with a fair wind...'

'There could still be a pursuit.'

'How many boats leave this harbour before the sun is up, a hundred, two?'

'Fishing boats.'

'In the dark, no one will trouble to comment on a larger vessel, a not much larger vessel.'

The look in Kasa Ephraim's eye was one that told the young man not to enquire too closely; someone would be bribed to look away, and he had no need to know anything of that transaction.

'Money?' Guaimar asked.

'That, honourable one,' Ephraim said, rubbing his finger and thumb together, 'we will come to. Now let us drink another goblet of wine to seal the bargain.'

They were on that second goblet of wine when the Jew explained his thinking. 'You need little money for the journey to Ostia and it is best not to have too much about your person in case someone is tempted to robbery.' Seeing Guaimar raise an eyebrow, he added, 'It is not a good idea to put too much temptation in the path of those who have little.'

'Even if you have engaged them to a purpose.'

'Even then! In Ostia there is a synagogue where you must wait. From there to Rome I will arrange. You can call upon the people I deal with to give you gold, for north of Rome, and surely in Bamberg, that is what you will need. There is in the Eternal City a family called Pierleoni, once of my faith but now converts and immensely rich. I will give you a coded letter to them, and they, who know more than I do what will be required, shall ensure you are well supplied on my bond.

I will also ask them to give you access to their agent at the imperial court, in case bribes are required there.'

'And for this?'

'Look around you, honourable one, and you will easily see I am a man of business. Through the Pierleoni, I advance to you what you need out of love for a city more at peace than it now is. But, should you succeed, and should the Emperor place you back in your rightful position, I would beg to be given as my reward the office of collector of the port.'

'A handsome one,' said Guaimar, feeling cheated, which was risible, given the task he still had to perform. Yet the collector of the port was the most lucrative office in the ducal gift.

'Rest assured, honourable one, entrusted with that office we will have a bond. I will not cheat myself, but neither will I cheat my Lord.'

'And the smuggling which goes on now?'

'You have a sharp mind, as I suspected.' Kasa Ephraim smiled. 'We men are sinners, and when one sinner dies or is caught, another will take his place.'

'So it will continue?'

'Be assured it must continue, but also take my bond. It will not get worse and you too will find, should you come into your inheritance, that a flow of funds to do with what you wish can much enhance a man's power with those he must command, but dare not trust.'

* * *

The prospect of the departure of William and Drogo from Hauteville-le-Guichard was, like all family partings, full of false emotion: brothers not travelling joking how much easier life would be without their pesky siblings, no mention that, in a dangerous world where God moved in mysterious ways, to say goodbye to anyone going on a journey could very easily be a final farewell. William and Drogo were just as bogus in their display of extreme confidence; they too knew that to travel five hundred leagues, even on busy pilgrimage routes, to a place where they could only hope they would be welcome, was a daunting prospect.

As if to underline the need to go, they were barely returned from service with Duke Robert, when their father's second wife, the Lady Fressenda, was delivered of another boy child. Geoffrey de Montbray baptised him with the name Roger as soon as it was seen he would live, and, true to the family trait, he cried as lustily as all his seniors when his head was ducked in the church font. He too, God willing, would grow to impressive manhood.

The celebrations attending that event were only slightly marred by the proposed venture; neighbours came and admired the addition to the family, then drank too much of the contents of the family flagons; Tancred took his ribbing as an uncontrollable satyr in good heart until the impending expedition of his two eldest, combined with his consumption of an excess of apple wine, reduced him to maudlin tears.

That duty seen to, they had to be equipped for the journey, choosing the best horses with which to travel. Apart from their own destriers that they had trained from the foal, they needed not the swift coursers that had carried them to the battle, but mounts known for their good health and robust constitution. Pledges had to be made to certain people in Coutances, a promise of future produce from the demesne to gain in advance some more coin, this added to the little that the family itself could provide.

Each would take two extra packhorses laden with sea salt extracted from the pans the family maintained on the Normandy shoreline three leagues from their home, a good source of estate revenue and a very tradable commodity on the route they would travel: a peck of good salt was worth a meal in a land where it was scarce. The horses, once their loads had been used, could, if they were still fit animals, be traded for sustenance or a money payment.

A destination was another decision to be made and that involved much questioning of those who had returned from Italy and others who had any knowledge or connections there. In this, Geoffrey of Montbray, with his clerical associations, was most useful. The Church of Rome had a way of disseminating information denied to mere laymen:

priests and monks travelled to and from Rome, and papal envoys traversed the whole of the known Christian world carrying the messages and strictures of the various popes.

There were Norman forces in every part of Southern Italy, but the most successful seemed to be a knight from Alençon called Rainulf Drengot. He was no longer just a mercenary, but had acquired land as well, a heady prospect to the two young men intent on travelling, for they were not immune to the idea that they could gain glory as well as money in that fabled land said to have streets paved with gold.

Besides, Drengot would be the leader of the first Norman band they would encounter so it made sense to try there first. If he had no need of their services they could continue on to the Byzantine fiefdom of Apulia. At worst, their swords could be put to the defence of Calabria from the raids of the Sicilian Saracens. It never occurred to them that they would not find employment: Norman ability was too highly prized!

It was late autumn, bordering on winter, before all was in place. The morning they were due to depart William went to look out, for the last time, over the land that was still his to inherit, his mind whirling with thoughts. His brother was wiser and had declined to join him, insisting no good would come from standing in the freezing cold when there was a blazing fire in the hall.

The manor house, which was home to them both, stood at the top of the highest hill for leagues around, and from there Tancred could look over his demesne with a clearer eye at this time of year than most others. The abundant trees had lost most of their leaves and the higher branches were still white from the morning frost that clung to them. Trails of smoke rose from the homes of the tenants and serfs, who at this time of year were more concerned with gathering wood for their fire than farming.

The rolling landscape trended away in all directions, west to the coast, further south of that to the see of Coutances. Eastward lay the more settled and richer part of Normandy, the towns of Caen and Rouen, with their markets and multitudes, places William had visited but where he was never truly comfortable. To the north the de Hauteville land bordered on the extensive de Montfort domains, and in his mind's eye, for it was too far off to be visible, he could see the high, round, stone donjon of the kind which his father so envied.

It took only a glance to his left to see that which he wished to replace, the earthen mound atop which was a wooden tower and palisade. From there you could see more of the land; it was designed not for that but for the observation of approaching danger and defence from troublesome neighbours and others, like the piratical raiders of the offshore islands, ever bent on mischief.

Not wishing to go indoors, he plodded through the mud and climbed the slippery wooden treads to the heavy tower gate and, entering the circular edifice, went still further to stand on the stoop that overlooked the spiked tree trunks of the palisade. He had been standing there a while, he knew not how long, when the deep voice surprised him.

'I brought you your cloak.'

Engrossed, he had not heard Tancred approach, and realising how cold he had become he gratefully accepted the heavy deer hide garment he had brought.

'The prospect of the journey troubles you?'

'Leaving this place troubles me. I have known little else.'

'You know I pray you will return.'

For a man not given to emotion, unless drunk, that was as close as Tancred was ever going to get to saying how much he loved his eldest son. And William knew what hopes he had harboured: of a day when a de Hauteville, he most of all, would be the man chosen to ride at the right hand of a Duke of Normandy, the man their liege lord trusted to command his familia knights.

'Duke Robert must be well on his way to Jerusalem,' William said.

'I fear he has much for which to ask forgiveness,' Tancred replied.

That had, in discussion, led to the conclusion that the rumoured murder of his brother must have some truth in it. Robert, a man not known for excessive piety, going all the way to Jerusalem, hinted at such a grave sin.

'Can God forgive a transgression of that magnitude?'

'Your cousin of Montbray would tell you He can.'

'And you, Father?'

'All I know is this. It would break my heart and my beliefs if it happened with any of my sons.'

'And when Duke Robert returns?'

'Pray God he marries and breeds an heir, for if that boy William succeeds him, even if he is grown to manhood, it will not go without challenge.'

'From us.'

'No. I could no more take up arms against the wishes of my liege lord than do so against my own sons. I respected his father too much and I gave my word when in his service to be loyal to them always. But others will.'

'You will be asked, as I would if I were here. Our connection to the ruling house is too well known.'

Below, they could see the family servants leading out the already laden packhorses, which gave Tancred a good excuse not to answer. He pulled from inside his jerkin a small folded piece of cloth and pressed it on his son. There was no need to explain what it was – the blue and white colours identified it as the de Hauteville lance pennant.

'I hope and pray one day you will go into battle under this, our family standard. Now, let us go down. The time has come for you to be on your way.'

It took a seeming age to get everything ready, to check the horses, even if servants had already done so, to ensure that nothing had been left to chance or worse, left behind, for they must, if they did get to Italy, be equipped with everything they needed. Naturally the whole family was on the stone-flagged pathway that bordered the front of the manor house to say farewell, and each embraced the pair, saying words that were whispered hopes. Tancred was naturally last, but he did not embrace his sons, instead he called forward Geoffrey de Montbray, before commanding them to take out their swords and kneel. They knew, without being told, how to use the hilts of those weapons.

'Swear before this priest, your cousin, on the Holy Cross, that never will you raise a weapon, nor bring harm in any other way, against your own blood.' Both, heads bowed, murmured the response, before kissing the joint between hilt and pommel. 'Now stand, and take my hand like the men you are.'

That they did, clasping Tancred's arm to the elbow. There was no kissing, no embrace, as that completed, they sheathed their swords and mounted their horses. 'Now go, and God be with you. And above all, my sons, remember you are de Hautevilles and make me proud.'

Geoffrey de Montbray was still praying, head bowed, when they were out of sight. Everyone else bar the head of the house was either joking or choking but trying to hide their emotions and baby Roger, having picked up the mood, wailed like the infant he was.

Tancred had gone indoors before he lost sight of them and his whole family knew he wanted nothing more than to be alone, for they, like he, doubted he would live to ever see their faces again.

CHAPTER SIX

Guaimar of Salerno was deluded to think he could get away quickly, or undetected; in organising his escape the Jew would not be rushed and weeks turned into months of frustrating delay, which put in peril the whole affair. His patrimony was like every city, a place of rumour, gossip and downright betrayal if some citizen suspected there might be a reward for information.

Though the late duke had been respected, and there was always appreciation for a handsome young heir fallen on hard times, there was also in many hearts a residual dislike of the whole Lombard race – with their north European background – who had lorded it over the local populations of the land they had conquered and resided in for five hundred years, without ever assimilating. Their masters required them to pay taxes and to fight when they disputed with their enemies, other Lombard nobles, or even the mighty empires whose world they straddled. Minor offices they could hold, but never were they allowed real power, and just in case they should rebel, which they did often, the Lombards had their hated Norman mercenaries to keep them in place.

What shocked Guaimar was not that some Italians were prepared to betray him – he had grown up in Salerno – but he learnt that the gossip of impending flight was emanating from Kasa Ephraim. The Jew had insisted no more visits be made to his house, but he did send round written instructions with a different body every time on how matters should proceed. Sealing a letter in reply, the young man demanded he explain his betrayal.

The response was blunt, informing him that he was being naïve. He could barely move without news of his activities coming to the attention of the Normans occupying the Castello de Arechi and through them the Wolf. He was well known all over Salerno and he had neighbours, as well as those who observed him in the streets he used frequently.

Osmond de Vertin was not so well supplied with men that he had enough to place permanent guards on his doorway or that of anyone else suspected of fermenting trouble, but he had his informants and, by their very nature, these would be people unknown to Guaimar, and just as importantly, neither he nor Ephraim knew how numerous they were.

He and his sister must be prepared to walk out of the door of the humble gatehouse they now occupied with not a single possession. Any preparations they made would be observed, indeed, he did not know if they could trust even the servants they employed – like Berengara's maid and his own attendant valet – those who supplied their food, the people who cleaned their house or the priest that confessed their sins, and he would, by following the instructions he had to burn every note from the Jew, cause some suspicions to be raised.

...You may hear it said, it could be whispered to you by someone loyal to your house, that your intended flight is known about, that the horses and supplies being gathered at your father's old monastery are no secret. They are not to me, since I have arranged for them in your name and likewise sent ahead to various places on the route to the Apennines to arrange accommodation. Thus, it is to be hoped that the Normans will be guarding the routes out of the city to the east, while you are choosing the northern path skirting Capua...

He had to admire Ephraim then; even in a letter to him he would not break the true method intended. The Jew was not even prepared to trust his messenger!

Matters are in hand for the night of the new moon in

January, when there will be little light. A man you have never before seen will come to you to lead you, and he will ask you to follow the Star of David. Do as he says.

In the days before their flight, various souls came to the villa and each one took away with them a bundle. No words were exchanged, just a note saying to trust this fellow, which left Guaimar with no choice; he had no idea where their possessions, packed by his own hand without even telling their personal servants, were being taken, or how Ephraim would get them aboard a boat. There were his clothes, but more importantly there were the dresses his sister would need, those carefully stored in chests for the day she returned to become once more a lady of the court. These she would certainly need; there was little point in turning up in Bamberg with her in rags when she needed to make an impression.

'Brother.' Guaimar, who had been looking out onto the street trying to work out who might be informing on them, turned in surprise to see Berengara standing with a velvet bag in her hand. 'I have brought you my jewels.'

'Your jewels?'

'Those few I managed to smuggle from the Castello when we were thrown out.'

Looking at her, he saw in those great almond eyes the distress the mention of the name of their old home still caused.

'What would I want with your jewels?'

'You are, I think, going away.'

Guaimar had told her nothing, his reasoning being that she might be alarmed at the risk, but then it occurred to him that he had been as close mouthed as the Jew. Had he kept his plans to himself from fear that she might inadvertently disclose them? He walked over to where she stood and kissed her on the forehead.

'Do you think I would go away without telling you?'

'I would say that you might have to.'

'And leave you to face the wrath of Pandulf?'

Her face puckered up with determination. 'If I must face that then let it be. Our father must be avenged.'

'My word, sister,' said Guaimar, chucking her chin, 'you are valiant.'

The voice became a hiss, and the eyes actually blazed in a way Guaimar had not seen since they used to scrap as children. 'Do not seek to belittle me!'

'I don't,' he replied, surprised and well aware that, even if it was unintended, that was exactly what he had done.

'Then take these jewels and sell them. There is a Jew near the marketplace called Ephraim who will give you money in exchange.'

'How do you know of a Jew by the marketplace?'

'Bricee told me.'

'And why did your maid tell you that?'

'The town is full of rumours that you intend to flee to Byzantium to seek assistance to get rid of Pandulf.'

'Is it?'

'So Bricee said!' she insisted. 'She also said the only way you will get clear is with a bribe. Everyone knows if you want the services of a Norman you buy it.' She pressed the bag towards his hands. 'Do so with these.'

About to tell her she was wrong, Guaimar stopped himself, but in doing so he wondered at what he had become. Ever since he had spoken with Kasa Ephraim he had been forced to examine the past both of himself and his house. If his father had business with the Jew that gave him funds, what were they for? Secret pleasures, possibly, but more likely his dealings provided money with which he could bribe people. To find out what? Local dissent, information of plots being hatched, even the placing of spies in the households of his perceived enemies and, even more troubling, those he called friends. What would Berengara say to find out the father she thought a saint was almost certainly very far from that?

He loved his sister in a way that was not possible of expression, and he also felt a duty to protect her that went with his position as her elder sibling, but he must hold to caution, as surely his father would have done. Could he trust her not to let something slip to Bricee, a woman who had been with the family for decades and had served Berengara as almost a surrogate parent when her own mother died? He could not even tell her she was coming with him, so he held out his hand and took the jewels.

'Thank you.'

'It is no more than my duty,' Berengara replied, with a determination that made her look younger, not older, than she was. For a long time, Guaimar had not seen that face; it was one he remembered well, of the sister who never hesitated to stick out her tongue at him just after it appeared.

'If you need directions to the Jew,' she added, 'Bricee will give them to you.'

Again he questioned what he was turning into, for he knew, as a subterfuge, he would indeed ask her maid that question.

The last note from Kasa Ephraim came two days before the new moon, and told him that all was in place, while he was off to Capua to present himself to Prince Pandulf, with the hope of becoming the Wolf's man of veiled and discreet business. He did not say that, when the absence of Guaimar and Berengara became known, there could be no safer place to be than in the man's actual lair. The last two figures on the note were an eight and a bell, to tell him at what time to expect his messenger to call.

Osmond de Vertin, on the night of the new moon, as soon as it was dark, sneaked a troop of his men out of a side gate of the Castello de Arechi. He was in high spirits, for he not only knew that Guaimar was going to seek to get away, but he knew, from a variety of informants, precisely the route he intended to take. He could have stopped him at his own front door, but he decided not only to let him get to the monastery and the ready pack animals assembled there, but to be on his way.

The Norman wanted to take him when there was no doubt about his intentions, on the road leading to the main pass through the mountains to the east, and with all the possessions he had so carefully accumulated. There would be no return to Salerno for the snotty little swine. Osmond would take him straight on to Capua, to be handed over to Prince Pandulf and his torturers, so that the names of all who had assisted in this undertaking could be dragged out of him.

As he rode ahead of his men under a starlit sky, he wondered what reward Pandulf would think appropriate for his success. He knew in his mind that, if asked to name what he desired, he had a ready answer. Guaimar would die, either under torture or in a deep dungeon in years to come. His sister, however, would still be alive. She was young, beautiful already, and would ripen superbly under the hand of a lusty husband. That would, to the Norman captain who had once carried her as a child, be a fitting reward.

* * *

The man who came at the appointed time said only the password and nothing else. Guaimar had told his sister only minutes before that they were leaving, and when she spoke of packing something suitable he told her she would find the chests that held her better clothes empty, and why. The look she gave him then was one to make Guaimar uncomfortable, which made him realise that Berengara had grown in more than just a physical sense: she was developing a deductive brain as well; she knew he had deceived her.

They exited in their cloaks, hoods up, to streets that were dark and deserted – people lived by the sun and mostly slept when it was no longer light. Their guide walked just enough paces ahead to be visible but, as Guaimar knew, also far enough to disappear if they were intercepted by the Norman garrison. A tallow wad showed in the odd window, but mostly they made their way, moving downhill to the port, through a silent city.

Was it quieter than usual? There seemed to be no revellers out at all, and Guaimar knew that was unusual. Had he not been a party to many a noisy drinking bout with his friends in the taverns that lined the edge of the port when still the ducal heir? He found he was sweating, and he knew it was brought on by fear. Odd, when he took Berengara's hand to reassure her, it, unlike his own, was dry.

Having reached the edge of the quay, their guide

stopped and indicated they should go down in a decked boat bobbing on the very slight swell that came through the harbour entrance. There was no one on deck to greet them; indeed the boat seemed deserted. The last thing their guide did was to press a very small purse into Guaimar's hand.

'To use when you get ashore in Romania.' Then he was gone.

Lord in Heaven, Guaimar thought, even this fellow does not know where we are going. It then occurred to him, given the cunning of the Jew, that perhaps he did not know either. There was little headroom under the deck and no sign of anyone to sail the boat, which induced in the young man a feeling of impending betrayal. Was all this an elaborate ploy; would they sit there till daylight only to find the quayside lined with Normans when the sun came up?

Time passed with neither he nor his sister having any idea of how long they sat in the dark, but it was hours, time in which Berengara prayed in a soft voice. Then there was shouting, faint but clear, the noise of many voices. The sound of bare feet on the deck above their heads, as well as the way the vessel dipped and moved, made Guaimar's heart contract with terror, but then he heard the faint creak of ropes, along with whispered instructions and he understood the crew were aboard, having waited a long time to make sure that he and his sister had not been followed; that way, if they were discovered and exposed, they could claim ignorance.

A lantern was lit, which cast a sliver of light into the space where they were huddled, and immediately after the whole boat began to rock and creak as it left the shore. All the two young escapees could do was imagine every possible scenario. A crack made them jump until Guaimar whispered he thought it was a sail taking the wind. The fishing fleet must be on its way out, and each would have a lantern at the stern. At the end of the mole there was a permanent Norman guard, but this happened every morning except Sunday. Were they too bored to look very hard?

Lots of shouting went on around them, faint through the planking but raised voices nonetheless, then from above their heads the voices of the men in whose hands their fate lay, shouting insults to the guards on the mole, of the sort that were returned in kind with no hint of rancour on either side. Berengara fell against him as they hit the first real wave, and as the boat began to rock up and down, he whispered in her ear.

'We are safe now, sister, we are safe.'

That was the first time she retched, but not the last.

Osmond de Vertin began to fret as the night wore on, then as the grey light began to tinge the sky he began to shout in frustration. By the time the sun was above the Apennines he was raving at his men, cursing them for fools. He had already seen that the undulating road from Salerno, though full of carts going into town with produce, was barren of folk leaving. Mounted and riding furiously, he made for the monastery, to find the monks at lauds, having had their breakfast. There was no sign of Guaimar, his sister, or a loaded packhorse and the response of the inhabitants to his threatening questions met with looks of ignorance.

Osmond was no fool; he would not have risen to his present position if he had been a dolt. He was well aware that he had been tricked. First he sent off messengers to Salerno; a party was to set off north, and seek information, with the instruction not to be gentle.

'Demand of the peasants if they have seen Guaimar; if they so much as shrug, whip them till they speak.'

Sensing the monks were secretly enjoying his discomfort, he bade his men dig a pit and start a fire with the monastery's own logs. The Abbot, a venerable old man, was seized, then roped about his feet, his waist and his chest, before a lance was rammed through the ropes and he was lifted by two strong men who advanced with him suspended towards the now blazing logs.

What could he tell them? No horses had come from the old duke's heir, nor any clothing. Osmond was incensed enough not to care; to him the old man represented all those educated swine who could read and write and talk in high Latin while laughing at his ignorance. He ordered him seared, and the two men holding the lance moved him over the flames, which immediately began to burn his flesh amid his hellish screams.

Half the watching monks were on their knees praying, the rest were crying for mercy for their Abbot. Osmond signalled that he should be taken away from the blaze before the ropes burnt through, not from compassion but so that he could be held up to see what had been done to his mortified flesh. There was his face burnt beyond that which could be recognised, his simple garments scorched off his body to reveal flesh blistered and peeling from his aged frame. Was he dead? He might as well be; there was no recovery from such mutilation.

'Every one of you will face this, unless I get an answer,' he bellowed. 'And if you die in the flames I am sure that Christ will welcome you into the Kingdom of Heaven, for you will have faced the fires of Hell on this earth.'

It was one of the servants who spoke up then, coming forward at a grovel, to say that various people had come from Salerno over the past weeks with horses, but they had taken them away again. Others had come with bundles of clothing, as gifts to the monastery, which were still lying untouched.

'Show me,' Osmond barked.

He took his sword to the wrapping, and being sackcloth it parted with little effort. The clothes inside were the garments of a rich woman, dresses and the like, of velvet, one or two trimmed with ermine. For Osmond de Vertin it was like a stab at his hopes; when the servant, ordered to hold them up, did so, he recognised the garments that had once graced the sylphlike young body of the girl, now grown to woman, he had decided days before would be his wife.

The servant should not have looked at him questioningly, nor sought to smile in the hope of reward. Osmond saw it as mocking, and with a scream he stuck his sword into the poor fellow's ribs, and hauled hard to pull it up through his heart.

By the time he got back to Salerno, having left the roofs of the monastery buildings blazing behind him, and the Abbot dead, he knew that Guaimar and his sister had got away, maybe going north without using roads, probably by sea. The fishermen came in with their catch for the day to be questioned, and even with two who had protested hanging from a warehouse gantry, and the entire day's catch floating in the harbour, the others, kneeling and pleading for mercy, had nothing they could tell him.

One fellow was held upside down above the harbour

waters and interrogated about the chances of catching a sailing boat that had been at sea since daybreak. Despite being ducked and near drowned half a dozen times he still insisted that the chances of finding a boat at sea were close to impossible. He survived, wet but breathing, too stupid to know that another answer might have saved him his ordeal, without knowing how lucky he was.

It was the way his men looked at him that really troubled Osmond. Normally respectful, they were now giving him the glances a fellow throws to a dead man. He would have to go north himself and tell Pandulf what had happened. Could he stop at Aversa and plead with his old leader to intercede, and if he did what could Rainulf say to the Wolf to assuage his wrath? The Normans were careful never to sacrifice each other, but was this an error too great to forgive? And there had been bad blood in Aversa at Osmond's desertion; would Rainulf Drengot, even if he begged on his knees, just throw him to the Wolf, for Pandulf to do with what he liked?

CHAPTER SEVEN

The plain stretched as far as the eye could see, flat and fertile, dotted with small windmills, the strips of cultivation full of people working to plant their spring crops. The two riders on the road between the River Volturno and Naples attracted attention, but what looks did come their way were far from friendly; to the people toiling in fields they were clearly not of their kind and the differences extended beyond mere occupation. They were tall, blue-eyed and fair in a world where the people were generally dark, small and swarthy. That height difference was more obvious when they dismounted to walk their horses and they towered, one of them excessively so, over those with whom their animals shared a trough.

Any greetings offered were ignored and not just because they were in barely comprehensible Latin.

Habit made the peasants of Campania cautious, and these giants were armed with big swords and sharp knives; if the locals carried anything they were farming tools. Close to, it could be seen that the faces of these strangers did not take well to the climate, and in places the reddened skin had peeled. Both kept a leaf in their mouth to protect them from a burning overhead sun that would blister an exposed lower lip.

To look at the horses was to know these men. Those on which they rode had the height and fine lines of an animal bred for swift movement. The first-led horses were sleek and well cared for, those behind a last pair of pack animals. As well as the slung pouches containing the riders' possessions, there were lances, helmets and shields strapped to the animals' sides, the whole assembly identifying them as men whose trade was oppression. The one word spat out was never said in their hearing, only when they had passed by: Normans.

Their destination was a square tower of white stone rising out of the waves of heat that made the ground ripple. Soon strips of farmland gave way to green pasture, and endless paddocks full of horses, which were the subject of close scrutiny, for the de Hauteville brothers had grown up surrounded by equines in all their forms. The railed fields each had a thatched byre into which the animals could retire from rain or, as they had now, the mid-morning sun. Haystacks were liberally dotted between these paddocks and the air was full of that sweet smell of piss and dung, which was ever present where horses were kept in numbers.

Past the paddocks, running towards the tower, there were lines of round huts with pointed thatched roofs set around a huge barn; the inhabitants, if there were any, inside in the shade, that is, with the exception of the tribe of near-naked children who stopped playing to look up at these passing strangers. The cries they emitted brought to the door of one hut a short, round, black-haired woman.

'We seek a knight by the name of Rainulf Drengot,' said William, in Latin.

The response was a lazy hand waved in the direction of the tower. It did not get them a greeting of any kind, nor a smile: if anything the look was one of suspicion from a woman with hard eyes and little humour. Long before the sun had caught metal atop the castellated donjon, lance tips most like, and looking hard into the glare, now they were near, the brothers could see the helmets of those set to watch out for approaching danger, men who must have first seen them, on so flat a landscape, a good half a league away.

The sound of clacking wood and grunting came to them as they cleared the huts and that revealed a large, fenced-off and sand-filled manège equipped with low poles set up as jumps, some followed by deep ditches, and thick upright baulks of timber showing

the cuts where they had been smitten by hundreds of
sword blows. Lance targets stood at the end of long
balancing poles, while in a line shields stood at the
height they would be when held by a foot soldier, next
to a circular wood target marked with roundels. In the
middle, two lines of tough-looking men were practising
swordplay with round wooden staves.

Activity ceased as they rode past, every eye
examining these newcomers, stares that were returned,
but they did not stop, instead riding on to the square
tower. Close to, this donjon did not look so white: the
stones were streaked with the effects of age, moss was
thick at the base, the mortar at the joins of the blocks
was crumbling and there was some blackening around
the door to show that at some time a fire had been lit
at the base in an attempt to burn out the defenders.
This was a fortress that had stood for tens of years,
perhaps hundreds, perhaps long enough to have once
been occupied by Roman legionaries.

The heavily studded door, topped by a carved
armorial device, was now open; attack the place and
the ramp that led to it would disappear inside, while
the door would be slammed shut. Several floors below
the living quarters of the defenders it would be the
well that guaranteed a steady supply of water, stalls
for horses and a byre for animals which would be
kept alive to eat, just above them the storerooms full
of hay, oats, pulses and peas, enough to keep fed the

knights who would man the walls.

As the brothers dismounted a figure appeared in that doorway, which immediately brought half a dozen lean hunting hounds out from under the ramp where they had been dozing, not least because the fellow observing them had in his hand a piece of leg bone on which he had been gnawing. As broad as he was tall, in a fine surcoat decorated with a coat of arms, the man eyed them up through what appeared to be slits in his deep-purple face, making both brothers conscious of how they must appear: weary, dust covered and in garments that, after five months of travelling, were close to threadbare.

'William and Drogo de Hauteville,' William said in French, his voice rasping in a dry throat, 'seeking to take service with Rainulf Drengot.'

The bone was tossed aside, which sent the dogs scurrying to fight over it as the fellow responded in the same tongue. 'You are Norman?'

'We are.'

'From?'

'Hauteville-le-Guichard, where our father has his demesne.'

'I do not know it.'

'It is in the Contentin.'

William was aware that some of the men they had passed had left the manège to follow them and were gathering to listen to the exchange. Though he did not turn to look he heard the growl in his brother's throat and assumed he had. Drogo, amongst his other faults, was inclined to brawl, almost without cause being given and quite impervious to numbers, so he whispered a caution to tell him to stay still.

'A land of rough folk, the Contentin, I'm told,' said the fellow at the top of the ramp. 'Ill-mannered and quarrelsome.'

'Others may have told you that it is a land that breeds good fighting men.'

'What others would they be?'

'Duke Robert thought us the best.'

'How can I ask Duke Robert? He is dead.'

'God rest his soul.'

William crossed himself as he replied; they had heard in Rome that their one-time liege lord had died on his way back from the Holy Land. They had also heard that the whole of Normandy was in danger of disorder over the succession. It made no difference to him and Drogo; they were too far south and too strapped for the means of existence to think of turning back.

'My father, brothers and I fought under his banner at Bessancourt when he aided the King of the Franks to bring his rebellious brother to heel.'

'Before which, I am told, he named his bastard son as his successor.'

Even if he had worries about how such things might

affect his family, it was not the way William wanted this discussion to go. 'If you know of that battle you will know that we Normans won it. Henry, King of the Franks, could not have done so unaided. The men of the Contentin were in the front rank.'

'Duke Robert was a fool to name his bastard as his successor and an even bigger fool to die while he was still a child.' The man waited to see if William would respond to that, in fact, display his own feelings on the matter; he waited in vain. 'So once you fought for Duke Robert and now you would like to fight for me?'

'If you are Rainulf, yes. We were told by those who have returned to Normandy that we would be welcome.'

'More than welcome,' hissed Drogo. 'Embraced.'

Rainulf looked over their heads at the men to the rear. 'What do you say? Shall we try out these Contentin ruffians?'

'Try out?' demanded Drogo.

Rainulf looked past William to his brother, not in the least upset, it seemed, by Drogo's angry glare.

'Many men come here from our homeland and claim they are doughty fighters. Most are, some are not. It is best that we find such things out before our lives might be forfeit for an error of judgement. Behind you, in the manège, we can carry out all the tests we need to see what you are made of, both on foot and mounted. So, let us see your mettle.'

William was surprised. 'Now?'

'I can think of no better time.'

'Our horses need rest.'

Rainulf smiled for the first time, but it was not warm. 'If you can assure me that when I fight I will do so rested, then I will let you have that. But if you ask those fellows behind you they will tell you that Campania is a place of snares and ambush, where trust is a virtue that can get you killed, a place where a morning friend can be an afternoon enemy. So, it is best to be ready to do battle in an instant. You have your swords, and I see your lances and shields. All you need do is don hauberks and helmets and move your saddles to your destriers.'

'A little time, perhaps till the sun cools?'

Rainulf shook his head. 'Prepare to show us your quality, or prepare to ride out of here.'

By the time they had donned their mail and helmets, and moved the high-formed saddles to the destriers, Rainulf Drengot had arranged for another eight riders to be made ready. There was no need to explain to a Norman knight what was required – the basic fighting unit, the source of the success of their cavalry arm, was a convoy of ten lances which, unlike the mounted knights of other forces, operated as a disciplined unit and could be multiplied by joining several convoys together.

Drogo and William were separated. On one side of each was the shield of an unfamiliar neighbour, on the other their own shields touched that of another rider, neither of whom looked in their direction. Like the brothers, their animals were especially bred for the task, steady and fearless; they would have been constantly put through their paces against false shield walls so that facing the real thing became familiar.

Back in Hauteville-le-Guichard there was a valley field where they had practised these very same skills. Neighbours had often come to joust and train just as the de Hautevilles had gone to them. No festival gathering at the nearby cathedral town of Coutances had been complete without a show of equine and armed skill that, with spirited young men pitted against each other in what was supposed to be mock combat, had quite often descended into a brawl that drew copious blood.

On top of that there were the endemic disputes with other landholders, the containment of uprisings against ducal authority, on whose side Tancred always placed his duty, and the task entrusted to all the knights in their area when the bells sounded in alarm: the defence of the coast of their part of the Contentin; there was nothing unfamiliar in what they were being asked to do.

William and Drogo had one major problem: their destriers had not been in training for all the months they had been on the road, so they were skittish and harder to control than normal when harnessed, and set next to unfamiliar mounts they did what all horses do: tails stiff and high, stepping like dancers, they tried to assert dominance and that did not go unchallenged, so there was much biting and some flying hooves that, had they made contact with human flesh, would have at the very least broken a bone. Strong hands and many a hard slap on the neck were required to keep them under control and get them into line, and even then they were disinclined to settle.

Thus their performance was far from perfect as they manoeuvred, riding from one end of the manège to the other, first at a walk, then at a trot and finally at a canter. At the command all ten lances should have turned left or right as one, or reversed their course and retreated in unison. The best that could be said was that it was untidy. Norman cavalry could pretend flight, a tactic that often broke an otherwise solid line of pikemen who could not resist the urge to pursue and once the defence was fractured the Normans would swiftly reform and attack again. An attempt at that left William and Drogo lagging behind.

Reformed and cursing, the next manoeuvre went better as a touch of fatigue made their mounts more malleable. The whole convoy attacked the shield wall, first with lances couched, each one hitting a guard of wood and leather in a tattoo of sound before turning to the right and rising on their stirrups so that their shields protected their flank. They could then employ their swords to smash at the same targets and, being upright, their blows were delivered with great force. To follow came the same attack but this time with lances raised above their heads. Again they stood upright, controlling their mounts with their thighs, shields held forward with reins in the same hand, while they jabbed over the shield wall at straw bales, which represented the holders of the line or those who made up the second rank.

In a third attack targets had replaced those bales and they were required to accurately cast their lances as spears. The final mounted acts were individual, hacking at those great baulks of timber as they rode past or aiming their lances at the hanging targets, the one and only time they put their horses into a gallop. By the time that was over the horses were near to being winded.

'Dismount,' shouted Drengot.

Weary and sweating, William and Drogo complied, aware of two things. What their father had told them about fighting in southern climes was true, for he had fought the Moors in Spain to keep open the pilgrimage route to Compostela. Wearing a hauberk, cowl and a metal helmet made a man sweat copiously. The second was, though they were not going to openly admit it, that they were tired and near as rusty in battle practice as their mounts.

'Let's see your sword work,' Drengot ordered, signalling forward a couple of big fellows with the round staves that were used for practice.

'Should they not be mailed too?' asked William.

The reply was more of a sneer than an answer. 'I'm not testing them, fellow, I know they can fight.'

Wearing only padded leather jerkins the opponents would have an advantage in freedom of movement denied to the brothers, and that showed quickly as they feinted with their staves, only to draw the pair forward, and to a gale of laughter they cracked them both across the helmet, making their heads ring.

'Step back, Drogo,' William ordered as their opponents attempted another ploy to embarrass them, this time trying to thwack their shins.

They had fought together since they were boys, as much with each other as anyone else, and they knew one another intimately. William de Hauteville was not obeyed because he was the older brother; he was obeyed because Drogo knew he was twice the fighter in combat than he was himself. In unison they took two paces back and created enough space to draw on the men intent on making them look like fools.

'Now!' was the single word of command and the two mailed brothers came forward again as one, staves swinging right and left which forced their opponents to parry, before the weight of the blows then obliged them to step back. A man advancing generally has the advantage of one retreating and Drengot's mercenaries were forced to defend themselves. They were no fools either and soon they made enough telling sweeps to hold their ground. It then became a contest of strength as the staves were swung, under, over, right and left, with occasional jabs, four pairs of eyes locked on each other seeking to detect where the next sweep was coming from.

'Keep going, brother,' Drogo called; he loved nothing more than fighting, if you excluded bedding women, a pair of traits that had caused them no end of trouble on their travels.

William barely heard him, he was breathing so heavily, while concentrating on his opponent, a shrewd swordsman. What told in the end was the sheer size and muscular power of the oldest of the de Hautevilles, for having manoeuvred his opponent into a position where he had to hold his weapon horizontal in defence, the downward stroke of William's weapon had behind it so much weight that he smashed the stave in two.

Shocked, his opponent quickly stepped back out of harm's way. William did not desist, he turned on Drogo's man and with cruel intent and his brother's assistance drove the fellow to his knees. Unaware of a loss of control, Drogo had raised his stave high and was about to seek to smash the fellow's skull, when Drengot's barking voice brought him back to the present.

'Enough!'

Slowly he walked towards them, they leaning now on their staves and sucking air into aching lungs.

'So, you can fight, you Contentin ruffians, at least on foot, though I think you are dolts mounted.'

'Our horses are rusty,' Drogo insisted. 'Give us a few days to train them up and you will think otherwise.'

'Perhaps,' Drengot replied, with the air of a man who did not want to be convinced. 'I will tell you how it is here. We are mercenaries and when we are not fighting we are training to fight. You will be paid whatever you do and allowed to plunder as long as you don't steal that which is mine by right. If I say kill, you do not hesitate, nor do you take the life of anyone who might provide ransom. I have the right of life and death over you. Serve me well and you will prosper, betray me and I will strip the skin off your bodies with hot pincers. Is that a bargain you accept?'

'Yes,' gasped William, removing his helmet and woollen cowl to reveal hair plastered with sweat.

'If you die I will bury you with honour, and take steps to let your family know so they can say a mass for your soul. If you lose a horse or equipment through carelessness you must replace it, if you lose it in my service I will provide you with a mount from my stud or a weapon from my store.'

'Would it be possible to have a drink?' asked an equally sweating Drogo.

Rainulf indicated over his shoulder to some servants who had come to watch and a ladle of water was brought from a covered barrel, both brothers supping greedily.

'Go to the armourer tomorrow and get him to punch some holes in the rear of your helmets. You cannot fight in this climate without it, or your head will fry. And always wear a bandana underneath to keep the sweat out of your eyes, otherwise you will be so misted up you will be bound to die from being blinded.'

'Anything else?' asked William.

'Yes. Get out of that mail.'

'We need to wash.'

'There is a stream fifty paces from the back of my donjon. You might wish to cool yourself in its waters.'

'We must look to our horses.'

'It is good that you look to the comfort of your mounts before your own. Perhaps you are true Normans after all.'

For the first time Rainulf Drengot favoured them with a genuine smile as he shouted to the servants behind him, who had fetched the water, pointing to the now hitched but still sweat-streaked destriers. 'Get these animals seen to, groomed, fed and watered, but have care which paddock you put them in.'

'We too have not taken sustenance since sun up,' Drogo said.

'Then I bid you enter my dwelling, for there is food and wine on my table.'

'Thank you, my Lord,' William replied.

'I have a desire to hear of the fight at Bessancourt.'

That was as much of an acceptance as they were going to get. William nodded and put his arm round the shoulder of Drogo. 'Journey's end, brother.'

'Thank God, Gill, you have no idea how sick I am of nothing but your company.'

CHAPTER EIGHT

They were shown to one of the round, earthen-floored huts, an empty one, in which two more women, with similar colouring to the one they had first seen, were busy stuffing palliasses with fresh straw, prior to putting them on two low, wooden-framed cots; apart from those the place was bare of furnishing, but someone had brought the packs off their horses. Seeing Drogo's eyes drawn to the rear of one of the woman bending over, William spoke loudly.

'It might be best to find if she's already got a man, brother, before you exercise your charms. We've done enough fighting for one day and a dip in cool water will do you more good.'

'Allow me to judge what I want to dip,' Drogo replied, reaching out to stroke the woman's posterior. The speed with which she spun and slapped him, and the weight of that slap, made Drogo wince and William laugh.

'What makes you think she needs a man?' Drogo complained, rubbing a cheek made even more red than that achieved by the work of the sun, this as the woman went back to stuffing straw. 'If we'd had to fight her this day we'd be lying in the sand. So, how do you find Rainulf?'

'A hard taskmaster, I think,' William replied.

With some care the two women, task finished, manoeuvred their way round the walls to the exit, leaving the brothers to remove their hauberks. The place had been occupied before; there were nails hammered into the walls on which to hang possessions, and these soon had on them helmets, shields and mail, with both stripping to the waist, removing leather jerkins that had become almost as heavy as the mail, so filled were they with perspiration.

'That was tough going.'

'We're flabby,' William insisted. 'Properly battle hard we would have seen off those two in no time.'

'They should have beaten us.'

William scowled. 'They didn't because they were not good enough. Given we were not good enough either, that bodes well. Now let's wash.'

Drogo wrinkled his nose and glanced around the walls. 'I wonder if I can get one of these to myself. Then I won't have to smell your armpits all the time.'

'I hope you do, brother, because your grunting while you are belabouring some poor wench is hard to sleep through.'

Drogo grinned. 'It's the screams of pleasure that keep you awake.'

'Pleasure? I always thought they were cries of pain and regret.'

Washed and in smocks that were, if not fresh, at least not more worn than a week, the pair found the paddock where their mounts had been put to graze, pleased that they seemed to be doing so peacefully, and not in any way challenging any of the other horses. Gentle calls brought them to the rail and they could see they had been well groomed too, the dust of the day brushed out of their hides. Both had words to say to them, the kind of endearments even hardened warriors make to animals they have known since they were foals. Neither brother was soft about horses; they had a purpose and they must fulfil it or be replaced, but a bond between rider and mount was an aid to the way they behaved when they were required to perform the duties for which they had been bred.

'I think they will relish a chance to stay in one place,' said William.

'They and us, brother,' was the reply, as he nuzzled his head into his horse's neck. 'Now I think we should go and attend our new master.'

'We're mercenaries now, Drogo. Rainulf is no more than our paymaster.'

The sun was well past its zenith by the time they were ready to climb the ramp in the square tower, yet it was pleasant to enter a cool chamber where the walls were covered with tapestries to make gentle what was bare stone. The place had about it an air of luxury and there was a pair of servants too, who produced bowls of water in which they could wash their hands, as well as cloths with which to dry them; which was a surprise to a pair unaccustomed to such refinements.

Rainulf, having greeted them, had gone to the head of a stout wooden table and thrown himself into a high-backed chair, from which he eyed them in silence. By the time they joined him he had emptied one goblet of wine and taken a refill, William reckoning he had just seen the source of the man's high colouring. The table had a joint of lamb half consumed, fruit in abundance and bread that, when picked up, was floppy and fresh. Drogo was first out with his knife, hacking at the meat and, once he had carved some, filling his mouth with both that and wine, watched by an amused host. William took more care, accepted a goblet of wine and drank deeply but once. His carving was careful, and the consumption of meat was accompanied by equal amounts of fruit.

He could not help but feel that something was

wrong. In his twenty years, and as the eldest son of a Norman baron, he had been a guest in many a neighbour's home, and, just as in his own, every meal was an affair of many folk and abundant food as long as the land had been fruitful; no one feasted at all when it was not. His father had also taken his heir to the nearby castles of the regional counts where in great halls the lords of those places were wont to show their wealth by feeding a multitude, down to and including their serfs.

Yet this Rainulf, with a numerous body of men in his service, had the air of a man who commonly ate alone, and at a board that would easily accommodate twenty. It could not be from lack of provisions: the fields through which they had passed that day and the one before were in his fief and they were fertile. They had seen vines aplenty, crops in abundance both in the ground and on trees, as well as plentiful sheep, pigs and cattle.

'More wine,' Rainulf said, indicating to his servants to top up his guests, one having done so for him. 'So tell me, what brought you here?'

'Is it not enough that we have come?' William replied.

'I find it helps to know something of those in my pay.'

It was Drogo, through mouthfuls of food and wine, who named one of the two paramount reasons: a patrimony too small to support the number of sons their sire had fathered.

'Neither of us hankered after the role of running a petty barony in the bocage. We have worked ploughs, we two, as well as wielded weapons.'

'So you are not running from your neighbours.'

'It is our neighbours who fear us,' William replied, 'not the other way round. But when you have carried a lance in battle, to return to husbandry is disagreeable.'

'A good enough reason,' Rainulf agreed. 'There is no other?'

Both brothers allowed themselves a small shake of the head. The other reason, which had to do with the bloodline of their mother, both William and Drogo would keep to themselves.

'The country we passed through seemed quiet,' said Drogo, the enquiry muffled by his full mouth.

'For the moment there is peace.' Seeing Drogo's face register disappointment, Rainulf laughed out loud. 'But it never stays long like that. Eighteen summers I have been here and not one has gone by without a quarrel from which I have been able to prosper. And if it is too quiet, we have ways to ensure we do not go without.'

'Such as?' asked William.

The question seemed to annoy Rainulf; his face went a deeper shade of purple and the eyes, already hard to see, seemed to slip deeper into the fold of the flesh surrounding them.

'You will discover that in time,' he rasped, holding out his goblet for a fourth refill. 'Now, tell me about Bessancourt.'

'William will do that,' Drogo insisted.

Which his brother did, for he was a good storyteller and he had, many times, told his tale coming south to willing listeners in the various pilgrims' hospices in which they had found a place to lay their heads. Rainulf interrupted occasionally to ask a pointed question or two, mostly about how the Frankish milites had performed, never without supping from his goblet, and he forced William to be quite exact in his description of how they had first retreated, then were able to reverse that and resume the attack.

'They must have been well led.'

'They were beaten,' William insisted, as the servants lit candles, mildly distracting him as he came to the end of his tale: candles cost money and he was more accustomed to smoky tallow. Whatever else Rainulf was short of – like company – it was not money.

'The enemy horse were broken and suddenly with them in flight it was clear that we had the power of decision. Duke Robert did not rush; he ensured an organised line before calling for the advance, so that the King of the Franks could be in no doubt as to the person to whom he owed his triumph. A number of the enemy pikemen formed up to defend themselves, but for all their bravery the battle was lost. We hit their line like a great rolling rock smashing a haystack.'

'That, brother, is too poetic.'

William smiled at Drogo. 'Is it? Almost the whole of those who stood to defend themselves paid with their lifeblood. Behind them panic took over as each man sought to save himself, and that included the King's rebel brother.'

'I hope he flayed him alive,' said Rainulf.

'No,' Drogo hooted, 'he made him Duke of Burgundy. He gave the Frankish half of the Vexin to Normandy for a battle that he did not need to fight.'

'Some men will forgive their brothers much.'

The look in Rainulf's hooded eyes then was a curious one, which was not helped by the way his gaze was fixed on William. 'You describe the battle well.'

'Thank you.'

'Let us hope you get a chance to do for me what you did for Duke Robert.'

Over the days that followed the brothers discovered how well organised Rainulf was: there was accommodation for up to four hundred knights, the great barn for communal eating and feasts, a proper stud to provide a steady supply of mounts, mendicant monks from the monastery at Aversa to see to the ailments of men and horses, a nursemaid equally versed in remedies to care for the women and children.

The balance of mares to stallions and good animal husbandry ensured a steady supply of foals, and extensive ditch work and careful attention to paddock numbers, fed by windmills, gave all the mounts good pasture, while the fecund fields of the Aversan plain provided fodder in abundance, the peasants taking away as rich fertiliser the dung that littered the fields.

There was a blacksmith who doubled as an armourer to maintain weapons and keep the fighting mounts shod while the Norman leader had even engaged the services of a scrivener so that anyone unlettered, wishing to send written word back to Normandy, could do so, through the auspices of a Jewish trader, who would also commute money through mysterious channels, this gained from both normal service and plunder.

Guaimar had grown to manhood in some luxury, but he had never seen anything like that which attended the family of Pierleoni. They lived in a villa that had once been the property of a wealthy Roman senator, a haven of arboreal peace in the teeming city which surrounded it. There were fountains set in mature gardens, cool, tiled and colonnaded courtyards from which to stay out of the sun, endless rooms in which to take repose and a whole tribe of hosts who could not let their legions of servants do enough for these two young unfortunates from the south. Yet the walls that faced the city of Rome had been fortified and armed retainers made sure that no one could breach the peace of this fabulously wealthy family. It was such a relief to come to this after their journey.

Sailing in a boat normally used for limited coastal trading had been damned uncomfortable out in deep waters. It had taken every wave in full measure, the bow lifting and dropping, the vessel pitching from side to side at the same time as the single sail reacted to the unsteady wind. Guaimar had been sick the first day, but had recovered; not so Berengara, who had lain below the deck the entire journey in a state of wretched distress, in the now fetid space, while her brother had sucked in fresh sea air and tried to hold conversations with the trio of taciturn Italian sailors who had helped them escape. Initially he had been fearful of them, for they looked like a bunch of cut-throats, until it finally dawned on him that the reverse was true: they were in some dread of him.

Even in clothes that had suffered from his previous confinement, he had still looked, with his build and features, like authority to these fellows, the kind of person, in Salerno, they would have avoided like the pestilence. He had assumed the Jew had paid them well for the service, and he had extracted from them the reason why they were out of sight of land – the need to avoid curiosity from boatmen from places like Naples and the various offshore islands by which, in the distance, they took their bearings.

The young man did not think it wise to point out that the mere knowledge of such places as Ponza and Palmerola, the last small island now a smudge over the stern, was telling evidence, in a boat this size, of the occupation they followed. What did they smuggle? It was not a question he could ask.

It had been a shock to find they had no possessions, not so much as a change of clothes, something Guaimar had kept from his sister; she was suffering enough. He had to assume that Ephraim had seen the necessity of using those as a blind. The purse he had been handed was far from heavy and, standing in the prow, looking north, he had worried as to how they were to clothe themselves for the onward journey to Bamberg and he had felt like a vagabond when a velvet-clad and scented representative of the Pierleoni came to the synagogue in Ostia to fetch them. His sister felt that more than he; since the age of ten she had been fastidious about her appearance.

Now, as they prepared to depart from Rome after a stay of two months, they were better dressed than they had been at home. It seemed there could be no service to which they were not privileged: clothing of the very best run up by tailors and shoemakers brought into the villa for the purpose, servants to dress their hair and attend to their skin and nails, any amount of scents with which to grace their bodies and travelling chests provided, with the ducal crest of Salerno picked out in proper colours, for their onward journey.

They had enjoyed sumptuous meals as well, and the last of these before they departed was attended by the whole extended family, including one son newly introduced, Ascletin, who would accompany them. He was only a year older than Guaimar, but already a bishop with a very high opinion of himself, loudly delivered. Toasts were proposed both to their prospects and to future prosperity. Well-mannered, Guaimar was bound to respond and thank them, and say that if the House of Salerno could ever be of use to the House of Pierleoni, then it must be taken as a given that whatever aid was requested would be provided.

'Most comforting to know, young friend,' replied the head of the house, Francisco Pierleoni. Then he turned to Berengara. 'And can I say how pleasant it has been to have a lady of your beauty grace our table.'

Berengara was maiden enough to blush at the compliment, but very slightly, for she took it as her due, and it had come from a man old enough to be her great-grandfather. The murmur of approval for the remark, from the younger males, sons, cousins and well-born adherents at the table, was more pleasing.

Francisco Pierleoni was a man of whom they had seen little, his absences explained by the very busy life he led. Guaimar had been tempted to enquire what business he had been about, but his first tentative foray had met with such a sharp rebuff that he had since desisted. He guessed that the family was deeply involved in the affairs of the City of Rome and even Guaimar knew that to be a tangled affair. There were other families in the Holy City equally rich, some more powerful than their hosts, and they were, as a matter of course, at one another's throat.

All had bands of heavily armed retainers; each one had a section of Rome, one of the hills usually, that they considered their fiefdom, populated by mobs which, for the distribution of money, would emerge from their slums to attack another rabble rioting at the behest of a rival family. Rome was a place into which flowed money from all over the Christian world. It was the home of the Papacy, that fount of enormous wealth provided by tithes, as well as splendid offerings so that masses could be said for the rich of Christendom. It was also a place rife with simony, where ecclesiastical offices were bought and sold. Inconvenient marriages could be dissolved if the payment was high enough, indulgences granted for the most terrible of sins.

So, to the great families of Rome, the holder of the office of pontiff and thus the key to the coffers was a matter of great import, the easiest way to profit – in commissions, offices and downright theft – being to have a member of your own tribe on the throne of St Peter. Opposing that were not only the other families but the cardinals and archbishops who staffed the Curia, as well as the abbots of the great monasteries.

They would wish to place in the position a man who would meet their needs, which were not always those of the flocks they claimed to represent. Finally, in that mass of conflicting interests came the Emperor of the West and no Pope could maintain an office that he did not support: try as they might, and they had tried very hard indeed, the Roman families and the high church clerics had not been able to wrest from that source of power the right of appointing whomsoever they wished.

Guaimar had been granted an audience with the present incumbent, Pope Benedict, ninth of that name, in the great Castle of St Angelo, which overlooked the Tiber. A stout fortress and well protected by the Pope's own guards, it was the only place in the city where the Pontiff could feel safe. From the noble, if impecunious, Roman family of the Tusculam, he rarely ventured out of St Angelo, for when he did so he risked being attacked by the paid mobs of the other great magnates.

The rumours surrounding Benedict were those that attached to any pope; he had not taken Holy Orders before his accession: he suffered from every carnal excess, from pederasty, through multiple concubinage, to dabbling in alchemy and black arts that involved communing with the Devil, the only certainty being that he was not a woman, given that every incumbent since the scandalous Pope Joan had been obliged to be carried head high over his cardinals to ensure his genitalia were external.

Given all these supposed sins, Benedict had turned out to be a surprisingly gentle man. He blessed Guaimar's purpose but refused to accept that the Bishopric of Salerno could not meet its obligation to the Holy See. Indeed money, or the lack of it from the duchy, had dominated the conversation. Pandulf was damned not because he was a rabid despoiler of other people's property, but because his incarceration of the Archbishop of Capua had stopped the flow of tithes from the whole of that diocese, and seriously impeded money from others.

This Pope had seemed to Guaimar a nervous fellow but, of course, having been elected, he had been subsequently deposed, twice and violently, by families who opposed his elevation, which had seen him a prisoner in his own castle. And it was obvious to Guaimar that while he presently occupied the Holy See, his grip was yet tenuous: it was quite common for the Pope, any pope, to be besieged in St Angelo or chased out of the city altogether if two or more of the Roman clans combined against a choice sanctioned by a distant emperor. Benedict might have the power of the Almighty himself at his disposal, but he had no real force he could depend on apart from his papal guards unless the great families of Rome chose to support him.

Perhaps Guaimar's Pierleoni host had been party to that! It was hard to equate this lined, benign-looking old patriarch, with his heavily lidded eyes and large Levantine nose which showed his racial antecedents, with the kind of mayhem that was endemic in the streets beyond the walls. But one only had to see him prepare to depart the villa, through heavily studded gates that would not have disgraced a stone castle, to know that he took much care for his person.

His carriage was heavy and made of thick timber; crossbowmen sat with the driver and hung on to the postillion. Armed riders went ahead with their swords unsheathed while more brought up the rear, making Guaimar wonder if he was, in this peaceful domestic setting, actually in one of the most dangerous places in the world.

'My son, Ascletin, is, as you know, to accompany you to Bamberg. I have no doubt you will be given audience with Conrad Augustus, and I also have confidence that he will listen to what you say.'

'I require him to act, sir.'

Francisco Pierleoni nodded at that, but Guaimar thought it was less than wholehearted. Conrad could not march an army south without passing through

Rome. Was that a welcome prospect for his host, given the Western Emperor was the final arbiter of who sat on the throne of St Peter?

'In your discussions with him he may ask you for your impression of my family.'

'They will, sir, be wholly approving.'

'I would particularly ask you to recommend to Conrad my son. He will, of course, meet with Augustus himself, on family and other business, but a word of praise from a Duke of Salerno...'

'I am not yet that.'

The response was quite sharp; there was steel beneath that benevolent exterior.

'You are, young man, despite the actions of the usurper. In short, you are the legitimate holder of the title, the holder of an imperial fief, which makes you the equal of those who have raised Conrad Augustus to his pre-eminence. He will listen to what you say. Your words, for all you are a young man, will carry weight.'

The old man stood, and everyone else did likewise. 'You depart in the morning, and I will not see you after this. May God speed your journey and attend your purpose.'

'Thank you, sir,' said Guaimar, as the Patriarch Pierleoni smiled at Berengara's curtsy.

'And, when you return to Salerno, you will say, for me, a welcome to an old friend who has brought you to my house.'

Was it part of their religion, Guaimar wondered, to
keep secret everything? The old man would not even
use the name of Kasa Ephraim in his own house, and
to a guest who knew him well.

The convoy of coaches that departed next morning
was in itself impressive. Berengara had been allotted
a conveyance of her own, with two maids to attend
to her needs. In front of that, Guaimar and Ascletin
travelled in the kind of coach used by the Pierleoni
father, and it was just as well protected for between
them sat a small chest full of money. Before them
those mounted men were there to clear a route
through the teeming streets, while at the rear, in front
of the armed retainers who rode guard, was a heavily
laden cart bearing all they now possessed, plus the
son's baggage, as well as gifts for the Emperor and
the various court officials that attended upon Conrad
Augustus.

As they made their way through the streets leading
to one of the great gates that would take them north,
they passed ancient temples now dedicated as churches,
and buildings falling into ruin as the stones were
stolen by the populace; Ascletin was busy distributing
small coins to an endless series of grasping hands, the
owners of which, out of sight, called out a blessing and
a hope that he would one day occupy the office of the
Bishop of Rome.

If Guaimar was in any doubt as to what he was supposed to ask Conrad Augustus, these outpourings of pious anticipation in return for money, accompanied by the look Ascletin gave him, dispelled it.

CHAPTER NINE

CHAPTER NINE

A little more than a week passed before William de Hauteville's fellow mercenaries began to avoid him in one-on-one fights in the training area. He was there first every morning, working with a pair of heavy rocks he had found to rebuild his strength to that which it had been when he had left the family home, and that was formidable. Drogo was hard to beat, his brother near to impossible, susceptible only to a piece of clever guile, and even then his opponent had to be lucky. For such a big man, half a hand taller than anyone else in Rainulf's band, he moved with grace and speed on foot, and with deadly control mounted; his destrier having also been put endlessly through its paces so that it, too, had been brought back to peak performance.

Drogo had caused a different set of problems,

and since unsupervised fighting with weapons was forbidden in a society of high-tempered young men, it was his fists of which they came to be cautious. Usually jolly and full of tart good humour, he was nevertheless easily slighted, this younger brother, ever ready to take umbrage and throw a telling punch without warning. But it was his attitude to the womenfolk in the camp that touched many a raw nerve: he saw them as common property; his confrères did not!

Most of the men had a local concubine to look after them, and several had bred children. It was galling the lack of respect Drogo showed these women, waylaying them in his heavily accented Latin and seeming to seek their favours, acts which were not always unwelcome, for he was a handsome devil with a beguiling smile. Not that their own men respected them: the women they kept were as good as slaves, but they were damned if another was going to be allowed to treat them with regard.

Rainulf had just over three hundred lances under his command, split into three companies, each with its own captain, and it was telling the way none of these men were overkeen to have the brothers under their command, seeing in them a threat rather than an asset: in William someone with an innate ability to lead others, someone who might usurp their position rather than enhance it, for if no one was keen to do mock battle with him, they found him easy to deal with otherwise, while Drogo could cause internal squabbles.

Rainulf still trained himself, so he could ensure that others stuck to their task, but it was clear he was past the actual prime of his fighting life. He too had once been the best; he could not have risen to lead these men if he had not, and it was with mixed feelings that he watched the way the men he commanded began to naturally defer to William de Hauteville, rather than to those he appointed to lead the companies.

'Send him away,' said Odo de Jumiège, Rainulf's senior captain, a much scarred veteran and second in command of his force. 'His brother too.'

'You fear him?'

'I think perhaps you should fear him, Rainulf.'

'I wonder. He seems to have no side to him.'

'None he is showing now. What he will be like in time is harder to say.'

'Perhaps we should test him.'

'How?'

'That is easy, Odo. I will make him responsible for his brother's behaviour. If he turns out to be more loyal to his blood than to me, it will mean he cannot be fully trusted.'

There had been no more private dining with Rainulf – in fact there had been few words exchanged since that first night – and William had discovered that he kept his men, even his captains, at a certain arm's length, perhaps to underline the fact that the service they gave was moneyed not feudal. Nor did Rainulf reside in that square tower, using it only as a place from which to command his forces; he lived in a more sumptuous villa on the edge of Aversa, all marble, murals and mosaics. This he shared with his much younger wife, Pandulf's niece, in what was said to be a stormy association.

Given they trained and ate with the men, some of whom had been in Campania for years, William and Drogo soon learnt about the world into which they had ridden as well as the man who commanded them. Rainulf too had come south with an elder brother, one Gilbert, who had been killed at a great battle on the field of Cannae in Apulia. There the Normans and their Lombard paymasters, who were fighting to gain independence, had suffered the same fate at the hands of a great Byzantine host as the Roman legions had suffered at the hands of Hannibal of Carthage.

Before Cannae, the Norman mercenaries, faced with Greek or Lombard opponents, had always been victorious; not this time. Constantinople deployed against them not only a good general with a substantial army, but a weapon equally as potent in battle as the Normans: the Eastern Emperor's Varangian Guard, men from the land of Kiev Rus, of the same Norse stock as themselves who, unlike the opponents they normally faced, did not break or flee, but stood their ground and used the great axes, which were their principal weapon, to deadly effect.

Chastened, the Normans had retired to Campania, to take service with new paymasters, but some had returned to serve, as mercenaries, the very Byzantine General who had defeated them, such was the volatility of life in these parts. Over the days that followed they struggled to get to grips with the seeming chaos of Southern Italy, and perplexing it was: a land of shifting fiefs, of claim and counterclaim, peopled by Lombards who ruled a mixed Greek and Italian-speaking population, with feudal oversight claimed by two emperors.

On the eastern side of the Apennines, directly opposite Campania, lay the Principality of Benevento, nominally a papal fief but one that was a cause of endless dispute. Below and to the east of that stood the Byzantine provinces of Apulia and Calabria, collectively known as the Catapanate, which, under a good ruling proconsul, was a land of peace and prosperity, the Adriatic and southern coasts dominated by great, near-independent trading ports like Bari, Brindisi and Taranto.

Threatened – and these proconsuls and ports often were by Lombard uprisings, Saracen raids, and even the odd attack from the Western Emperor and the Pope – they presented a formidable foe, as long as the leader was competent and he was given an army. Generally it was the opposite: there was either no one in office or some venal satrap given the position by court intrigue, which made febrile that which was unstable. Constantinople was far away and it was a place too often ruled by emperors who were weak or self-indulgent, which fired endlessly the dreams the Lombards had of a kingdom encompassing the whole region. It was in pursuit of that very dream they had been beaten at Cannae.

It took many repetitions to get hold of what was a mass of confusion in terms of allegiances and ownership of land and titles, just to comprehend that the Campania region alone contained three distinct fiefs: Naples, Salerno and Capua. The lords of these territories were rarely associates, never friends. They sought constantly to undermine their neighbours, not difficult since each province was riven with petty baronies that were forever transferring their allegiance and often in conflict with each other and what passed for the centre of power.

'My head is spinning, brother,' Drogo complained, after one lengthy explanation. 'This part of the world makes the Contentin look like a haven of order.'

'It's perfectly simple, Drogo, if you would listen.'

If Drogo loathed anything, it was times like these when his brother began to use his fingers to explain something, as though he was an idiot child. He understood that Rainulf's present paymaster, and so ultimately his, was the Prince of Capua, and really that was all that mattered. That Rainulf had betrayed another magnate to get his fief meant nothing: that same duke had at one time bribed Rainulf to betray the Prince of Capua. It was the way of this world and the only common goal of the mercenaries employed was that they should prosper.

Capua was, at present, dominant, and that ensured a steady flow of money as they carried out whatever commands were issued by the rapacious prince of that fiefdom. If thunderbolts of approbation at his depredations came from the Pope in Rome, as well as the Holy Roman Emperor in Germany, who might claim to be titular overlord of this part of Italy, it mattered not at all unless it was backed up by force. Strictures from Constantinople counted for even less.

All that required to be understood was the fact that the Lombards were treacherous, greedy, unreliable and given to rebellion, as were their subjects and it was those traits which kept the Norman mercenaries regularly and gainfully employed.

Rainulf sought out the brothers later in the day. They were working in one of the paddocks used for the training of fighting horses, an activity which took place in the early evening when the sun had lost its strength, both with animals not long risen from being colts, seeking to teach them to respond to the command of the thigh alone, no easy task given they were still not fully trained on the reins. It was work that required endless patience: there was no way to force a horse into compliant behaviour, they were not like dogs, they had to be won over by constant repetition and a firm hand regularly applied, and even then only certain animals had the aptitude to face the kind of dangers to which they would be exposed in battle.

Rainulf, like every other Norman, bred his mounts with passion and made sure they were looked after, given they were the key to battle success. So he watched with interest as the de Hauteville brothers put these tyro destriers through their paces, gently cajoling them, occasionally hauling them up with strength to remind them who was in charge, trotting round the paddock standing upright, reins lightly held, pressing with one knee seeking to turn them left or right. You could go through this for weeks, months even, get it right, then find that the horse on which you had expended so much time in training would shy away from the danger of a shield wall, or pull up rather than jump a ditch.

To an experienced eye it was clear Drogo de Hauteville was better at the task. Not that his elder brother was poor, just that Drogo seemed to have an affinity with these equines greater than William.

Indeed, listening, it was obvious that it was Drogo who was proffering advice, the precise opposite of what took place in the manège where they trained to fight. On their own mounts, now resting after their morning exertions, both seemed equal, but not with animals yet to be taught. Judging by the sweaty state of the horses, they had been at their training for some time, and they called a halt before tiredness in the animals made them cantankerous.

'Drogo,' Rainulf said, as they came to the rail, leading the sweating mounts. 'Oblige me by seeing the horses to their fields. I wish to have words with your brother.'

There was a slight feeling of anger in Rainulf's breast when Drogo hesitated, waiting until William nodded that he should comply; he was a man who expected to be obeyed, not to have to have his orders – and it had been an order however gently couched – approved by another.

Waiting till Drogo was well out of earshot, Rainulf spoke again, aware, close up, just how much taller William was than he. 'Your brother seems to be good with horseflesh.'

'I have never met one better.'

'I saw you deferring to him just now.'

The way Rainulf said that, as though it was odd, made William question the statement. 'Why should I not?'

'You are the older.'

'By a year, Rainulf, which is not much, and be assured I will happily take instruction from any man who is my peer in anything.'

'Including me?'

The clear blue eyes hardened at that. 'You have come to talk to me for a reason; you have sent my brother away, I think because he is the reason.'

That piece of perspicacity caught Rainulf out. He had intended to talk for a bit and bring the subject round to Drogo, but he had found this de Hauteville too sharp for his game, which made him wonder if perhaps Odo de Jumiège had been right. Should he be cautious of this man, for there was no doubt, in close proximity, he had a commanding presence?

'He is trouble, your brother.'

William smiled at that, which was just as disconcerting, given there was a reprimand implicit in the words. 'He is his father's son.'

'You will forgive me if I say that makes no sense to me.'

'If you knew my sire, Tancred, it would make perfect sense.'

'But I do not.'

'Drogo is my brother, but there are ten more of the same in my family, as well as three sisters. My father, and Drogo has inherited it, has an unbridled appetite...'

Rainulf interrupted. 'You sound as though you do not respect your father.'

'I respect him and love him, but I would wish him less fertile. The only peace my mother got, God rest her soul, was when he was away fighting.'

'Your mother is dead?'

'She is, but he wed again, and I have a raft of half-siblings.'

'Away fighting?' Rainulf enquired. 'Fighting who?'

'The Moors in Spain, the Parisian Franks as well as those on our border with Anjou. He even went to England once, to help put a king back on his throne.'

'Ethelred?'

William nodded. 'You see, he was as active on the field of battle as he was in the bedchamber. He was much admired by Duke Robert's father, as a soldier.'

'If, as you say, Drogo is like his father, I need you to rein him in.'

William laughed out loud, and it made no difference to his humour that he saw the way it annoyed the Lord of Aversa.

'Why do you laugh?' he snapped.

'You came here a long time ago, Rainulf.'

'So?'

'Do you remember that journey?'

'That does not tell me why you laughed.'

William, though he was looking at Rainulf, was back on that long road south. The first thing the brothers had discovered was that they came from a race that was unpopular; it was better to deny they were Normans – hard, given their size and colouring – than admit to it. That they should not be loved in Frankish Anjou was accepted; the Angevin territory bordered on Normandy and had suffered much from incursion, though not without an equal amount of retaliation.

It was when they came to cross the Loire at Tours that it really struck home. The locals had memories that went back two centuries. Viking raiders – and the good folk of Tours saw no distinction between a Norman and a Norseman – had sailed up the river and inflicted on the city all the rapine and mayhem for which they were famous. To the inhabitants, it was as if it had happened yesterday.

Even the monks in the local hospice had treated them with a very unchristian reserve; they did not believe them to be true pilgrims, given the number of mounts and their nature – that was made obvious by the way they indulged others who were genuinely on the road to various shrines, pilgrims from as far away as Denmark, Caledonia, Hibernia and England. Too many Normans had passed this way claiming the status, when truly they were on the way to fight and that was before Drogo was caught in the nunnery, which led to much shouting, the drawing of swords in a place of sanctity, followed by a hurried dawn departure. It was that memory which had made William laugh, along with Drogo's justification for his actions.

'I feel sorry for them,' he had insisted, when William castigated him for the twentieth time. 'They don't want to be in a nunnery, it's their damn families who have put them there.'

'They put them there to keep them chaste, not for the likes of you to deflower them.'

'Deflower? There wasn't a virgin in sight.'

'No doubt you tried them all?'

'Not even I am that stalwart, brother, though I confess, if I could have stayed, there were enough covert glances to make me think I could have died happy, and some of those from aged creatures who you would think past such impious thoughts.'

What to say to Rainulf: that Drogo had an appetite that made his own father look tame? That was unfair to Tancred who had never strayed from wedlock in his carnality. His second son could not see a wench without trying to have his way with her, and many a fight had he been saved from, merely because he had so many brothers who would take his part, even when he was clearly in the wrong. There must have been fathers in the Contentin who heaved a sigh of relief to hear he had gone south, just as there were those in that same part of Normandy with numerous bastards at their hearth, the paternity of which could be, with some certainty, laid at Drogo's door.

In Tours he had climbed the nunnery walls to get at his conquests, and insisted they stay for extra days, with the excuse that the horses were fagged, only for his brother to find out the true reason when the hue and cry broke out, caused, Drogo had insisted, by the jealousy of some fellow engaged on the same mission as he, who opened the door of a paramour's cell to find him on top of her. As trenchant as his activities, were his views on the subject of nunneries.

'Me,' Drogo had added, 'I would shut them all. It's one thing for a man to renounce the world and become a monk, but to force a woman into chastity is wrong. Mind, there were a few black habits sneaking about as well as my cuckold. I wasn't the only one favoured with a bit of warm flesh, the hypocrites.'

William had ventured to advance the concept of family honour, even although he knew that Drogo had never let an insult to their name pass, knowing he was wasting his breath. Drogo would never change, and in truth, what he had said about nunneries had a great deal of validity. Certainly there were some young women who elected to become Brides of Christ, but for the majority they were incarcerated against their will because of some transgression real or imagined, and perhaps only on the possibility of sin.

Or they were widows; their late husbands' families wanted them out of the way, and on many occasions it was more to do with an inheritance than any notion they might cause disgrace: a woman in a nunnery was not likely to remarry. Then, of course, there were the wives who had cuckolded husbands powerful enough to do with them as they wished. They, according to his brother, who had made a habit of night-time excursions in every place they had stayed, were the most needing of his attentions.

Looking at the man who now employed them he was tempted to relate the tale he had recalled, but he decided it might not sit well with him. 'Why did I laugh? One day, Rainulf, you must let me relate to you Drogo's adventures and you will laugh too. I assure you it will be a long day. If his seed is any good you will be able to trace his route back to Normandy by the bastards he created.'

'It is that very thing about which I need to talk. Now he is here and he is causing trouble. He will not desist from disquieting the women of other men.'

'So?'

'He might be killed for this habit.'

'I think you have already observed, Rainulf, that is not easy. So what do you want from me?'

'To make him your responsibility.'

'And if I decline?'

'I like trouble with my enemies, not with my soldiers.'

William said nothing for several seconds, just

holding Rainulf's gaze. The inference was obvious: either rein in Drogo or saddle up and depart.

'How do your men come by their women?'

'Mostly they buy them. There is always a peasant with too large a brood willing to sell a daughter.'

'Then I must ask you to advance the price of one and the time to find him a concubine. The only way to keep Drogo out of that kind of trouble is to give him something to occupy his attention.'

Rainulf thought for a moment then nodded. 'The price is not high, but any woman who comes here cannot be the kind to cause trouble. If your brother buys, it must be on the arrangement that the girl can be returned.'

William decided, as he saw Drogo coming back to join them, that such a sanction was not one to pass on to his brother, otherwise he would try out every wench in Campania. Besides there was a more pressing concern.

'And I will need another hut in which to sleep.'

'That can be arranged when you return.'

'Return?'

'Yes,' the Lord of Aversa called as he walked away. 'You are about to earn your keep.'

CHAPTER TEN

William knew he was under scrutiny. The men on this expedition were all mercenaries of long experience; he was still, though popular, the newcomer, perhaps with a chance to show his peers that the tales of the fighting he had done in the past were not boasting but true. It was also significant that Drogo had been left out; separating them had been deliberate.

Bringing up the rear of the party he was enveloped in the dust of a dry autumn. There had been no rain for weeks and his surcoat was covered in so much dust that the red and black colouring that now identified him as one of Rainulf's men was quite hidden. Once more, he had a leaf in his mouth to protect his lower lip, and on his head he wore a straw hat bought in Aversa. But it was battle service, so his helmet was to hand, hooked over his saddle, while under the mail hauberk, even at this early hour of the morning, his body ran with sweat.

Both dust and heat eased somewhat as the company left the flat agricultural plain and moved up into the rocky foothills and a cooling breeze, manoeuvring up a track that previous downpours had scarred clear of earth, the metal on the hooves occasionally ringing as a foot struck bare rock. Far ahead, in the clear air, the higher hills rose all the way to the forbidding mountains of the southern Apennines, set in a bluish haze like jagged broken teeth. Somewhere between there and where they now rode lay the place where he would be tested.

The duty on which they were engaged was a common one in this world: a vassal had refused to meet his obligations, declaring that he was no longer subject to Capuan rule, but instead claimed his fief was held from the papal enclave of Benevento, and thus his sovereign lord was the Pope. It was an excuse, of course, a pretext to avoid payment of his feudal dues. For this fellow, the Lord of Montesárchio, the problem was simple: the Pope was in Rome and lacked an army, while the Prince of Capua had Rainulf Drengot in command of several hundred armed and brutal war lovers only too keen to collect what was owed, and more besides.

William had been told there was a good road from Aversa to their destination and he assumed, since no one bothered to inform him, they were taking a route through the hills in order to effect surprise. They had been riding for more than one glass of sand when Odo de Jumiège, the captain of the expedition, called a halt by a gurgling stream. This ran through a glade of decent pasture, which also provided shade from some trees. The horses, once watered, were hobbled and left to graze, and the men looked to their own comforts, those needing to piss careful to do so downstream of the place where the horses might again drink.

None of the men would themselves drink water in a land so abundantly supplied with wine and several, having eaten fruit and dried meat as well, lay down to nap, using their saddles as pillows. William was about to do likewise when Odo approached and ordered him to stand as sentinel on the route they would take.

'Our Lord of Montesárchio must anticipate that his impertinence will not go unpunished, and he is a bold fellow who claims to command fifty fighting retainers. Make sure it is we who surprise him and not the other way round.'

There was no choice but to do as he was bid, even though it was absurd to think their enemy would come so far, at least ten leagues, to attack them. He, along with the absent Drogo, might be confused about the tangled web of local vassalage, but he knew too much about basic tactics to be fooled by such a command. This Lord of Montesárchio had a defendable tower:

he would stay in that and hope that an assault would be reckoned too much trouble. No one in their right mind took on Normans in the open, even when they outnumbered them two to one.

The reason for Odo's action was not hard to fathom: he had not taken kindly to the inclusion of the brothers de Hauteville in his command. He had men he trusted, men he had fought alongside before, who knew his commands and would obey them without question. These newcomers had an air of superiority about them, even if they seemed able fighters. William particularly acted more like a leader than a supporter, which clearly irked the captain. Thus he ensured the elder brother ate the dust of his fellow mercenaries and he would, at times like this, be denied rest; if he was inclined to insubordination, the sooner Odo found out the better.

The station William was required to take, at the crest of a slight rise, had no shade, and so was uncomfortable as the heat of the day steadily increased. Equally tiring was the glare of the sun on a landscape of grey rock and tree-filled valleys. It was those on which he kept his eye, looking for any signs of human movement, like startled birds rising into the sky in sufficient numbers to denote a strange and powerful presence, aware that he used to do this at home when trouble threatened. For a moment he was back there, standing atop the wooden tower that overlooked the family manor house, and the woods he was examining were not those of Italy, but the thick forests of the Normandy bocage. Sometimes, in high summer, it had been this hot.

Many times on the road south he had wondered if they were doing the right thing, only to come to the same conclusion on each occasion: there was no way of knowing. As his cousin of Montbray would have said, their lives were in God's hands. All they could do was to follow his ways and keep their souls fit for salvation. The recurrence of that thought brought forth a wry smile: Drogo was certainly doomed to eternal damnation.

They had gone to pray for the soul of Duke Robert when they heard he had died, though Drogo had insisted he did not deserve their supplications, but William had, in part, been seeking some sign of what he should do. Through his mother, he had some claim on the ducal title; one that could be challenged, certainly, but valid nevertheless. Would the Norman barons accept Robert's bastard as his heir? Hands clasped in prayer, he had deduced some would and some would not. There would be trouble in his homeland and that posed for him a question: was that where he should be?

That his father had entertained high hopes for all his offspring was no secret; he spoke of it often enough, but he had held the highest expectation for his eldest son. The way Duke Robert had rebuffed him before Bessancourt had wounded Tancred, for William knew his father had never had aspirations that any of his five sons by his first wife should aim for too high a station. He had raised them to serve their duke not displace him, based on the oath he had given to the duke's father always to serve his heirs. To Tancred, that oath was sacred.

Were there now, at this very moment, men trying to engage Tancred in revolt? They would be wasting their time, and not just because of given oaths. For all his paternal fecundity, Tancred was not a power in the land; he could field his feudal obligation of ten lances but no more. Certainly he had friends, but what he would have now would be men with much more land and authority than he seeking to use him, and if William had still been at home they would have tried to engage him as a figurehead, the aim being to depose his bastard namesake. Once that was achieved, it was impossible to believe they would bow the knee to a de Hauteville. It would be folly to suppose otherwise.

Thanks to Geoffrey de Montbray, the de Hauteville brood were better educated than most of their contemporaries. Tancred had fought alongside Geoffrey's father, his brother-in-law, and had been present when he was killed by a Saxon axe while helping to regain the English throne for King Ethelred. He had raised the boy and helped him to the priesthood not just as an act of family duty, but to have at hand someone lettered and well read who could minister in the Hauteville church and also act as a tutor to his sons. His nephew had repaid him handsomely.

There was no escaping his teaching; no excuses were acceptable. Thus all those down to children too young to tutor could read, write and speak Latin. They had been taught a fair amount of history, culled from the manuscripts that Geoffrey had seen as he studied for his office at places like the great Abbey of Cluny. They knew their catechism and their Stations of the Cross, just as they knew that if they needed intercession in any of their affairs, only prayer could provide it. But if Geoffrey taught them one thing above all others, he taught them to think.

'Are you asleep?'

Odo de Jumiège's hard tone interrupted this string of thoughts and reminiscence, but it was not enough to make William turn round.

'I was tasked to watch the approach, and that is what I am doing.'

'A glance behind you might have shown you we were breaking camp.'

William did turn then, and he stared just as hard at Odo as the captain was glaring at him. 'Just as it might have made me miss something important.'

'Get saddled up and mounted.'

'And my station?'

'Where do you think?' Odo growled.

William sprang to his feet so quickly, to tower over Odo, that the captain, who was as tough as boots, actually recoiled a step. 'As you wish.'

Needing to assert himself, Odo barked, 'I don't wish, I command.'

William smiled then, in the same way he had once smiled at Duke Robert, which was insulting and deliberately so. 'So you do, Odo.'

Again bringing up the rear, William was at least, now they were in wooded country, spared mouthfuls of dust, but he was not spared the thought that he would have to do something about the man Rainulf had put in command of him. He was not given to disobedience, but neither was he given to buckling under domination. The difficulty was, how to go about it: in a troop of twenty-five knights, most of whom would be loyal to their leader, to raise a sword could be suicidal. A fight with Odo held, for him, no terror, but if they all took their leader's part...

Most of the men Rainulf employed came from the same source: a land full of warriors with not enough wars to fight, added to endemic malcontents, content to live a good life off the backs of their liege lord's subjects and the purloined property of his enemies. They were tough and far from gentle, so there was no appealing to them for fairness; the only thing they would respect was martial prowess. But then William de Hauteville had a different thought: he knew Odo to be tough, but was he clever? In short, could the captain be outwitted?

Such considerations sustained him throughout a day of much riding, walking, and frequent halts, through a night when the provisions from the panniers on packhorses were roasted or boiled and consumed, and throughout the next day until they finally came in sight of the fortress of Montesárchio.

The sun was high in the sky, but the Normans were hidden from any sentinels, sat in the deep shade near the edge of a forest to observe the high central tower and flanking walls. The packhorses had been left back in the woods, along with a couple of trussed-up foresters they had encountered who, free to run, could alert their quarry. Two men had been detached to care for them and every man looking out at their objective was now fully ready for battle, lances in hand and helmets on, all bearing Rainulf's colours.

It was really a small castle of cream stone blocks set on a hill shaped very like the conical helmets they wore, with the stronghold on top, served by a steep, winding causeway. William's first thought was that even in an undulating landscape the mound was unnatural: it was just too much of, and too high, a protrusion. Possibly it was a strand of volcanic rock, they were after all in a land of live and extinct volcanoes, but he doubted it.

To him, it looked like something that had been built up deliberately to house a tower from which most of the surrounding ground could be observed, not least the old Roman road which ran straight back to Aversa. Not that his view was sought: Odo's idea was to emerge from the trees and rush the place, trying to get up that causeway to the heavy wooden gate before it could be shut in their face.

William, being one of the half a dozen men detailed to attempt this, was surprised no one questioned what was an absurd command. The distance was too great, at least seven hundred paces, and that was just to the bottom of the causeway. Gallop across that space and their horses would be slightly winded; to then force them up a steep slope, which looked from here to be made of loose stones, was going to be hard work. They would do it, but not at speed, and if the defenders had crossbows, both mounts and men would present perfect targets, and be outside a gate which had been slammed shut well before they could get to it.

Twenty-five lances could not attack and subdue a place like this. It had been designed to withstand a siege, and everything about the fortress was given to that – the cleared flat farmland between these woods at the base, with not even an olive tree to hide the approach – the way the stone buildings of the town, with their red-tiled roofs, had been also kept away from the access route. The only notion William had was to wait until nightfall so that they could get under the walls on foot and in darkness, to perhaps surprise the garrison at first light if they opened a gate they were bound to shut at night.

He did not propose this for the very simple reason he knew he would be ignored. He was the last person Odo de Jumiège would take advice from, and the rest of the men were indifferent. They would do as they were told, and if it failed so be it; William had already overheard enough talk of how they generally went about their business in such situations.

All would be spared if the castle surrendered, the Lord of Montesárchio alone being taken to face Prince Pandulf, along, of course, with his coffers. If they refused to surrender, the Normans would threaten both the lord and his vassals down to the meanest peasant with the most horrible death, and if necessary sit down to starve them out, cutting the vines and olive trees in the surrounding farmland, destroying any seed so that nothing could be sown in the next season, and living off the crops in the fields or storerooms, even if it took months, with an occasional hanging, drawing and quartering below the walls of one of the townsfolk to remind the garrison of their forthcoming fate.

The idea of building ballistae and knocking down the walls, or sending over the top tight bundles of fired and oil-soaked straw, was not the Norman way; they were cavalry not artisans. Of course, messages would be sent back to Rainulf to ask if he wished to speed matters up, but hope rested on the reluctance of the men of the garrison to sacrifice their blood for a result which could only be gainsaid if a force came to relieve them, and no such force existed.

Odo waited until the sun was sinking in the west, in the hope that, behind them, it would give those rushing the place a few extra seconds before discovery. Then he ordered them to stand by, and after a few moments, with their mounts now stamping impatiently – for trained to war, they knew what was coming – he gave the command to attack. The progress to the very edge of the trees was not hurried, there were too many loose branches and unseen hazards on the uneven ground that could cripple a horse, but out of the shade and with nothing but strips of farmland before them the riders kicked their mounts into a gallop.

There was no ordered line in this: it was who could get there fastest that counted and in such a situation William de Hauteville's great height and bulk counted against him, so much so that he cursed Odo's spite in choosing him. This was a task for the lighter lances, the men who bore down least on their animals, for quite apart from their own weight the horses had to bear the burden of the fighting equipment they wore and carried. Soon William was bringing up the rear, and no amount of spurring could make his horse go faster. He could hear the sound of a blaring trumpet and knew the defenders had seen the approach and were raising the alarm.

The first riders were halfway up the steep causeway before he got to the base, while beneath him he knew his mount was breathing hard. It took heavy spurring to get him to begin the ascent, and even then his hooves were getting poor footing on the loose surface. Up ahead he could see the gate was shut and the way barred, which made him wonder at the stupidity of his confrères to keep going in the face of a defence they could not hope to breach.

They were milling around on the flat ground before that gate when the first great stone came over the crenellated wall. It missed them all but set their horses off in panic, which had them rearing and bucking, hard to control, as more stones followed. William hauled on his reins to halt his mount; there was nothing but death or a maiming to be gained by going further and he was yelling for those under the hail of stones to pull back. One stone took a rider right on the crown of his helmet, leaving William unsure if he imagined or actually heard the man's neck snap. Another hit the ground in front of a horse and, bouncing, took its fragile leg, bringing it to its knees and throwing its rider.

The men under that assault were fighting their

animals not the enemy, for if their mounts had been trained for combat they had not been trained to withstand this. His own horse was using the slope to back up, only his hold on the reins keeping its head facing what was going on above. Only when he saw that three riders had got out from under the hail, did he let it have its head, and it was round and slithering away from any danger as soon as he did that.

The first crossbow bolt hit the ground in front of him, and it was only an automatic reaction that made him press hard to alter his mount's direction. Shoulders hunched, he felt as if he was naked and there was no point in slowing or turning to see how the others were faring; the only place of safety was out of range. On the flat ground again the going eased, but even well winded his horse did not slow, for in its brain it had its own set of demons from which to flee.

Four men and five horses made it back to the woods, the riders breathing as heavily as their mounts. One of the attacking party was certainly dead, another probably so and they could see the wounded horse struggling to stand while the defenders amused themselves by trying to kill it, and the rider it had cast off, with more stones. Glaring at Odo, William was presented, at least in what he could see, with a face utterly indifferent to what had just occurred.

He heard his captain order one man forward

with him, and as they rode towards the base of the causeway, Odo dropped his lance and attached to it a strip of white cloth. Walking his horse halfway up he stopped and began to shout, the words he used floating back to be just audible to his company, who had emerged from the trees, most leading their mounts, to show their number – to William, another error: they should have stayed hidden so that the defenders had no idea of what they faced.

Odo's demand was straightforward: surrender the fortress and the body of the Lord of Montesárchio, and the garrison would be spared; refuse and they would face siege and assault, and no quarter would be given once the inevitable happened. In time-honoured fashion, when refusing such a demand, Odo was greeted with boos and whistles, while several of the defenders climbed onto the parapet and turned to bare their arses.

'Then I ask to be allowed to collect the bodies of my men,' he called.

A single voice answered, and the men at the edge of the woods strained their eyes seeking to see the man whose surrender they sought. It was a high voice, near girlish, that told Odo his wish was granted. That brought from him a wave of an arm and, obviously prearranged, four of the still-mounted men detached themselves and rode forward. Odo himself had dismounted and gone to look at the bodies, perhaps hoping that one man was still alive. Following that, he went to the horse with the broken leg, and gently lifting its head, he took out his knife and cut its throat.

'Looks like we're here for a while,' said one of the men beside William.

'Let's hope there are some decent women in the town, then,' replied another. 'I'm sick of that bitch I bought last year.'

'There'll be a few bitches in this Montesárchio sick of us afore this be over.'

'Best get digging first, to bury our own, and we'll need a priest.'

'Two men dead an' for a daft notion.'

'That's Odo. If he has a brain, it's in his arse.'

Saddened as he was, William felt a stirring of relief in overhearing that conversation: he was not alone!

CHAPTER ELEVEN

Guaimar did not like Ascletin, and he liked even less being cooped up in a travelling coach with him for days on end. The Pierleoni son had only one topic of conversation: himself, and it was one he was happy to talk about endlessly. All his actions were brilliant, all his friends adored him, his family were amazed at his perspicacity, his fellow clerics at his grasp of the intricacies of Holy Scripture and, of course, his parishioners were in awe of so elevated a personage holding the office of bishop.

His diocese was the mountain town of L'Aquila, perched in the high Apennines, on the direct route from Rome to the Adriatic. He had never actually visited the place, though he was happy to take what revenues came his way to help fund his true purpose in life, which was to pursue the Papacy and thus elevate the name of the Pierleoni to rank amongst the highest in Christendom.

In this he was naturally backed by his family's wealth, but Guaimar soon discerned that the Pierleoni, when it came to money and influence in the city of Rome, were way behind the other leading families who could trace their roots back not decades, but centuries. Ascletin might call them arrogant; they probably behaved as if he and his tribe barely existed.

He also seemed acutely aware that his family's conversion from Judaism to the Latin faith was a drawback; he felt he needed to stress their adherence to Christianity and he did so relentlessly, and always with praise for the far-sightedness of his grandfather, a wise, nay brilliant, man from whom he had, of course, inherited those desirable attributes. It was all too desperate in its constant repetition and insistence, made worse by the slow rate at which their convoy was travelling and by his continuing habit of treating Guaimar as if he was a youth in the presence of an adult.

The road to the imperial heartlands of Germany was the best maintained in Italy, and one of the most travelled, studded with comfortable inns and religious establishments where those who had the means were happy to stay. This was diminished somewhat by the fact that they were buffeted about in a coach; on horses the party could have managed twenty leagues a day, with a stop every fourth day to rest the animals. In this caravanserai, with teams of six animals per coach needing constant replacement, ten leagues was a matter of some exhilaration, a lot less being more common, which promised a month cooped up with this terminal bore.

On their too frequent halts, nothing but the best was good enough for the party: the Pierleoni son was intent on impressing everyone with his fabulous wealth, and he planned his stops in advance, sending ahead a rider to the next place of rest to ensure that they knew who was coming, and also to make certain that food of the required standard was produced.

He had another worry, one he was gnawing on now: Ascletin had designs on his sister, and being the self-centred creature he was saw none of the disapproval in her eyes that his slimy attention produced. He was the type to think everyone smitten by him, and not just the fair sex. Every owner of an inn, every abbot at the monasteries at which they rested, all the monks, and even the Archbishop of Milan, when they had stayed at his palace, was expected to be stunned by this paragon.

It was in a tavern in Verona that he had overheard Ascletin telling one of his family retainers, one of a tribe of valets brought along to see to his personal needs, in a voice brimming with confidence… 'I will have the lovely Berengara, who is so clearly attracted to me, but not until I see how her brother stands with the emperor.'

Passing outside the door of the buffoon's chamber, Guaimar had to stop himself from pushing open the door and thumping him on his clerical ear. Berengara, though polite, loathed him, and even if she had not, the assumption that he could have his way with her at a proverbial click of his fingers made her brother's blood boil. But he had to calm himself – Berengara would be polite because they needed his aid; he could do no less. This restraint was made more difficult by Ascletin's next remark.

'No point in wasting my charms on a nobody. I will only grace her with my seed if her brother stands in some regard with Conrad Augustus. If the emperor shows he is inclined to aid the young booby, he will be a person whose support might be worth a lick of attention. At present he is nothing but a bore and I am stuck in my coach with him all day. The blessed fellow will just never shut up!'

'The Papacy must be brought into the present age,' Ascletin insisted, at the end of a long repetitive diatribe.

Guaimar had only been half listening, but the remark dragged him away from his concerns regarding Berengara, to leave him wondering if this was the first or the fiftieth time he had heard this in the last three weeks. He had developed a look and a persistent nod that persuaded Ascletin he was paying attention when actually his mind, as it had been just now, was elsewhere, and it was easy to pick up the thread if his fellow-traveller ever posed a proper question; all he had to say was 'But surely you have a solution' to set him off again.

'This notion that a Pope cannot be elected unless he is approved by the Western Emperor is absurd!' Guaimar waited for what was sure to follow, and he was not disappointed. 'Not, of course, that I would ever allude to that in the presence of the present incumbent. It would not do to have him in opposition to my ambitions for Holy Church.'

Why is it, Guaimar wondered, that this pompous fool thinks me so indebted to his family that I might not tell Conrad this myself? But, of course, he would not, for the election of a Pope was such an affair of arcane rights and privileges – as well as an occasion for an outbreak of furious violence from competing centres of power – it was a field best kept well out of.

'Do you not agree, Guaimar?'

Forced by the directness of that question to look at Ascletin, he altered his stock response slightly. 'But I know you have the solution.'

'Holy Church must elect the man to lead it,' Ascletin declared, 'not a lay emperor. Only then can the factions come together to agree on the candidate.'

'Absolutely,' Guaimar replied, moving aside a heavy curtain to look at the snow-capped mountains that enclosed one side of the Brenner Pass.

He also saw the faces of those peasants, male and female, holding large, flat, wooden shovels, whose task it was to keep the road clear of snow, and he wondered if that was a feudal service demanded of them or one for payment. Very likely it would be the former: in these parts there was no planting and sowing the fields in the winter season and he had already observed their cattle were kept out of the cold in barns, so whoever was their lord and master would not want them idle. Peasants with nothing to do became troublesome.

How different this was from Campania, where in parts near Vesuvius you could sow and reap four harvests a year – two was common throughout. Here, they depended on one. That blessing of climate and soil was, of course, part of Campania's curse as well. Being so fertile it was also a land that produced much in the way of riches, a territory people would fight over to control. He was on his way to bow the knee to Conrad, but he could just as easily be on the way to Constantinople on the same errand.

'A convocation of cardinals, abbots of the great monasteries, and archbishops, should elect a Pope.' Ascletin was asserting this, as though such an idea was original and his own, instead of one advanced by everyone who opposed imperial intervention. 'And there should be no intrusion into the deliberations by the factions of Rome.'

Even that blatant piece of hypocrisy – he meant everyone except the Pierleoni – could not divert Guaimar from the thought which had hit him like a thunderbolt. It is not pleasant to realise you have made an error, and one so profound as to undermine your entire purpose. The Emperor Conrad had to be persuaded to come to his aid, made to see that the removal of Pandulf was essential, and the only solution to that problem was a military one. Strictures not backed by force would carry no weight whatsoever, but what would persuade the emperor to act when he had not done so in the past, even although the depredations of the Wolf could not be a secret.

Guaimar was now back in the archbishop's palace in Salerno, and he realised he had acquiesced too easily in the cleric's insistence that seeking help from the Eastern Empire was anathema. Both the courts of Bamberg and Constantinople were content to protest their rights as suzerain as long as neither sought to enforce it and the air of seeming harmony which they projected was a mask. There was deep mistrust between the two halves of the old Roman inheritance, but inactivity was the response: you stay out of South

Italy and so will we; you ensure stability on one side of the Apennines, and we will do so on the other.

Conrad had made an error in releasing Pandulf, and before he would do anything he would have to first admit that. He had not done so up till now, even if it was obvious, so what would change his mind? Conrad would not move unless he felt threatened!

Guaimar nearly said those last words out loud, so obvious was it to his now troubled mind. He should have sent to ask the Eastern Emperor for help as well, and damn the fears of his archbishop, for there was one truth that never evaporated: both emperors would dearly love to take over the whole region, east to west, if they thought that they could do so and hold it without endless conflict. The next problem to surface was how to alter what was a cardinal error.

'... No, I must take care with Conrad Augustus to give him no inkling of my thoughts.'

God Almighty, is he still talking? Guaimar wanted to scream.

'This, of course, will not be a problem. When he sees the power of the intelligence he has to deal with, I am sure I will have this so-called Augustus eating out of my hand.' Ascletin leant forward over his chest of money to impart, again not for the first time, his conclusion. 'I do not expect, of course, to be the next holder of the papal office, but the one after that, young Guaimar. That I think will be mine.'

Looking into Ascletin's face, Guaimar thought he might have a solution.

The cries of the escorts were enough to alert everyone to the approach of their next stop and his fellow-traveller began to preen himself in a plate of highly polished silver; he wished to be seen at his best.

When told of Guaimar's plan, Berengara was entranced, but was wise enough to insist they rehearse the thing before carrying it out, and her brother was, although initially sceptical, made wise to the fact that she was correct when he stumbled on the words he needed to use. The other thing his sister said was equally true: just because he had realised his error, there was no need to correct it that second.

If sitting listening to Ascletin's witterings had been hard before, it was doubly so when impatience was added. The temptation to blurt out what had to be delivered with guile was nearly overwhelming, and lasted until they reached Innsbruck, where they were once again the guests of an archbishop. In a palace that would not have disgraced an emperor, the perfect setting was found for the argument Guaimar and Berengara needed to construct. The rooms were vast, and so were the connecting corridors, high ceilinged and given to echo. Placing themselves within earshot of the apartments allotted to Ascletin and ignoring any passing servants, their raised voices carried a long way.

'I absolutely forbid you to mention it.'

'For what reason?' Berengara demanded.

'Telling Conrad such a thing will ruin what we are trying to do.'

Berengara had placed herself so she could see Ascletin's door, and she nodded sharply to her brother to let him know it had opened a fraction, so she cried, 'It is dishonest!'

'It is necessary. If the emperor finds out we have sent a mission to Constantinople as well it will ruin everything.'

'Why?'

Guaimar dropped his voice, hoping he had done so enough to have their eavesdropper straining. 'The archbishop was adamant. Only the Western Emperor should be approached. To send for help from both could render useless our hopes. I need you to swear you will say nothing.'

'Swear? Do you trust me so little?'

'Berengara, a chance remark, a word let slip, and we will be undone. Conrad Augustus must come south with his army and get rid of Pandulf.' Now he raised his voice again. 'There is no chance of him doing that if he thinks we will take help from the Byzantines as well. When I swear allegiance to him, as I must, he will have to be convinced that it is inviolable.'

'What if help comes from the east as well?'

'What do we care who rids us of Pandulf, as long as we have Salerno?'

'You will have Salerno.'

'And you, my dear sister, will have a husband that goes with your station as my relative.'

They began to walk away from Ascletin's door, still arguing, their voices fading until they were far enough away to collapse in a fit of giggles.

Ahead lay many more days of having his ears assaulted by his travelling companion, but it had been noticeable on that first morning after their ruse that Ascletin wore an expression on his face even more smug. They came to Bamberg eventually, through a week of snow, to find a town smaller than half a dozen they had passed through. Conrad had set up his court here because it was a fief of his own house and the palace of his predecessor and uncle, a move probably not popular with those who had to gather to elect and anoint a Holy Roman Emperor: the great magnates of church and state who represented half of Europe.

As a court it was far from magnificent, and away from the blazing fires that filled every chamber it was freezing. Outside the trees sagged under the weight of snow, and every morning, if the sun shone, great sheets would fall from the steep roofs of the buildings. Every one of Conrad's courtiers dressed in heavy fur-trimmed garments indoors – including his chamberlain, from whom Guaimar had requested an audience – and thick furs if they ventured out of doors, which they had to do often, given their master was a slave to the hunt.

Guaimar found himself mounted and chasing stags, wild boar and wolves as Conrad and his fellow madmen raced their mounts across a snow-draped landscape or through dense forests, hoping that by doing so he would circumvent the strict protocol of the court and win a face-to-face meeting with Conrad. He hoped in vain: the emperor was always way out in front, and rode his mount with a total disregard for his own well-being. Many a fellow hunter found the going too hearty, and some who tried to keep up paid for it with badly broken bones. It was the weather that saved Guaimar from this: a week slightly warmer which produced a thick mist, one that simply would not clear. Finally, Conrad found time to welcome him officially.

Whatever else the imperial court lacked it was not servants and the chamberlain was as efficient an official as the job demanded. Guaimar had been greeted by his ducal title as well as all the family claims, however arcane, and because of the rank both he and Berengara held, much to the chagrin of Ascletin, had been awarded the kind of apartments that went with superior status. Now, emerging from those, both were dressed in their very best clothes, and Guaimar could look at his sister, nearly a full year older than she had been at the time of their father's funeral, and see that his suppositions had been correct. Her figure had filled out and her face had lost what trace of youthful puppiness it had retained. She looked wonderful.

He was nervous; so much depended on what was about to take place, and try as he might he could not disguise it. This time it was Berengara who tightly held his hand, as they made their way through the chilly corridors of Conrad's castle to the imperial audience chamber. Two pikemen in steel helmets and metal breastplates stood guard at either side of the closed door – no one in freezing Bamberg left a door open – and as they composed themselves to enter, as though by some osmosis the doors opened and a voice rang out.

'His Grace the Duke of Salerno, and the Lady Berengara.'

The room was crowded and warm, a wave of welcome heat that enveloped them as they entered to face a sea of enquiring eyes. Here were the nobles of the empire, several red-capped cardinals, princes, dukes, counts and margraves, all of whom seemed to have about them an air of certainty of their status. Guaimar knew that whatever plea he made to Conrad would be examined by many of those present; these were the men who advised the Emperor in council.

The crowd parted, to reveal at the end of a passage of magnates a heavily built man, who stood with his legs set in a way that, allied to the hands firmly resting on his hips, seemed to demonstrate his power. Here was Conrad the Salian, Duke of Babelsberg and the Lord only knew of how many more fiefs, King in Germany, and the Holy Roman heir of Charlemagne the Great. He had the ruddy face and substantial build of an outdoor man, topped by a mane of pepper and salt hair. The look aimed at the two young nobles was not friendly: it seemed to ask what dared them to enter his presence.

Guaimar's mouth was dry, his heart was pounding, but he did notice as they made their way forward that these great men to either side executed a bow, not to him – they saw themselves at least as his equal – but to his sister, each one receiving a smile and a nod of gratitude. In front of Conrad, Guaimar bowed low, Berengara executing a deep curtsy, which brought Conrad forward, to hold out his hand and raise her up.

'You have brought me the flower of Salerno, I see.'

His voice was deep, composed of gravel, and seemed to come from his belly rather than his throat. As Guaimar replied, the emperor was still looking at Berengara.

'I bring you the loyalty of Salerno as well, sire.'

The benign look evaporated as his gaze turned to

Guaimar. 'I am glad to hear it, though I had no reason to fear it was in doubt.'

There was a sting in that: previous lords of Salerno had flirted with Byzantium, which had required Conrad's Uncle Henry to enforce his rights with an army.

'I am sure Prince Pandulf has sent you many such messages protesting that you are his true liege lord as well.'

'He has.'

'Just as you, Conrad Augustus, are wise enough to know how false they are.' Receiving no reply, just a less-than-engaging stare from a pair of steely grey eyes, Guaimar knew he had to say more. 'It is no duty of a loyal servant of the empire to steal from another, no part of a loyal servant of the empire to people his dungeon with his subjects.'

'Unless they are disloyal, boy! If they are that, then let them suffer the fate they deserve.'

Guaimar made a point of stiffening his body, and holding the imperial eye. Even though Conrad was twice his girth, his voice did not lack equal force.

'I think, your grace, that my true title is not boy, but Duke Guaimar.'

The two held a look for several seconds – it seemed to Guaimar like a lifetime, for he had issued a direct challenge to his suzerain, which could prove totally fatal to his hopes. He was inwardly cursing his own inability to bend to another's will, and then Conrad laughed.

'Well, Duke Guaimar, you must tell what is happening in Campania that warrants you travelling all this way to confront me in my own court and, I may say, show scant regard for my imperial majesty.'

'I cannot but believe, sire, that you know that as well as I do. No man could hold your title and be a fool as well.'

Conrad was still smiling when he replied. 'You are not lacking in impertinence.'

'I believe my station and my duty oblige me to speak truthfully to my sovereign lord.'

'Very well, Guaimar, we will talk a little. My chamberlain will arrange it.' Conrad's attention, as he said that, had moved back to Berengara. 'Now you, young lady, must tell me how you find my little court.'

It was smoothly done, the way the emperor detached her, and left Guaimar standing virtually alone in a crowded room.

CHAPTER TWELVE

It was a thoughtful Norman captain who oversaw
the burials of the men who had died under that hail
of rocks, though Odo de Jumiège sought to display
indifference. The priest, dragged from his church,
performed the service with a tremble, as though he
expected to end up in the grave with one of the bodies.
William, though he prayed for the souls of these men
who were strangers to him, studied the faces of the
other mercenaries to see how they reacted to the loss
of two of their number, not least because of the manner
of those deaths.

Following on from the burials, it was too late in
the day to do more than take over the best house and
stabling in the town with a clear view of the fortress,
throwing out the inhabitants, raiding others for the
means to feed both horses and men and to see what

valuables the locals had been foolish enough not to bury.

There was little of that, this being a part of the world often in turmoil, with a population who took up their possessions and made for safe places, deep pits or hard-to-find caves, as soon as disorder threatened. They would have known of their lord's defiance, would have known too that it would be likely to bring retribution, so anything worth stealing was long gone. The mercenaries were unperturbed, and William discerned from their talk that they were well versed in the art of torturing those who looked prosperous, to force them to reveal their hideouts.

William waited to hear what Odo had in mind regarding Prince Pandulf's renegade but he waited in vain. Their captain was too concerned with his belly and making sure that he had a woman, willing or otherwise, to warm the bed he had commandeered in the stone house closest to the causeway. His sole act was to arrange the guard who would keep watch on the actions of the Lord of Montesárchio in case he attempted to essay from his fortress.

As one of the first set of guards, William looked up at the stout walls and the torches that illuminated the area below them – Odo was not the only one wary of a surprise – trying to guess what the fortress contained. How many men? Did they have horses? If they had oil to soak flaming torches did they have enough and the necessary cauldrons to pour over the heads of attackers? That would make what happened with the hail of rocks look like child's play.

He was convinced they would have to assault the place, and he suspected Odo thought the same, but how? The slopes of the pointed hill on which it stood were steep, maybe too much so to get even a decent foothold carrying ladders – they might very well need those just to ascend, and once below the walls there would be no protection from above. To attack that way was just to provide easy targets.

That left that concourse before the gate, at the top of the causeway, the only flat piece of ground from which an attack could seriously be mounted. The man set to repulse them would know that too, so there he would have his best defences: his crossbowmen, more heavy stones, perhaps boiling oil and, if there were horses inside, the ability to suddenly emerge and mount an attack on men who would, of necessity, be fighting on foot.

They could put together a rough-hewn barricade, one that protected not only their front but their heads, one that they could manoeuvre onto the concourse, perhaps using it to set fire to the wooden gate. But that, stout oak studded with bolts, probably many hundreds of years old and thoroughly seasoned, would take an age to burn and the defenders would pour over water, as well as keeping wet the interior face.

Stay too long and the roles would be reversed: fire would rain down on them and force a withdrawal. It looked as though the only hope, as some of the men had accepted, was a lengthy siege, which was galling given the very idea was what the man they had come to capture would have calculated. He would have made sure he could hold out for months in the hope that either boredom, events elsewhere, or sickness, drove his besiegers away.

Such speculations helped the time pass, and after the glass had run twice he was relieved, grateful to get out of his hauberk and helmet and rest his weary limbs, for it had been a very long day. Sleep came swiftly, even if the room, too full of humanity, was hot, and he was surrounded by the stentorian snores and endless rasping farts of his fellows; sleep in which he dreamt of things cool, of the river back home in which he had swum, engaged in water fights against his brothers. They had also fished with rod and cold tickling hands.

The yell brought him awake immediately, though for a moment he had no recollection of where he was – in Hauteville or Italy – but that kind of alarm was one he had grown up with; in uneasy times Tancred too had mounted guards, day and night, in his wooden tower, to warn of any approaching threat. All around him men were on their feet, reaching for their weapons, shouting to rouse themselves for a fight; there was no time for mail, only his sword, shield, helmet and ability.

The sky was grey, the colour of the earliest dawn, just light enough to make clear the situation. Odo might have little in the way of brains but he was a fighter, already engaged by the time the group of which William was a part joined him. He was yelling the orders to form a line and hold it, at the same time as defending himself against those trying to kill him. This was where the endless training on which Rainulf insisted paid off: there was no panic, none of Odo's men were looking for a way to get clear or avoid their duty, only for a way to join without compromising a man already fighting.

William was with them, shield held firm, sword swinging, concentrating on his front and right, leaving the left side to the man who had taken up station next to him, all around the shouts of attackers and Normans, the ring of metal on metal and the thud as a weapon smashed at the hardened wood and leather of a shield. Even as he fought, parrying jabs from a pike before taking a mighty swing to decapitate the head, William was thinking this should have been foreseen.

The pikeman was now jabbing with the remaining wood, and with just enough light to see the fellow's eyes, he knew he was desperate, not looking to keep contesting the ground with this giant but looking for a way to get clear and leave his opponent to another. William pulled back his sword and the fellow turned to withdraw, he had had enough. That was fatal: the sword came forward with all of William's weight behind it and took him between the shoulder blades with such force that the sound of breaking ribs was unmistakable.

There was no time to care, there were others to take on, not least the man battling his right-hand neighbour. He ceased his activity when William's sword cut through his mailed arm so deeply as to nearly sever it. Odo was yelling orders again, a slow rhythm that saw his Normans take one step forward, hold that gained ground, engage swords with their enemy to beat them into yielding once more, then take a second step as soon as the defending line showed the first hint of weakness. The aim, to impose themselves so thoroughly that sooner or later the resistance was bound to break.

It takes very few men seeking to save themselves to render useless the efforts of their fellows. Two or three who valued their lives more than their duty pulled back further than was prudent, creating dog-leg gaps into which the mercenaries could impose themselves, taking in the side men now defenceless as they fought those before them, cutting down at their necks, jabbing swords under their raised arms, or slicing at the tendons of their legs to bring them to the ground, before a heavy sweep to smash skin and bone and finish them off.

It was hard fighting. William's rasping breath came and went from a bone-dry mouth in which his tongue seemed to have turned to leather. But he could feel that beneath his feet they were off the flat ground and on that sloping causeway. It was a long way up to the castle gate but that must be open. If they could break through and get behind the defenders now inching back, they could bar their inevitable flight, and if they were lucky, do more and get inside the walls.

The men before the Normans knew they were losing; they too could feel the sloping ground under their heels, which would tell them how far they had so far retreated. At some point their line would have to rupture. Would the men fighting alongside William have the breath left after their exertions to get in amongst them, indeed to get ahead of them?

The need to order this fell to Odo, but there was no way fighting in a single line he could control the action, so William found himself, with great difficulty, not only fighting but trying to shout to his nearest companions what was attainable, just in case they had not seen the possibility for themselves. He had no way of knowing if they even heard, never mind saw the sense, he was too busy stabbing, parrying with his sword and thrusting with his shield. If he looked either way he would leave himself exposed to a lunge

from the more than competent opponent he was now
engaged in trying to beat.

The fellow had a sword arm nearly as strong
as William's own, and he had real ability with the
weapon. He had got through William's guard once and
sliced through the jerkin and skin of his upper arm,
but fortunately not enough to cut tendons. There was
no pain, that would come later, but William knew that
it was bleeding, though not how badly. With his next
thrust he nearly skewered him through the belly and
only a sudden and powerful drop of William's weapon
saved him. That put both hilts in contact so it became
a test of strength as the two combatants swayed back
and forth.

Had he been up against a man of lesser build his
assailant might have prevailed, and in his eyes, now
that the morning light had strengthened, William saw
at first that was what he expected. But that look
faded as his opponent realised he was up against a
fellow who had more than enough strength to match
his own, that the only hope he had was to put distance
between them once more so his sword work could keep
him in the fight.

If those eyes told William of his concern they also,
in flickering at the wrong moment, told him the man
intended to disengage, so that when he stepped back
suddenly, hoping that William's own forward pressure
would make him stumble and render him defenceless,

he found that the sword he had in the air ready to slice down and deliver at least a disabling wound was in the wrong place for the thrust of the one that came up under his neck, taking him at the point where his mail joined his flesh. The blade went through with such force that the helmet protecting his head lifted with the top of his skull, and what light had been in those eyes went out.

The rush to get away was as sudden as the initial attack. No order was given; it was just a realisation by those backing up the slope that if they did not go now they would die on the loose gravel. They did not quite act as one, which was costly, but it was close, a collective loss of will that had the Normans looking mostly at retreating backs. William was not looking, he was following as fast as his legs would carry him, waving his sword and yelling, hoping some of his fellow mercenaries would see the sense of what he was about.

Unbeknown to him, Odo was badly wounded. He had kept fighting to the last, ignoring a gash in his side, using all his energy as well as the power of his voice to keep both himself and his band of men going forward; when the enemy fled, he did not have the strength to go on. He fell to his knees, only his sword jammed in the ground keeping him from toppling over completely. Thus half his men hesitated, unsure without commands what to do, one or two close to him trying to give him succour, while the other half, hard by where William had been fighting, were scrabbling after the escaping defenders who were rushing for that open gate and safety.

William's shouts must have penetrated Odo's brain, for he raised his head, needing to rest it on the hilt of his weapon, saw what William was about, and with one last surge of strength ordered, in a bellow, those close to him to go in support. Thus the Normans were in two groups and that was not good. Someone on the castle walls, possibly the Lord of Montesárchio himself, was yelling instruction to stand and fight. Few obeyed, but the lack of cohesion was enough to check William, then those in his wake, and the mercenaries were engaged in such disorder the threat of being taken individually in flank now rested with them.

William had his sword over his head, swinging it left and right with such force and speed that no one could live within its arc. The space he needed to create only need last seconds, enough for his confrères to form some kind of line, as well as a few more to allow to join the men Odo had ordered to support him. By the time they arrived William's shield was a shredded mess, indeed one of his newly arrived companions saved his upper leg, if not his life, by jamming his own shield in front of William's lower body as a defender struck at it with a lance. Off balance by his thrust, a blow to the exposed rear of his neck felled the holder.

The gate was no more than ten paces distant, yet it seemed like ten leagues, so desperately did the defenders, who should not have turned to fight in the first place – whoever had issued that command had erred – sought to create for themselves, a second time, a gap in which they could escape. Those who had made the gate were not prepared to wait and over the heads of the men he was fighting William could see that those inside were trying to close it.

Once that fact became known to the men who would be left outside, who knew that surrender was not a choice, panic set in: they broke and ran like scared deer, with the Normans stumbling along behind them slashing at their backs. That was when the stones began to rain down again, thrown with complete disregard concerning whom they might hit and maim, those trying to get to safety and the Normans pursuing them. Enough got between the two closing gates to stop those inside from forcing them shut, and William yelled for everyone to get with them, not least because under the gateway there was enough of an overhang to protect them from the falling rocks.

It was an irony only to be thought on later that the men seeking to open the gates were on both sides of the contest, both equally desperate to achieve the same result, and their combined weight was achieving that which no one entity could have done: the gate was giving. Over their heads, only because of his height, William was able to jab his sword through the increasing gap, slashing at hands that were wrapped around the stout, metal-studded wood of the doors, as well as the heads of those foolish enough to place them in the opening.

Sliver by sliver it opened, and lances and pikes jabbed in return were killing friends not foes, for the men who had come out to fight formed the bulk of those pressed against the stout oak. William was yelling again, in French, his throat feeling as though it was full of sand, so painful was his breathing, as he sought to coordinate the heaves of his fellow Normans. Now everything was being thrust through the gap: swords, pikes, lances, knives, flaming torches that took men in the face and reduced them to screaming wrecks as they were blinded. But it was to no avail, and in another act of collective despair, realising their efforts were fruitless, the defenders inside the gates suddenly gave way and they swung wide open.

Few of those who did not run fought, many dropped their weapons and their bodies and pleaded to be spared while the rest raced to find some place where they might be safe. There was no time for quarter, and Odo had, in any case, withdrawn it when they spurned his offer of terms. William and the men he led into the castle were outnumbered, they had to be, so mercy was in short supply as those who had given up died lest they recover the will to fight. Some did that, individually, on steps and in doorways, but it was the action of the doomed.

They died not to defend the Lord of Montesárchio, but themselves. William found him in what passed for the great hall of the castle, flanked by six of those men who would have made up his personal retainers, his body knights, lined up in front of their liege lord, swords unsheathed, ready to sell their lives. This was their sworn duty and a thing, had there been time to do so, to be admired.

Before them, once William had been joined by his confrères, stood a line of mercenaries, not one of whom was without a wound. William knew that blood was dripping from the back of his sword hand, not a great deal, but enough, just as he knew that he was not alone, the men alongside him now being in the same state as he. Their chests were heaving from the exertions they had made just to get to this point. They wore no mail and every sword they bore had the deep indents on it of having encountered other unforgiving metal.

These men they faced, these familia knights, were not only wearing mail, they were fresh and untried. Hardly able to get out the words, so breathless was he, William knew that if they fought them, perhaps he, certainly some of his companions, would die or be maimed, and for what? The final result was a foregone conclusion, and only an attachment to their sense of honour was at stake.

So he looked between them at the dark-skinned man, whose flesh was so smooth, his being so unblemished and his clothes so fine, he had to be their master. He held himself well; if he was afraid of death, there was nothing in his demeanour to say so.

'You are the Lord of Montesárchio,' he gasped.

There was a long pause, as if the man he addressed was unsure of his own identity.

'I am.'

His body knights did not move, did not show any sign of preparing to engage, and that was good. 'We come from Prince Pandulf of Capua, who demands you both acknowledge him as your true suzerain and wait upon his person.'

'I have refused to surrender my person once.'

William knew what he meant by that; the laws of how a siege was conducted were well established and this man knew them only too well: no quarter should be given, he should be cut down and his knights with him. With his breath easing, if no less painful in his throat, William replied.

'Then I make you the same offer now.' He was aware that he was subject to much scrutiny from his fellow mercenaries – it was not his place to say such words – but not one of them protested or intervened. They had gifted him the power of control. 'If you will do so, and the men who now guard you put up their weapons, you and they will be spared.'

'Who makes this offer?'

'William de Hauteville.'

'You do not command the force that demanded my submission. He named himself as Odo de Jumiège.'

'Odo is our captain,' William replied, without being certain of the grounds he had for his confidence, 'but in this hall I have all the authority I need.'

'And how can I be sure that Odo de Jumiège will accede? And behind him stands Prince Pandulf.'

'It makes little difference. You can die now, or take a chance of life. I offer you only what I can.'

The man was looking into William's eyes over a distance of ten paces. Was he seeking reassurance or looking for a trace of reserve in his adversary, a reluctance to fight? It was because of the steadiness of his own look that William saw him accept the offer before he spoke, and he felt a deep sense of relief.

'Put up your weapons.'

William felt the tension drain from his body, as he had them disarmed, then he addressed their master. 'You must prepare yourself to accompany us to Capua.'

Odo had been taken back down to the house he occupied and was in a bad way, his wound too grave for him to be moved. William, since no one else in the band seemed keen to take the responsibility, had the locals send for a mendicant monk to look to his needs, and once that Benedictine had examined the invalid and pronounced it safe to move him, he was taken up to the castle to occupy the quarters of the late owner. Only then could the monk look to the needs of the other Normans, William included. Following on from that came more burials, a common pit for those who had defended the castle, individual graves with crosses for the half-dozen dead mercenaries.

Then he called the Normans together and asked them about electing a temporary leader. That led to much shuffling and mumbling, but not to anyone putting themselves forward. For the first time in many months William felt like the elder brother he had been in Normandy. There he had faced the same desire that he should make any decisions that were not the lot of his father. Because of that, he felt no scruple in assuming command; if anything it came naturally to him.

The priest was obliged to say a mass for all the souls of the dead in the local church and two days were spent ensuring that all was secure, and counting up the value of everything the castle held, from the contents of the coffers, what arms and mail had been captured, horses, fodder, food and wine, down to the last vessel of lamp oil; Rainulf, the man to whom William would report, would want to know, so that he could claim his due reward from Pandulf.

William de Hauteville also used part of that time

to find out which citizens were respected in the town and to question them, his aim being to find out what they thought of their captured lord. The opinion was not high; though they feared the Normans and what they might bring in the way of tyranny, it was obvious that the man being taken away was not revered. What he said to them was a mixture of reassurance and threat.

Odo would have to remain, and since he was too comatose to make decisions, William made them for him, leaving ten of the remaining Normans to garrison the castle, safe in the knowledge that there were no forces left in the Montesárchio fief to attack the place, and in any case it was still well stocked for a siege.

'But,' he admonished them before he departed, 'you are small in number. Do not treat the local townsfolk badly, for you will depend on them for much. The lord we have taken prisoner had a heavy hand, and he was not loved. Perhaps if he had been the men we fought would have defended his person better. Do not make the same mistake as he.'

That done, he rode off out with the remaining seven of the men who had come to this place, to take the prisoner to meet his fate.

CHAPTER THIRTEEN

The party had been observed from the top of Rainulf's tower – seven Norman knights, a prisoner, and a string of several dozen packhorses, so by the time they rode into the encampment the whole of the remaining force of mercenaries were gathered to greet them. That Odo de Jumiège was missing, and William de Hauteville was riding at their head, set up a buzz of speculation, but most eyes were drawn to the downcast figure of the Lord of Montesárchio, who had been obliged to ride on a donkey so small that his feet touched the ground. William had done this so that when departing his domains, which they passed through on the old Roman road, those who owed him service, from the meanest peasant to richest artisan, should see how low he had fallen.

Rainulf was at the doorway of his tower again, the

height of that ramp enabling him to see everything over the heads of others, like Drogo greeting his brother warmly, the questions obviously pouring from his lips as to why he seemed to be in command, and just as ardently being answered. Annoyed, his voice came out as a roar that turned every head towards him.

'I think it is proper to report to me.'

William looked up; he had been bent off his horse talking to Drogo, and he gave Rainulf that lazy, amused smile which he suspected might infuriate him, as it had so many others. Judging by the deepening purple of Rainulf's face, he succeeded. Yet the look at that was fleeting; William dismounted, and bid the Lord of Montesárchio do the same, then, giving orders that all the contents of the numerous packhorses should be deposited safely in the tower, he led his prisoner to and up the ramp, and introduced him.

'Where's Odo?' Rainulf demanded, ignoring the man.

'In a cot, with a wound in his side that will take time to mend, if it ever does. I left him in Montesárchio with ten men to hold the place.'

'You left him?'

'I took command.'

'I cannot believe Odo gifted that to you.'

William had suspected that, for all his own dislike of the de Hautevilles, in the way he had been treated by his captain, the man might be acting on instructions from Rainulf. He was tempted to ask, just to force his leader to perhaps lie.

'He was in no position, Rainulf, to gift anything to anyone. I must tell you he may not survive. As for my being in command, the men you engage are certainly fighters, but few of them relish the idea of being a leader.'

'And you do?'

'I brought the men back, and your prisoner. What happens now is for you to decide.'

'Am I to stand here like some peasant?'

Rainulf seemed glad to turn away from a defiant-looking William and glare at the prisoner.

'Take what treatment you get and be grateful. You will rest here tonight, and tomorrow we will ride to Capua, where you can face your prince.' Then he turned back to William. 'And you will accompany us.'

'The wound is clean,' said Drogo, sniffing at the bandage in which the mendicant monk had wrapped it. Then he gently probed around the angry cut with his fingers, making his brother wince. 'Do you know what he used?'

'An infusion of herbs that stung like the Devil. There was the juice of a yellow fruit that he offered me to suck too. It was hellish sharp, worse than an unripe apple.'

'You should have asked him to give you some. It has clearly worked on your wound.'

'These monks share their knowledge. Rainulf's fellows will know of it. Right now, let the air do its work.'

'So you're going to Capua?'

The way Drogo said that did nothing to hide his envy; there had been plenty of that too when William had told him of the fight, even more when he had described the full coffers, stables and food stores of the Lord of Montesárchio, some of which must come to him.

'I shall ask that you accompany us.'

'Why?'

'I want to see if Rainulf refuses. If he does, that will tell us if he intends that we should never ride out together.'

'And?'

'If that is the purpose, we cannot stay in his service.'

The head in the doorway was there only long enough to pass on the message that Rainulf wanted to see him. Responding to the summons, William found Rainulf at his large table with the contents of Montesárchio's coffers spread out before him, piles of coins and valuable objects: plate, jewels and a gold crucifix that might well have been stolen from a church. Of the previous owner there was no sign.

'I take it you think you have done well?'

William shrugged. 'That is not for me to decide.'

'You should have killed him.'

There was no need to ask who Rainulf was talking about. 'Why?'

'Look at what is here before you. If only you and I knew…' Rainulf did not finish the sentence, because the implication of that was obvious too. 'And having paraded him through half his lands every one of his subjects knows you spared him.'

'So Pandulf will get to know?'

'That's right, and the Wolf will also find out how much he had in his coffers down to the last denier. Dead, we could have had half of this and he would never have known.'

'He surrendered.'

'Do you think I did not speak with him? You asked him to surrender, you allowed him to surrender, and all you did to his bonded knights was take away their weapons and send them away. Let me tell you,' Rainulf continued, his voice rising, 'William de Hauteville, you have not done well, you should have slaughtered every one of them!'

Given William did not reply, Drengot continued. 'Such notions as you displayed should have been left behind in Normandy. Here we fight, not for honour, but for profit.'

'You would cheat Prince Pandulf?'

William knew it was a feeble thing to say, and he deserved the sneering response his remark provoked.

'I would deceive a man who would sell his own mother. He would have given to me a twentieth of that which we gave to him. As it is, we can only take a tenth of this.' Rainulf was almost talking to himself, when he added. 'A man like Montesárchio can be expected to lie about a sum like that, but not half.' Then he looked hard at William. 'Learn, de Hauteville. Money!'

To conclude that Rainulf was greedy did not take William very far, after all he had the revenues of Aversa as well, but then he did have a large band of mercenaries to feed and occupy, as well as a paymaster who was no doubt slow to meet his debts. Added to that, from what he had heard of this Pandulf, from the men he had ridden with, and the prisoner they had taken, what Rainulf said about him was an understatement.

'I wish Drogo to accompany us to Capua.'

Rainulf did not answer for a while, playing instead with a gold coin. 'Why?'

'It would be of more interest to me, Rainulf, to know why not?'

The mercenary leader just shrugged. 'So be it, we leave at first light. Make sure your equipment is clean, I will need to present you to the prince.'

* * *

William paid a visit to the scrivener, to have composed a letter to send home to Hauteville. He could read and write, having been taught the rudiments of both by his Montbray cousin, but the fellow Rainulf kept, once a monk, had a gift for composition, which transcended William's ability to put in a missive words easy to find when speaking. Somehow the fellow seemed able to convey thoughts better than those who used his service, though William had asked him to avoid his more flowery allusions, knowing Montbray would smoke that the source was not his cousin.

There would be rewards from the spoils of Montesárchio greater than mere pay, and he wanted to have in advance the words that would tell his family not only of their progress in the fighting line, but the fact that soon there should be sufficient funds transmitted to pay for the next two brothers to join them. He had no doubt that Rainulf would accept them into his service; they were good fighters. He also urged Montbray to use the service in reverse, and let both him and Drogo know how things progressed in Normandy and, that done, he went to the hut of Odo de Jumiège, to perform a duty he would have undertaken earlier if he had not been summoned by Rainulf. Odo's woman, the mother of two children, must be told how her man fared.

What he saw in her black Italian eyes was fear, and

the way she clutched her children to her reinforced that feeling, for William did not seek to give her false reassurance. Her man may well recover and be what he once was, but the possibility of death had to be accepted, as well as the notion of a wound so serious: Odo might never be able to return to full service. Troubled as he left her, he wondered what became of the concubines of his confrères, for it was axiomatic that when men fought, some were severely wounded or died.

Outside Drogo's hut, he heard what had become commonplace: raised voices, as his brother sought to control a young and spirited girl, thinking it was remarkable how much, and how quickly, Drogo had mastered enough Italian to keep an argument going. Not wishing to enter, he just shouted the instruction for the next morning.

The brothers had passed through Capua on the way south, it being on the Via Appia and having the only bridge between the city and the sea, but they had not stopped, except to water their horses at the public trough. This time they rode in some splendour, William in a new red and black surcoat which, like the others, he had only donned on the limit of the city. Rainulf was more magnificent still, his garment bearing his coat of arms as Lord of Aversa. Not needing to humiliate the Lord of Montesárchio, he had been allotted a horse, though he arrived at Pandulf's palace covered in dust, his face growing more and more gloomy the closer he came to what could not be other than an unpleasant fate.

The gates and walls of Pandulf's castle were guarded by Normans, and it was pleasant to find themselves greeted in French and engaged in conversation by mercenaries who, they were eager to tell, had taken direct service with the prince. William was curious: given the numerous fighting men he employed, why had Pandulf not sent his own men to bring in their prisoner? But he decided against enquiring.

Also the look on Rainulf's face as he regarded these men was not one of fondness, and it was curious the lack of communication he had with them and they with him, given their shared birthright. It was Drogo, in his genial, chatty way, who nailed the reason: most of them had at one time served Rainulf, only to switch to a prince who paid a higher stipend and had no desire to depend on another for his protection.

In the courtyard they found the mounts of another party, the acolytes and donkeys that turned out to be those of the Abbot of Montecassino and, on entering the palace, they found that aged cleric in audience with Prince Pandulf, one that was clearly not proceeding well, given they entered a chamber in which voices were wont to echo to the sound of angry shouts. Marching behind Rainulf, William and Drogo had an arm each on the Lord of Montesárchio, aware that behind them came some of Pandulf's men.

'The Pope has no say in the matter!' Pandulf yelled.

The voice that answered was soft and emollient. 'We are all beholden to Christ's Vicar on Earth, and it is to him that any excess funds from our humble monastery must be commuted.'

'What you send to Rome is a pittance compared to what you bring in.'

'Nevertheless, we are not part of the diocese of Capua or any other.'

'And me, Abbot, am I nothing?'

'It is to be hoped, my Lord, that you are as much a son of the Church as you are lord of your domains. But I must say again, those domains do not include the Monastery of Montecassino.'

'You would deny me, Theodore? Might I remind you that the archbishop of the diocese you stand in is, at this moment, in my dungeon.'

'And he is in my prayers,' the abbot replied, his voice somewhat firmer. 'I do not seek to defy you, Prince. I merely seek to lay down to you the bounds of your fiefs. The monastery is church land: it is not subject to any temporal overlord, and never can be.'

Looking over the abbot's head, Pandulf saw Rainulf and his party, and quite naturally his eye was drawn to the man who had defied him. 'He is in your prayers, Abbot?'

'As is any soul in distress, and the archbishop must be.'

Pandulf walked past the elderly abbot and called to him over his shoulder. 'Then cast your eyes on this creature, Theodore, for he is in distress now, and will be in more before the day is out.'

Pandulf was now close to Rainulf, William and Drogo, though he had eyes only for Montesárchio. He was smiling, William thought, as though he had just been presented with his favourite dish. Then he leant forward and spat full in the prisoner's face.

'On your knees, pig.' Both the brothers eased their grip and the man sank to his knees. 'Now on your belly and kiss my foot.'

'My Lord...'

'My foot,' Pandulf insisted, sticking out a soft leather boot.

'I seek forgiveness.'

'Perhaps the abbot here will forgive you.'

Montesárchio extended his body to kiss the proffered foot, only to be kicked hard in the face. William was watching him, at the same time wondering if his brother was thinking the same as he: that for all the smiling they were looking at a man who took pleasure in base cruelty.

'It will be some time before I do.'

Rainulf spoke up, his voice loud and confident. 'We have the contents of his coffers out in the courtyard, Prince Pandulf.'

The eyes shot up in mock horror and the tone of voice matched that. 'My dear Rainulf, I have omitted to greet you. Can you forgive me?' Then he stepped forward and embraced the Norman.

'You need no forgiveness.'

William had to stop himself from smiling then, not only because of the honeyed tone of Rainulf's voice, but in remembrance of his willingness to cheat the man he was no doubt flattering. They seemed a well-matched pair.

'But I do, Rainulf. What would I be without you as my support?'

Now it was a case, given the number of men he had of his own, of who was flattering whom.

'And you have come at a most fortuitous time, Rainulf,' Pandulf added, putting a lazy foot on Montesárchio's neck, then pressing hard. 'I have here, as you can see, Theodore, the Abbot of Montecassino, in the hope of reminding him of his obligations to Capua, and do you believe it, he denies it is owed. Some nonsense about the Pope in Rome and the emperor in Germany, leaving me at a loss to know what to do about it.'

'Perhaps our business,' Rainulf replied.

'Yes, my friend.' Pandulf turned, looking directly

at the abbot, and said in a calm voice. 'You must take precedence over a mere monk, however much he thinks himself elevated by his office.'

'I am proud to be a mere monk, Prince Pandulf,' the Abbot Theodore replied. 'If I have any elevation it is only that given to me by my fellows of Montecassino who honoured me by electing me to lead them.'

'How humble, Theodore. I have a feeling that perhaps your humility could do with a touch of assistance. But that must wait, we have a recalcitrant vassal to deal with, who at least knows his place.' Turning back to Rainulf, the smile came onto his face like the light from a lantern. 'Let us see what this wretch has been seeking to keep from me.'

The wretch was left kissing the floor, with one of Pandulf's Normans, at the prince's instructions, pressing a lance into his back.

It was in another, more private chamber that William and Drogo emptied the contents of the panniers they had brought from Aversa, and though the treasure was enough to please any man's eye, it was telling the way it affected Pandulf. He grasped and caressed the gold in a manner almost sensual in its intensity. As he was doing this Rainulf was relating what had occurred, making sure to claim any credit for himself, leaving William to wonder why he had not done as he had said: he had quite deliberately not introduced either him or Drogo. His next words solved that question.

'I have left a small garrison at Montesárchio awaiting your pleasure.'

Pandulf observed the way Drogo looked at his brother, and his eyes registered the surprise in the younger de Hauteville face, and that made him look next at William, who was wearing that amused half-smile.

'It can be held?' he asked.

'Easily, though it may need more men, which I am happy to provide...'

'I shall provide them, Rainulf,' the prince said quickly, picking up the gold crucifix and kissing it. 'After all, given this, and what look like healthy revenues, keeping a garrison there will not be a burden.'

'No,' Rainulf growled, clearly not happy. 'And the Lord of Montesárchio?'

'Can taste my hospitality and learn his lesson. One day I may restore him, we shall see.' Then he looked up at William, who towered over him. 'Who are these fellows you have brought with you, Rainulf?'

'New recruits, the brothers de Hauteville.'

'And you were at Montesárchio?'

'One was,' Rainulf said hurriedly, 'William here.'

'I know of the place. Not an easy one to capture.' His hand swept over the table. 'I had not expected to see this for many months.'

'We were lucky, my Lord. The defenders sought

to surprise us on the very first night. They forgot we were Normans. We managed to fight our way into the castle before they could reclose the gate.'

'Truly, Rainulf,' Pandulf said, his eyes still fixed on William. 'You are a wonder.'

'I know who to pick and when, sire,' the mercenary leader replied, which was as close as he was going to get to an admission he had not been present.

'This must go to my chamberlain to be counted. I cannot reward you until that is done.'

'Of course.'

'But,' Pandulf said, picking up a clutch of several gold coins, 'I think your valiant fellow here deserves an extra reward.'

'Very generous, Prince Pandulf,' Rainulf said, without any conviction whatsoever, as William accepted the money. As a message it was as plain as a pikestaff: should the brothers seek service in Capua, they would be welcome.

'Now, Rainulf, I must return and see what I am to do about this damned abbot. We will speak later.'

When they emerged from the private chamber, instead of following Pandulf, Rainulf silently indicated they should follow him. He took them through the castle to one of the outer walls, and then down a winding set of stone steps, which became increasingly damp. The smell of rot increased as well, with Rainulf telling them, in a voice that echoed off the now dripping walls, that through the green slimy one they were passing lay the River Volturno.

At the bottom of the steps they came to a chamber into which daylight would never penetrate, with cells along the inner wall and, in the floor, square openings covered with heavy bars. A partially crippled individual grovelled to Rainulf, who bid him take one of his keys to lift the grill of one of these oubliettes, and then to fetch a torch. That brought and the grill lifted, Rainulf beckoned to them once more, bidding the brothers move forward to peer in.

The creature chained to the wall was naked, his body a mass of open sores. At his feet was a flat board on a rope that went up to a pulley where the floor joined the grill, obviously the method by which he was fed. The man looked up with pleading eyes sunk into an emaciated face, his hair, which would have been white had it not been so full of filth, hanging down his back.

'This is Osmond de Vertin.'

'Norman?' asked William, as Rainulf nodded. 'What has he done?'

'He failed.'

'You?'

'No. He was my captain once, in a post of honour, but he elected to leave my service and join Prince Pandulf. Osmond failed his new master. He sought his own advantage and as you see he has earned his own reward.'

'Why are you showing us this?' demanded Drogo.

Rainulf was looking at William when he replied. 'You are ambitious, you two, I can smell it. I thought it would do you good to see the cost of failing a man who has just tried to bribe you to join him.'

'The men he employs?'

'Many of them were once in my pay, yes.'

'You have influence with this prince. It shames you that he has this man in here.'

'It pleases Pandulf, and that is all that matters. Now I must go and see what the Wolf intends to do with his troublesome abbot.'

William and Drogo, once they were back above ground, were sent to the kitchens, to get food and wine, so missed what happened in the great hall. Rainulf told them on the way back to Aversa.

'Abbot Theodore can argue till his face goes blue, and quote Holy Scripture all day. The Prince of Capua claims he is the rightful suzerain to the monastery lands, so he will be forced to agree.'

'And if he does not?' asked Drogo.

'Then he will need all the faith he has in God. Pandulf will not be gainsaid. He will have the revenues of Montecassino, whatever it takes.'

Rainulf was right: the news filtered down to Aversa. The Abbot of Montecassino, having made a second visit, was thrown into Pandulf's dungeons, stripped by the prince of his title. The monks voted for another abbot, but Pandulf just ignored the appointment. Word also came from Capua that men were needed to help Pandulf assert his rights to the property of the abbey, the reward promised being in sequestered land instead of money payment. This request was not put to Rainulf, indeed much effort was made to keep him in the dark, but he knew what was afoot when men began to leave his band and head north.

'The promised rewards are good,' said Drogo, as he groomed a horse; he always with an ear closer to the ground than his brother.

'You think we should join Pandulf?'

'Do we owe loyalty to Rainulf?'

'No, Drogo, but a man who throws into a dungeon an abbot of such age is not one I would wish to take employment with.'

'Not even for land of your own?'

'No.'

As a conveyance, a servant-borne litter was a rare enough sight to raise the eyebrows of William and Drogo, though it was noticeable that many of their fellow mercenaries knew what it portended: the arrival of the Jew. Those with no interest in the services he provided shrugged and carried on with their training, but others began to put away their weapons, the first of those making for their huts.

The arrangement meant that the Jew, after he and Rainulf had sorted out their own business, took over Rainulf's quarters, and was given a list of what was due to each man. If they had acquired any extra of their own they tended to exchange that in Aversa, and as long as it was not property that should have been declared to their leader, nothing was said. The Jew would then undertake, for a fee, to get an agreed sum back to Normandy, by methods regarding which no one enquired. No doubt Rainulf knew, and that sufficed.

The Jew, who introduced himself as Kasa Ephraim, William found a pleasant individual, with a relaxed, reassuring voice, a man accustomed to calming the fears of fellows nervous of parting with possessions seen as hard won. He had his fee from Montesárchio, which was substantial, added to the gold with which Pandulf had sought to bribe him and Drogo, which should meet the obligation he had made in the letter he had had composed by the scrivener, yet he would have been the first to admit that the handling of money was to him a strange thing. Coin had been rare in Normandy; barter as a means of exchange was more common.

'Will they actually see gold?' he asked.

'They will, as long as they journey to Rouen to collect it, for the people I deal with would not travel with such in a place where they could be robbed. The risk of that must fall to those you send to. All they will get is a message saying there is a sum to collect.'

'No one will rob them!'

Having counted out what William gave him, Ephraim responded with a slip of paper on which he had written the sum that would be commuted. 'If you take this to the scrivener, he will tell you what my charge is for the service.'

'I can read it,' William replied, in a voice that showed he was not entirely happy to see a third of his funds go in payment.

'You read?'

'And write.'

'Many of your fellows do not,' Ephraim smiled, 'so I see I must explain to you the price of the service I offer. Understand that all these messages must be sent many leagues, and those who carry them must be paid. The person who will give out the money on my bond must also earn from his endeavours. However, if you are unhappy, I will happily give you back what you have brought and leave you to seek some other means of transacting this business.'

'No,' William replied. There was only one other means: he or Drogo going all the way back themselves.

'I did forget to add, that I too am a man of business. Some of what you pay will come to me.'

'You have others waiting,' said William, determined not to show gratitude.

* * *

He was summoned to attend upon Rainulf once the Jew had left, not just in the litter now but with a strong escort as well, given the accumulated funds of the mercenaries was considerable. Sitting at the end of his table, as usual with a goblet of wine in his hand, Rainulf eyed him for a few seconds before speaking, and when he did his voice had in it a tone William had not heard before: the man was not gruff this time, he was almost friendly.

'It will not surprise you to know, William de Hauteville, that if correspondence can go to Normandy, it can also come back.' William shrugged, not sure how to respond. 'When new men come to me, I make a habit of sending home with my Jew to find out about them.'

'And this you did with Drogo and me?'

Rainulf nodded. 'I do not care if a man is a murderer, but I do care if he is a thief, for a man who steals once will do so again and that means trouble in a company like mine.'

'So you have found that you have no fears with us.'

Rainulf sat forward. 'But I have found out other things.'

William could guess what they were. 'If they do not trouble you, I would put them out of your mind.'

'What, your bloodline?'

'My bloodline is my affair.'

'Did you run away, de Hauteville, you and your brother?'

'No.'

'Yet when you heard of the death of Duke Robert you came on. Why not turn around and go home, or were you too afeared of a seven-year-old bastard?'

William smiled, which he was glad to see upset Rainulf as much as it had upset others. 'You said I should leave honour behind, Rainulf. That I will never do.'

'How noble.'

The smile vanished. 'The business you have mentioned is that of my family and it is none of yours, and think on this Rainulf: if I am not given to the betrayal of an oath my father made, one that I will not explain, my honour is an asset to you, as it is to any other lord.'

With that, William spun on his heel and stomped out.

The next piece of news to arrive told of the death of Odo de Jumière, and here the brothers discovered that, although Rainulf had a say in who stood to replace him, it was the men he would lead who had the final word. William was unsure if he was put up because there was no choice, or because Rainulf thought him qualified, but stand he did and his election was unanimous, word having spread of his leadership at Montesárchio.

Both brothers would have said that their relations with Rainulf were subject to a certain amount of strain, yet it seemed this elective elevation changed matters. Or perhaps it was the knowledge he had gleaned from Normandy, added to the fact that even after Pandulf had tried to bribe them, and the carrot of land had been dangled before them by secret messages from Capua, he and Drogo, unlike some fifty others, had stayed with the Lord of Aversa.

'Well, William de Hauteville, my Contentin ruffian, I long to see how you will handle your battaile.'

'I see nothing in the offing, Rainulf, that will give me the opportunity.'

The sunken eyes in that purple face looked serious then, and Rainulf looked over William's shoulder to the road that led north.

'Did I not tell you the day you arrived? Peace in these parts is a rare commodity, and my bones tell me that for a certain lord not too far distant, I might have come to be seen as a less than complete friend.'

'And Montecassino?'

Rainulf understood the nuances of the question; they did not have to be openly stated, but he did not reply, instead posing a question. 'What would you do?'

'I think the answer to that is obvious.'

'And if I ordered you to take part in its dismemberment.'

'Then I would refuse.'

Rainulf slapped William on the back. 'Good. I am glad to hear it.'

CHAPTER FOURTEEN

The Bamberg weather had cleared, the mist lifting as the temperature dropped on an icy east wind, and Conrad was off on his hunting again, dragging with him many of his advisors, which meant that the business of the imperial court, never rapid, slowed once more to a crawl. Several weeks went by while Guaimar waited for a chance to talk properly; all he got was the odd exchange in a chance encounter. Yet each night, in the great hall, lit by flaming torches and heated by blazing fires, a great crowd gathered to eat at the board of their regal overlord, a noisy affair in which normal conversation was impossible.

This Guaimar had discovered on sitting at the high table with Conrad Augustus before, especially when the emperor's attention seemed to be concentrated on his sister, who was always close enough to his person to hold a shouted conversation. Her brother was not quite below the salt; indeed he was seated at the high table, but so far from the centre as to drown out any plea to Conrad. In the end, he had to appeal to Berengara to see if she could arrange a private interview, since when she called upon the emperor in his private part of the palace, he did not decline to receive her.

'I do hope, sister, that you have not gone too far in charming Conrad,' he said, when she confirmed that the emperor would see him the next day after mass, which, being Palm Sunday, meant not even he could justify going out to hunt.

'I do not know what you mean.'

It was the fact that she would not look at him which made him sound harsher than he intended. 'Yes, you do.'

The look he got in reply made him feel uncomfortable. Her eyes flashed with anger and her pursed lips were those of the spoilt child he so well remembered; if Berengara had anything of which she had reason to be ashamed, she was not going to gift him the right of chastisement.

'Why are we here?'

'You know that very well.'

'And what weapons do we have to bend Conrad to our hopes?' Guaimar did not answer; it was his turn not to look at his sister. 'Few, if not none at all, so we must employ what little we have which favours us. I am as wedded to the removal of the Wolf as you, but if you wish to know my every move, and imply that I am misusing what gifts God has given me, I am forced to ask you why you brought me here.'

'You know why, to aid me.'

'In what way?'

Guaimar avoided an honest answer to that; to admit he had hoped she would melt stony hearts with her beauty was tantamount to admitting he was prepared to act as a pander for her. 'I particularly wished to keep you safe from Pandulf. After what happened...'

Though she interrupted, it was not with any rancour; indeed her voice was soft. 'Please, Guaimar, do not seek to deceive me. We are both engaged in seeking the same outcome. You have your title and your wits, I have what you sought to use.'

'Has Conrad...?' He could not say the words.

'He has been kind, brother, considerate, and he has, thanks to me, acceded to my request that he see you.'

'The price?'

'Is one I am prepared to pay!'

'So it has not been forfeit yet?'

Berengara gave him a smile then, an enigmatic one that revealed to him that she too was growing up, as he had had to. She was no child now. What it did not do was answer his question.

* * *

Guaimar knew Conrad had been deliberately keeping him at arm's length, quite happy to talk in passing but never ready to sit, as he was doing now, and seriously discuss Pandulf or the situation in Campania. There was history here too, of course: Pandulf, for his previous treachery with Byzantium, had been a prisoner of his predecessor. Conrad had released the traitor on his accession, which he probably now felt to be a mistake, but not one to which an emperor could admit. The young man before him was asking him to alter a situation he had brought about.

So he listened politely while Guaimar enumerated the Wolf's manifest transgressions, which apparently failed to make much mark on the emperor's thinking. Not that he saw such behaviour as acceptable, it was just he could not be brought to see it as in need of remedial action.

'I had an audience with the Bishop of L'Aquila. In fact, he confessed me before mass this very morning.' Guaimar was not sure he believed that: Ascletin was so raw in the priestly line he doubted he knew the necessary words to say in a confessional booth. 'You travelled with him, of course.'

'And most pleasant it was,' the younger man lied.

Conrad looked at him quizzically then. 'Tell me, young Guaimar, you say you came only to me?'

'Yes.'

'Why?'

'I do not follow.'

'I am not the only source of redress, am I?'

'You mean Byzantium,' Guaimar replied, thinking it was Ascletin who had confessed in that booth this morning, not Conrad Augustus. The emperor sat back in his chair, making a gesture that demanded explanation. 'I agree, I could have gone to Constantinople, but I believe it was my duty to come here to my suzerain.'

'But you could also have sent to the Emperor Michael for aid, without actually travelling there. By ship for instance.'

He is stalling me, thought Guaimar; he is waiting to hear from his spies if Byzantium is prepared to intervene. The other thought he had was depressing: there was nothing he could do about it.

'No eastern emperor since the great Basil enjoys the reputation that you have, Conrad Augustus.' If he was flattered by comparison with the Bulgar-Slayer, who would have been a match for Charlemagne, Conrad took it as his due. 'The late Emperor Romanos was a voluptuary by all accounts, ruled by the whims of the Empress Zöe. Her new husband, Michael, is little older than I, and I cannot see him as your equal.'

'He is the brother of the eunuch who runs the court and that gives him power. Besides that, they say Michael is an ardent young buck and makes an old woman happy.'

'Competence in the bedchamber is not what makes a man great.'

Guaimar had replied tersely, annoyed by the way Conrad was taking the conversation. He had no concern for the carnal joys young Michael gave to a woman thirty years his senior and it was, he knew, just part of the game Conrad was playing.

'They have great resources, and a fleet that could put a force on Campanian soil in much less time than I can march there with an army, and they would dearly love to assert their authority there, as they have tried to do many times in the past. Even a youth and his frivolous old wife might be tempted by the prospect of detaching my imperial fiefs of Southern Italy from their allegiance.'

'Are you suggesting, sire, that I have come to the wrong place?'

Conrad smiled, like a man who had spotted a trap and knew how to avoid it. 'I am saying that your need is great, so perhaps it makes no difference who brings down Pandulf. You Lombards have bowed the knee to Constantinople before.'

'Not with much joy.'

That got a sharp response. 'My predecessor took an army all the way to the borders of Apulia to keep you free of the Eastern Empire, and it advantaged him nothing. I seem to remember Salerno sided with his enemies, and only acquiesced when faced by a host outside your walls too powerful to resist. The same blood flows though your veins.'

'I cannot answer for the actions of my predecessors. All I can say, sire, is no man likes to be a subject.'

'Yet you beg to be mine.'

'I beg to have righted a great wrong, and if the price of that is an acknowledgement of a title you already possess, then I am happy to accede to it.'

'You have still not explained to my satisfaction why you failed to send any request to Constantinople.'

Guaimar was hoist on his own petard and he knew it: he had tricked Ascletin, who had played his perfidious part and it had produced the opposite effect to that intended, making Conrad cautious instead of bold. There was no point now in telling the man the truth – he was not inclined to act regardless and anyway he would not now be believed, even if he had to try.

'I acted on the advice of my archbishop. Indeed it was only through his good grace that I could make the journey, for he funded it. You will readily understand his reluctance to have a Byzantine fleet in Salerno Bay.' Conrad's eyes bored into his, and they seemed to be saying that he had deceived him too. 'Am I to understand that you will not come to our aid?'

'I have not decided.'

'And if Pandulf takes Naples as well?'

'That may alter things, but we would have to see.'

'He intends to fight Byzantium.'

An inquisitive look demanded more information, which Guaimar supplied, and when he had finished Conrad actually burst out laughing. 'You will never learn, you Lombards. There's not one of you who is not wedded to betrayal.' He saw Guaimar about to protest, and he cut him off. 'And before you tell me that you are the exception, let me tell you that I will decide nothing until I know what it is I might face.'

'Berengara, I am bound to ask you how much influence you think you have with Conrad?'

'I may have a great deal, Guaimar, as long as he has not been gifted that which he so desires.'

So she was still chaste; her brother was not sure whether he was pleased or disappointed, and then he felt like a true scrub. As he asked the next question, so embarrassing to posit, he knew his face was slightly flushed.

'If you...would it? Do you think you could persuade... the emperor to act?'

'How tongue-tied you are, Guaimar, when talking of trading my virtue.' He could see by the wicked smile that she was teasing him, and she was enjoying it too.

'You would have to think Salerno worth the price.'

'Revenge,' she spat, 'is worth the price. Your father was my father too. The emperor wants to bed me, and my maidenhead is an added attraction. I think I could extract a promise from him to help us before it is surrendered. Could I get him to keep to what must be said in private after the event, I do not know.'

'How practical you are.'

'Does that disappoint you?'

'I still think of you as...'

Another snapped interruption. 'I am no longer your little sister, Guaimar. I know what must be done, and I will undertake to do it.'

'When?'

'Given his eagerness, as soon as his wife or one of his clerics is not looking, which is not often.'

'I'm sorry.'

'Why be sorry?' she replied coquettishly, 'I shall be like the mythical Helen, and launch a thousand spears, if I can hold him to his bond.'

'Damn that swine, I'll rip the skin off his hide. I'll sow him in a sack with a cat and snake and throw him into the nearest harbour.'

Both recognised the angry voice, shouting in the echoing corridor outside their apartments. Guaimar was convinced as he digested what was being said he was going to be the victim of those threats. The door was flung open with a resounding crash and Conrad stood there, his eyes on fire, boring into those of the young man.

'Do you know what that bastard has done?'

'Sire, I...'

'He has laid hands upon the Abbot of Montecassino, that's what he has done. He has thrown Theodore, a man whose election I personally approved, into his dungeons.'

By now Conrad was in the room, kicking any object that came within reach of his boot.

'When I lay hands on him he will wish he had never been conceived. I want you at my council in the morning. The host will be summoned and I will march south and crush that swine like a gnat.'

Then he was gone, still raging, still shouting, his voice fading as the distance increased, leaving them to exchange a look of relief.

'Well, brother,' Berengara said, 'it appears my virtue has been saved.'

'And by the Wolf himself, of all people.'

The door was flung open again, to be filled, once more, with Conrad's stocky frame and puce countenance. 'And by the way, you treacherous young swine, you can forget Byzantium. That Michael you call a callow youth has sent his whole fleet and army to conquer Sicily.'

'I did not set out to deceive you, sire...'

Conrad cut right across him. 'Of course you did, and if you had not, I would have had you for a fool.'

The so-called Empire of the West was nothing like that which had existed in ancient times; it was a loose agglomeration of states, the rulers of which elected one of their number to be Holy Roman Emperor. Conrad had his own lands and his own feudal levies, but to bring together an army large enough to subdue Pandulf, and stamp his authority on Campania, required the whole resources of the empire, and that took time to assemble.

Having got what he had come for, Guaimar was now suffering the tortures of Tantalus, so slow did it all seem, yet even he had to acknowledge that to march south with a thousand lances, and to gather more on the way, required an organisation of staggering complexity. The sheer provision of food and shelter for the men, and the amount of fodder and pasturage required for their mounts, beggared belief, and that only increased the further south they travelled and the greater the size of the host became.

Any plans that were laid had to do with that, not battle, and Conrad was in constant dispute with imperial vassals about the measure of their contributions in terms of lances provided, the money payments due after their days of feudal service had expired – as they must on such a campaign – the amount of forage and food their lands should provide as the imperial host crossed their domains, and that had paled when set against the prickly personalities and endemic feuding of powerful lords accustomed to be the masters of the world in which they lived.

The army camped outside Rome, and Conrad took the opportunity to enter the city and overawe both the leading families and the populace. Benedict, with imperial protection, was for once at liberty to travel around the city without fear of physical assault, and given such liberty, and the fact that he was as much in fear of Conrad as grateful, he was able to satisfy the emperor regarding any ecclesiastical appointments that were outstanding throughout his own domains; in short, Conrad got the archbishops he wanted.

Berengara had thoroughly enjoyed the progress, unlike her impatient brother. Still pursued by Conrad, and still denying him that which he sought, she was, as a seeming intimate of the emperor, also being fawned on by Ascletin and every ambitious noble in the imperial entourage. Many showered her with praise; the Pierleoni showered her with gifts, which she took with a smile that hid her deep dislike. When Guaimar sought to chastise her for this, he found himself put down like a disobedient dog; his sister was in full womanhood now, and not to be told what to do by her brother.

Finally, south of Rome, with the papal contribution of paid-for foot soldiers, as well as healthy contributions to the costs of the campaign wrung from the likes of the Pierleoni, military matters began to assert themselves. As they had marched, the news that had come from the south had not been good; they had barely left Germany before Pandulf had attacked

Montecassino and stripped it of its most precious possessions: priceless books, plate, church ornaments, as well as a considerable chest of money.

Then, having seized the extensive and well-cultivated lands the monastery owned, he had parcelled it out to his own Norman mercenaries, knowing how hard they would fight to retain it. A procession of monks had come to Conrad to tell him that hardly any of the original brotherhood was still present, so reduced was the monastery. One of the greatest abbeys in Christendom, a centre of learning to rival Cluny, had been practically destroyed, its buildings torn down, in an assault to rival any ever committed by the Saracens.

Conrad was no fool: he knew the Normans in the mass represented a threat to his whole campaign. He thought himself a good commander and he had under him a fine and powerful army, but time and again in this part of the world the Normans had triumphed in situations where they should have been crushed, this entirely due to their disciplined way of fighting. Given that, it made sense to consult the man who knew them best, despite his youth.

'The key is Rainulf Drengot,' Guaimar said.

Conrad's reply was telling. 'I hear that Pandulf's own Normans are numerically a match for Rainulf now. Indeed many of Drengot's own lances deserted him, tempted by monastery land.'

'Who commands them, sire, that is the important thing. Rainulf is a leader to be feared. Has Pandulf got anyone to match him?'

'If he has Drengot, he has his leader, and the man is attached to him since he betrayed your father.'

'What if he could be detached from Pandulf?'

'For money?'

'No. I have another prize that might tempt him.'

'Which is?'

When Guaimar outlined his thinking he could see that Conrad was impressed. He was promising no less than the settlement of endemic dispute, a way for Conrad to return to Germany with the very good prospect that neither he nor his successor again would have to bring a host south.

'Did you learn such subtlety at your father's knee, Guaimar?'

'I learnt much from him, it is true.'

'Like how to lie to an emperor?' Conrad was smiling as he said that, but it was not friendly, more enquiry. 'My spies in Constantinople told me that no request was sent there for help, information that reached me in Rome, and news confirmed by Pope Benedict's own informants at the Byzantine Court.'

There was no easy way to respond, at least not one which would not mark him out as devious, so he fell back on bluster. 'Then I am accused of being truthful.'

'So the Bishop of L'Aquila is the liar?'

'He is elevated enough a cleric to answer for his own sins, sire.'

'That is not an answer.'

'I cannot think of another.'

'Then think on this, Guaimar. Can I trust you?'

'I hope you do not doubt it, sire.'

'I always harbour such doubts. It is the price of the office I occupy. It is a lesson you should hold to if you truly wish to rule Salerno.'

'I am always eager to learn from such as you, sire,' Guaimar insisted.

'You are a Lombard, young man,' Conrad insisted. 'Lying is in your blood, so there is little I can teach you, but have a care when you lie to me. Now who is to carry this proposition of yours?'

'I am willing to do so.'

'The man may lop off your head.'

'If he is so inclined, I will have failed. Given that, what do I have to live for?'

'Don't go throwing away your life, Guaimar. Not even Salerno is worth that.'

'Not to you, sire. But it is to me.'

'I wish to accompany you,' Berengara insisted, not in the least deflected by her brother's furious shake of the head. 'You say it is dangerous, I believe my presence makes it less so.'

'And if we both perish?'

'Then it is God's will and so be it.'

'Berengara,' Guaimar pleaded.

'You took me to Bamberg for the same reason.'

Argue as he might, Guaimar could not shift her, so it was a small party that included her which left Conrad's camp, and made for a place where they could safely cross the River Volturno.

CHAPTER FIFTEEN

The sentinels at the top of Rainulf Drengot's tower again gave early warning of the approaching party. Even at some distance they could see this was a different kind of delegation to that which normally called on the encampment: one of the party was a high-born female and, closer to, the sight of the imperial banner held high by one of the armed, six-man escort made apparent the sense of something unusual.

Riding through the rows of round huts, they were scrutinised by every woman in the camp; likewise the mercenaries lined the rail of the training manège to watch them pass. By the time they arrived at the ramp leading to the entrance to the donjon, Rainulf awaited them, his dogs snuffling about his lower legs, in the company of his trio of captains, which now included, since the defection of another senior mercenary to Pandulf, the recently elevated Drogo.

It was obvious to both the youngsters that Rainulf had aged: what had once been a full face, albeit a high-coloured one, was now lined and there was the beginnings of a dewlap of flesh under the chin as well as large bags under the eyes. His hair was now more grey than black and thinner than the young man remembered, while his build seemed less solid. Where previously he had looked like a warrior to be feared he now had the appearance of an ageing man, whose watery eyes were staring, trying to make out who was approaching.

Guaimar was the first to throw back the cowl and reveal himself, which made one of the quartet stiffen, though it had no effect at all on the de Hautevilles. Rainulf gasped at a face he never thought to see again, before composing himself, but that was as nothing to the reaction of the four of them when Berengara dropped her own cloak to rest on the haunches of her horse. She had dressed her hair as well as plucked her eyebrows as if attending a court ceremony and had donned a low-cut gown that showed to full perfection the swell of her breasts. Two of the escorts Conrad had sent with them jumped down to help her off her horse, Guaimar dismounting on his own.

'Lord Rainulf,' he said, with a nod more than a bow.

The Norman looked at the bright-yellow imperial

banner, with the standing black griffin, the flag of Conrad the Salian, held by one soldier still mounted, and raised a quizzical eyebrow. 'I do not know how to address you under such a standard.'

'There was a time you would have been obliged to address me as Duke.'

'A time long past,' Rainulf replied. 'Let your name suffice.'

'Does that imply a welcome?'

'No, Guaimar, it does not. I shall, however, greet your sister as the Lady Berengara.'

The use of the names made William look harder at both; Drogo had never taken his eyes off the lady, mainly at what lay under her chin. There were not so many who bore those names, so their identity was obvious, and he had been told chapter and verse about the deposition of their father in favour of Pandulf, as well as just how much Rainulf had profited by his switch of allegiance.

'I come with a message from Conrad Augustus.'

Guaimar waited until that had the desired effect, waited till Rainulf could compose himself enough to respond, for, try as he might, he could not help reacting to that name.

'All the way from Bamberg?'

'No. Conrad is encamped near Castro dei Volsci on the River Sacco, and he has with him the whole might of his imperial power. I am surprised you are not aware of this, for I suspect Prince Pandulf might be by now, given he is not very far off from Capua.'

One of Conrad's acts had been to close the road to the south after he left Rome, in order that his progress should be kept covert. There was no way he could surprise Capua; they would know when he got close, but the less time they had to prepare the defences the better. In skirting that city Guaimar had been pleased to note than no one in the hinterland seemed aware of the approaching storm, but that could not last.

'And the message is?'

Guaimar ran his eyes over the trio of captains, recognising only the one, Turmod, the others being strangers, two very tall and imposing individuals with golden hair and big shoulders, so obviously Normans. At one time he had known all of those who served Rainulf close, indeed he had seen them as friendly adults who always indulged an impetuous youth. How easily they had turned into demons.

'For your ears only, Rainulf.'

'I might be disinclined to listen.'

'I have called you many things in my time, none of them to your credit, but I never thought you a fool.'

'Have a care, boy, or you might go out of here across your saddle instead of astride it.'

William was only half listening to the exchange, too busy examining the features of both Guaimar and Berengara. The young man was good-looking in a

Lombard way, with the same kind of complexion and hair colour as Pandulf, though without any attempt to beguile. He also seemed self-assured, but not so much as his sister, who wore the kind of slight smile that told everyone looking at her that she knew precisely the train of their thoughts – she knew of her own beauty. William speculated that if she had known Drogo's in detail she would probably have slapped him.

He did wonder what was wrong with Rainulf: these people represented no threat to him, and if they came as an embassy from someone like a Holy Roman Emperor then he should treat them with respect. It then occurred to him that Rainulf found their mere presence uncomfortable, a living and breathing reminder of the way he had betrayed their father.

In the months since his own elevation William had learnt a great deal about the Lord of Aversa, as Rainulf had learnt about him. A bond of trust had been established, not that such a thing led to an exchange of confidences, just to a sense of mutual regard. For instance, William had discovered the mercenary leader was not as thick-skinned as he liked people to think. He drank too much, and in part that might be for shame at some of his deeds, and right now he was looking at the reminder of one of the worst. Added to that, a man knows when he is ageing, knows when his physical prowess is diminishing at a rate which means things once seen as effortless seem to slip away and become a trial almost every day, just as he knows how apparent such a loss is to those around him.

Rainulf ate alone because in drink he became maudlin, and in that state he no doubt felt he would diminish himself in the eyes of the men he had to lead. He slept in his villa so that he would not be seen in a state of total inebriation, given his relations with his wife were stormy enough to drive him to the wine. He wanted a child; she denied him her bed and much as he would like to he dare not put her aside and marry another, for she was Pandulf's niece. He needed to be seen as still the puissant warrior, to be thought cold-blooded: a man who would not give way to a shrew, would not weep for a death, would not fear his own and would not consider any notion not motivated by profit.

In truth, he was as sentimental as Tancred: for all that tough carapace their father had presented, Tancred loved and was as proud of his boys as he was of his own title and his exploits in the field. What had it cost him to practically beg Duke Robert to take them into his trust? If Rainulf could not be said to love his men he cared for them deeply. He had probably done to the parent of these two what he thought necessary, but William seriously doubted whether he enjoyed the memory of it.

More telling was the fact that Rainulf was now

forced to be cautious. Word had come from the south of the proposed Byzantine assault on Sicily, to take advantage of a split between the island's rulers. The Emir of Palermo had been assassinated, following on from a rebellion led by his brother and a Zirid invasion by an emir called Abdullah from North Africa. The island was in turmoil as the Saracens fought each other, and so ripe for an invasion.

The payment for such service was high, the possibility of substantial booty even higher, especially if the excuse of aiding one emir against another could be turned into a full-scale reoccupation of an island that had increased in value since the Saracens took it from Byzantium. Unquestionably this was the ultimate aim of Constantinople. In short, it was perfect for a band of mercenaries not only at present underused, but also a way to stem, and perhaps reverse, the losses in men Rainulf was experiencing with the land inducements offered by Pandulf.

Yet it was the Wolf who made acceptance dangerous; his recruitment of Rainulf's men could only have one aim: to so weaken Rainulf that his position as Lord of Aversa became brittle. Pandulf, when it came to greed, knew no limits, likewise betrayal. In his meetings with Rainulf, at which William had now become a presence, the fulsome protestations of love and loyalty looked increasingly threadbare as the number of Normans engaged to Capua increased in direct proportion to

Rainulf's losses. Those coming south from Normandy stopped at the Volturno now – the rewards were greater – cutting off the numbers coming on to Aversa, thus increasing an imbalance which could only end in one way.

'It would make sense to listen,' William said, in a whisper, his mind racing with a complex set of calculations.

Rainulf did not respond, but William knew he had heard. He had come to rely on him, trusting him in a way he did not trust Drogo or Turmod, and in part it was his experience as an elder sibling that had gained him such faith. To be a big brother to such an unruly bunch as the de Hautevilles had required qualities that made him useful to his leader: a level head, the lack of a quick temper, a slightly jaundiced seen-it-all judgement that made light of things that breached the code by which the mercenaries lived, added to an ability to resolve disputes between fighting men in a way that left no rancour. The other thing was his utter lack of sycophancy: on more than one occasion he had pointed out to Rainulf, in private, never in public, that he was utterly wrong.

'Treat them as you would the man they represent.'

If Guaimar had not heard the whispered words, he had seen the lips move. He also saw, after a pause, how Rainulf nodded to this blond giant, and he wondered who was this man who spoke to the Norman leader in that manner; no one else Guaimar had ever known, the likes of Osmond de Vertin, Odo de Jumiège or Turmod, had dared to even look Rainulf in the eye.

'Drogo, Turmod,' Rainulf said, 'look after the escort. See them fed and the mounts cared for. You, Guaimar, I will allow into my tower, along with your sister.'

'I'd rather take care of her than the horses,' Drogo moaned.

Though he did not say it out loud, the words were expressed strongly enough to carry to the ears of Berengara. Her smile broadened, as if she was not upset, but Guaimar glared at him, which got him, in response, a very elaborate wink, as if both shared the truth implicit in the remark.

'William, you will join us.'

In the cool chamber of the tower, Rainulf offered them to sit, then ordered his servants to fetch wine and fruit. While that was happening he sat in silence staring at the young man, during which time William wondered what to say, as he tried not to be too obvious in his glances at the dark line of the sister's alluring cleavage. It was all very oppressive, with Rainulf clearly, by his stillness, seeking to imply before a word was spoken that, whatever this messenger from Conrad wanted to say, it was of no interest. Tempted to speak again, because it was mere posturing, William knew he should not; his task was to aid his leader, not to diminish him.

Guaimar broke the silence as soon as he had a goblet of wine in his hand, this while Rainulf was draining his.

'I am not sure I want to speak in front of...' The young man looked at William, as if inviting him to name himself. That was Rainulf's right, so all he got in reply was the amused half smile that, unbeknown to him, had once guyed another duke.

'This,' Rainulf responded, once his goblet was refilled, 'is William de Hauteville, and he is my right hand. What you say to me can be said in front of him.'

Two people reacted with disguised surprise: Guaimar because it underlined his opinion that the Norman mercenary had aged; in past times he had never needed another's counsel. William was astonished for another reason: although he knew he had become trusted enough to give Rainulf advice, the older man had never before used that expression regarding his standing. Berengara's reaction was different, a sort of coy sideways movement of the head and eyes, as if to say that he had, no doubt, gone up mightily in his own estimation.

'Conrad intends to depose Pandulf.'

'Does he?'

'He should hang, draw and quarter him,' spat Berengara, showing, both in the way it was said and the expression that accompanied it, a vicious side to her, up till then, amiable character. 'I would happily cut out his heart.'

'You would need a long blade to even find it,' said Rainulf, spluttering at his own jest.

'I would claw his eyes out with my own fingernails.'

Rainulf was still amused. 'Your sister is bloodthirsty, Guaimar. I sense that you are not.'

'I seek only the return of that which is mine.'

'Was yours,' the old man snarled. 'I took it away from you.'

'Conrad will give it me back.'

'And if I say that he shall not, what will Conrad do then?'

'He will add you to his enemies.'

'Look at me, Guaimar. Do you see me tremble?'

'You have come to offer something, sir,' said William, in an even tone, looking at Rainulf who, in nodding, gave him leave to continue. 'It would be best to get to that and stop this sparring, which produces nothing but bile.' Seeing Guaimar hesitate, he added, in a much harder tone of voice, 'You have come with an offer for the Lord of Aversa. Make it!'

'How do you know I have come to offer no more than the fact he might live?'

Seeing Rainulf sit forward to roar at the youngster, William held up his hand: no good would come from a loss of temper. It was pleasing that Rainulf responded positively, waving to William to carry on and burying his face once more in his goblet of wine.

'Allow me to speak for my lord. I trust that Conrad Augustus has a brain, and if he is possessed of one he will know that killing Normans is a vow often made and even more often regretted.'

'I would not regret it,' said Berengara, words which had her brother holding up his hand to restrain her. Defiantly she added, 'It would provide much pleasure to line the Via Appia with hanging Norman bodies, as the Roman general Crassus once did with the soldiers of Spartacus.'

'It would be a pleasure hard won, lady. We Normans tend to spill more blood than we lose.' As she made to respond, William talked right over her, addressing her brother. 'But you are not here to vent your spleen, however right you feel in doing so. I repeat what I said just now. You have an offer! Make it, let Rainulf consider it, and when he has decided on it, the response can be taken back to the emperor.'

'It's perfectly straightforward,' Guaimar replied, looking at the bloated, purple face of Rainulf. 'If you wish to keep the title of Lord of Aversa, you must loosen your ties to Pandulf.'

William was thinking this young man had a lot to learn. Before saying those words it would have been wise to find out from Rainulf what was his view of Pandulf at this time; he knew it was not high after the Wolf's depredations at Montecassino and it had dropped even more with his inability to go to war on behalf of Byzantium. He had also laid out on the table, without gaining any leverage, the very obvious fact that he was prepared to forget Rainulf's previous betrayal of his father, if he would change sides once more.

'So Conrad will reinstate you?' William asked.

'He has assured me he will.'

'And Capua? What happens to that after Pandulf is removed?'

Guaimar shrugged, but the answer was obvious: it would be joined to Salerno.

'Can you be sure of the emperor's word?'

'As sure as I can be of anyone's.'

'That does not take you very far,' William replied, with just a touch of asperity. 'But let us say you have the right of it, and you're installed as Duke of Salerno as well as Prince of Capua. You are saying you will confirm Rainulf in all his present lands and titles?'

'I am.'

'And I don't believe you,' Rainulf growled, before he leant forward. 'I think like a Norman, and I know a Lombard. You will say and do anything to get rid of the Wolf, but once he is gone, and Conrad is back in his German lair, my title would not be worth a pitcher of piss.'

'I will give you my word.'

'You can poke your word up your Lombard arse, begging your pardon, Lady Berengara.'

She looked as though she would like to put a red-hot poker in his, then twist it.

Rainulf was not drunk, but he was drink affected. It took less and less to get him to the point of a slight slurring and he was there now. And he was trying to rile this young man, to get him to lose his temper, but he failed.

'I am told Pandulf has so many Normans in his pay now, many of them your old levies, he could depose you if he wished.'

Rainulf belched. 'He knows better than to try.'

For the first time Guaimar raised his voice. 'He will try eventually, Rainulf, for I doubt he still sees you as an ally.'

'You know nothing.'

'I know he is wedded to treachery, and you are a potential victim, as I once was. But is it not odd that my sister and I have come to save your hide?'

'To strip the skin off my back more like, if that look on the face of the Lady Berengara is anything to go by.'

'A trade in insults will get us nowhere,' William insisted.

He was actually thinking hard on what Guaimar had just said, in fact an accurate assessment of the true situation in which Rainulf found himself, and the beginnings of a solution were forming in his mind, but it had to be one kept close. He gestured to the servants that they should leave the room, Rainulf indicating they should deposit the jug of wine by his right hand. No one spoke until they had gone.

'My lord would need some guarantees, and there is only one I can think of that will be acceptable.'

'And that is?'

'He must be confirmed in his title by the emperor,' he said softly, so as not to be overheard. 'Perhaps as a count in his own right.'

'That is to ask a great deal.'

'Is it? You say you wish to keep him in his title. I suspect when Conrad restores you, if he restores you and gives you Capua, you will acknowledge him as your rightful suzerain and he will, with some ceremony, confirm you in your title. Let him do the same for Rainulf and he will have imperial protection against you, and...' William looked at the still-peevish Berengara,'...your successors, as well as any other Lombard noble who wishes him ill.'

Rainulf nodded vigorously; what William had proposed was a thing after which any man of sense would hanker. Right now he was in possession of his fief, but he had come by it in dubious circumstances which meant only his military strength kept him in place. To be confirmed by the Holy Roman Emperor would make him legitimate: if he could get rid of Pandulf's niece, and perhaps breed a son with another, that child would be his lawful heir.

'Only Conrad can decide that,' Guaimar said.

'True.' William leant forward now, his voice remaining soft. 'Sir, I have no desire to diminish you, but you are a messenger. Therefore the response must be carried back to Conrad Augustus to get his answer. Your aim is to detach Rainulf from his allegiance to Pandulf. Give him the desire to do so and you will succeed.'

'And if I fail?'

'Then you will face, when you seek to besiege the Prince of Capua, a force of Norman cavalry at your back which will put in doubt the success of the whole endeavour.'

Guaimar made to speak but William stopped him. 'You may have the greatest host Christendom has ever witnessed, but we will call upon our brothers from all over South Italy to come to our aid, maybe as many as a thousand lances. I doubt Conrad wants to face such a force, as well as Pandulf and his Normans. Take it from one who knows, and I have no doubt Conrad knows this too, nothing is certain in war.'

There was bluff in what William had just said: Sicily was a more attractive prospect to the rest of the Norman mercenaries in Italy, but he imparted it with enough conviction to make it seem a real threat.

Guaimar sat in silence for half a minute. He did not know whether to be angry or impressed. He had advised Conrad to do the very thing this William de

Hauteville was proposing, the notion he had formed before he and his sister escaped from Salerno, the idea he had kept from the archbishop. But he had intended to tease matters out, and draw Rainulf into grateful acceptance of an idea that would seem to come to him with a flash of spontaneity.

Imperial confirmation would make him, as his captain so ably outlined, inviolable: no matter how strong he became once back in his seat of Salerno, he could never revenge himself on Rainulf without incurring the kind of imperial wrath which was about to depose Pandulf, but he had very badly wanted the Norman to be grateful to him at least. Had he been outmanoeuvred? He was not sure, but he was now certain there was no point in doing that which he had originally intended, which was to ride out of Rainulf's camp with the pretence of going back to plead with Conrad, then return to tell him that, after much argument, he had persuaded the emperor to agree.

'I have no need to take such a message,' he said finally, wondering, as he looked into the penetrating Norman's eyes, if the man ever blinked. 'It has already been conceded.'

'As I thought,' said William.

'You knew?' demanded Berengara.

'No, I did not know, but to detach Rainulf you had to offer him something he could not refuse, and, given he has much wealth, that was the only thing that made sense.' He turned to look to the top of the table, to where Rainulf was looking confused. 'I advise you to accept, and if you do, I suggest that it would be a kindness to offer these two visitors both a meal and a bed if they want one.'

Rainulf just nodded. Berengara looked as if she had bitten that yellow fruit the monk had used at Montesárchio to cleanse William's wound.

'I would give my eye teeth to see the look on Pandulf's face when he hears this,' she said.

'Let him hear it only when he sees our lances,' said William. 'I sent the servants out of the room so that they would not overhear. Not one of the men we command will be told of this till we turn up under Pandulf's walls.'

'I must tell the emperor.'

'No, your honour,' said William, giving for the first time some credence to his claimed title. 'It is I who will tell the emperor, and I will also tell him that the next time he will meet you and your sister will be under the walls of Capua.'

'You don't trust me.'

Rainulf laughed, his belly shaking. 'He is a true Norman, of course he does not trust you.'

'And now,' William said finally, standing up. 'I would like a few words with my lord, alone, while you are shown to one of our huts. I fear the accommodation you will be offered will not meet the standard to which you are accustomed, but it is all we have.'

'You have no idea, William de Hauteville,' snapped Berengara, 'of what we have had to live in these last few years.'

CHAPTER SIXTEEN

William rode out at dawn the next morning, accompanied only by Drogo, leaving behind him a camp speculating wildly about what was afoot. Like his brother, they were in ignorance, and try as he might Drogo could get no answers to his questions until the camp and Rainulf's tower was well out of sight. That was not just caution on William's part; he still needed time to think through what he was going to do, well aware that he had been lucky in his talk with Guaimar. Up against a more experienced envoy he would not have nailed things so easily, but he suspected the young man would learn: he had not been stupid enough to seek to string matters out when his ploy had been exposed.

William was in his prime: never had he felt more fit to be a leader and a warrior, and he knew Drogo was also at his peak, unlike Rainulf, who was fading.

Though he might have many years to live, his days of leading men into battle were numbered, if not actually over, and while nothing would make William disloyal to a man who had come to trust him, he had to consider, in a world where every creature was at the mercy of an implacable and mercurial God, as well as the vagaries of his fellow humans, what would happen after Rainulf was gone.

'The wine will kill him,' opined Drogo, when the thought was finally broached, 'though maybe if he can get himself a new wife, he might put aside the jug.'

'You think a woman can rejuvenate him?'

'It does wonders for me. That Berengara creature would make me feel like the Archangel Michael.'

'She's a fine-looking woman...'

'Ah hah!' crowed Drogo, who had often guyed his brother about his lack of attachments; there was a woman in Aversa he visited, but so infrequently that to Drogo it was like chastity.

'But, I think she might be murderous if crossed.'

'Take my word for it, brother, always choose a woman who might kill you, for such a creature will surely entertain you.'

'It's a wonder you're still with us.'

'I am fleet of foot. Now are you going to tell me where we are going and what we are going to do?'

'Let's walk,' William said, dismounting.

* * *

Drogo whistled more than once as his brother outlined what was about to happen, though he did have his own questions, and he was unaware that William was not telling him everything he had in mind.

'You're sure Conrad can win?'

'If his army is as large as Guaimar implied, he would beat Pandulf, and might do so even if we aided him.'

'I didn't like the idea of aiding Pandulf before you said that. I like it even less now.'

'This may have come just in time.'

'How so?' William looked at Drogo as though he was dense. 'You think we have to fear the Wolf?'

'Rainulf does, even if he has never openly said so. I do not know if we have to; remember, he tried to recruit us once.'

They talked of that; of the way Rainulf must now be seen by Pandulf, as leading the only force in Campania that could possibly check his ambitions, plus the fact that he was getting older and weaker in manpower, which made him obviously less able to defend himself.

'You've forgotten us.'

'No I have not, Drogo, but hand on heart, faced with Pandulf, and looking at Rainulf, how many of the men we lead might think it better to defect if it came to a choice?'

Drogo nodded. 'Too many, because the Wolf would come armed with all the gold he has torn from the throats of his vassals.'

William nodded; Pandulf was not called the Wolf for nothing. Rainulf excluded, he had taxed his inferior lords mercilessly, the likes of Montesárchio being sent back to bleed dry anyone with property, and they in turn bore down on their peasantry, robbed anyone who showed even a hint of prosperity. The man was fabulously wealthy and William was not about to castigate those who might desert Rainulf for a bribe. They were mercenaries: they fought for gold, which was why they had come all the way from Normandy.

'I'd rather go south,' Drogo said.

William looked sharply at him then; had he heard about Sicily? Rainulf had confided in him but no one else, but Drogo was just staring at the road ahead, his face bland.

'Do you remember this road when first we travelled it?'

'Do I?' Drogo groaned. 'I can remember my belly was empty and my arse was raw.'

'We have done well, have we not?'

That made Drogo look hard at William, being far from a fool. He knew by the look on his face that his brother was driving at something and he demanded to be told what it was.

'Rainulf came south how many years ago, less than twenty, and what has he achieved? Add to that what he will have if Conrad confirms and raises him to an Imperial Count of Aversa. When we rode here, we came with the intention of one day returning home, did we not?'

'We did, and before you ask me, I am not sure that now I would still wish to do that.'

'Because there is less for us in Normandy than there is in Italy.'

'By some margin, brother, unlike you, who had an inheritance to look forward to. I never had a spare piece of copper at home; I have a box of gold here, not much, but some, and so have you, and that is after we have sent back enough coin for father to build his stone donjon.'

William nodded, thinking, if he had an inheritance, it was not a great one. He could ride around Tancred's demesne in half a morning. As for a proper stone tower, that could not be built without ducal approval, which had been denied.

'There are things I miss,' Drogo added, 'but not having my arse hanging out of my breeches, and knowing that, despite our bloodline, we had nothing, and that was likely the way it was going to remain.'

It was not something of which they often talked, their connection to the ducal house of Normandy, the fact that they both had as good a claim to the title as the Bastard of Falaise who held it. There was little need and both knew everything, and had said it all too often. News had come from the Contentin, mostly discouraging to any hope of increased good fortune there.

Several barons had rebelled, seeking to put aside Duke Robert's bastard, and each uprising had been crushed with the aid of the King of the Franks. So much for Bessancourt; all Duke Robert had done, as Tancred had predicted, was to strengthen the entity that posed the greatest threat to Norman independence. William had felt the time had come to make a decision he knew he had pondered often and put off again and again. 'So you think we should stay?'

'I will, what you do is a choice you make, Gill.'

That was a tacit acknowledgement of William's prior claim, after Tancred, as head of the family. He would inherit the demesne, if he wanted to. Yet Drogo also knew his brother was not cut out for such a life, any more than he was himself. Yes, it was attractive if it could be extended, but the chances of that, given the present duke and his support from the Capetian King, were slim. In fact it was quite the reverse. At home, William would be drawn into conspiracies of the kind that had already failed. Instead of gaining more land and power, he might lose everything.

'You have said Rainulf is old, Drogo. It is also true he has no heir. What happens to the County of Aversa after he is gone?'

There was no need for Drogo to respond to that, for the answer was too obvious: the loss of Rainulf would still leave his men, and they had to be led by someone.

The heir to that, and quite possibly the title, was William.

'Do you trust my judgement?'

Drogo hooted, and leapt onto his mount. 'What fool trusts his brother?'

That reassured him: if Drogo had replied in a serious tone he would have been worried. He too mounted. 'Then, Drogo my brother, we must, before we go to see the Holy Roman Emperor, call upon the Wolf of the Abruzzi.'

The look Drogo gave William then pleased him mightily; his brother had no idea what he was about.

As they approached the centre of Capua, they could hear the labours being carried out to repair the defences long before they saw the men working on the walls: hammers hammering, levers being used to remove loose blocks of stone, with tackles rigged to fit replacements. No castle was ever properly maintained, such things were put off until danger threatened and many a fortress fell because time did not allow for it to be put into a proper state for defence. Pandulf was no different: rich he might be but he would hoard his money or use it to bribe and suborn, not employ it to ensure he had an impregnable place from which he could defy anyone who threatened him.

Carts loaded with hay and wine, others with wheat and oats, herds of sheep and lowing cattle were crowded in the open space before the castle gates, as the garrison tried to stock up for a siege. Given the number of fighting men working and manning the walls it was obvious that everyone had been called in from the countryside, some from their seized monastery lands; if the castle fell they could kiss those possessions goodbye.

As they forced their way through it was clear the fellow Normans who greeted them were nervous, even if they tried to be bluff and jesting. It was just as telling the looks the two brothers had got as they rode through the streets of the city. Pure hatred was the most accurate description: the good folk of Capua saw the Normans, any Normans, as the power that helped keep them under the thumb and rapacity of the Wolf. There would be no aid from that quarter, which meant the walls of the city, the first line of defence, could not be manned.

'We bring messages from the Lord of Aversa,' William called to the sentinels by the gate.

'He has heard then?'

'Who has not?' Drogo replied.

'When is he coming?' asked another, a fellow William recognised as one who had left Rainulf's service.

'As soon as he is ready,' Drogo replied.

'And before any damned emperor,' William added, before crossing himself by habit. He was still his father's son.

That got a sort of hollow cheer from the fighting men who could hear, leaving William to wonder what they had been told. Did they have any real notion of what they faced? If they did, would they desert Pandulf?

'No, they took an oath facing God,' said Drogo, when William voiced that possibility. 'They will keep it, as would we.'

They took their horses to the stables and gave instructions they should be fed and watered, then went in search of the Court Chamberlain.

'William and Drogo de Hauteville to see Prince Pandulf on a matter of great urgency, bearing the greetings of the Lord of Aversa.'

Previously the man's response would have been haughty; there was none of that now, he practically ran into the audience chamber, shouting who had arrived and on whose behalf. The brothers did not wait, they marched in behind him, to find the Wolf surrounded both by fighting men and courtiers, all of whom seemed intent on giving him advice.

'My good friends,' he cried when he espied them, coming towards them arms outstretched.

William went down on one knee. Drogo followed, whispering, 'What are you doing?'

'Trust me,' William replied, just before Pandulf's hand touched his arm.

'Arise, arise, you have no need to kneel to me.'

Odd, the thought came, how you always ignored me when I came with Rainulf. Upright, William looked the Wolf right in the eye. 'I wish you to have no doubt of the depth of respect in which we hold you, Prince Pandulf, and so does our liege lord.'

'Good. Rainulf sent you to me in my hour of need.'

'To assure you he is making ready to come to Capua with every lance at his disposal.'

'Will it be enough?' Pandulf asked, his face creased with concern.

'It is to discuss this that we have been sent to speak with you.'

Pandulf could not help himself; a look of deep suspicion crossed his face, before he wiped it off and replaced it with his worried smile.

'I think we need to speak with you alone, sire.'

'Yes, yes,' Pandulf cried, waving his arms at those who had previously surrounded him. 'Leave us, I must hear what the Lord of Aversa has to say.'

William waited until the room was cleared before speaking. 'He would have come himself, sire, but he must make all ready.'

'Tell me of his thinking.'

'He wishes first, sire, to know the size of the enemy we must face.'

'Not great,' Pandulf replied, his eyes suddenly bright with optimism, until he realised with all the activity of repair going on, such a response did not make sense. 'Large, enough to besiege this place, but, with Rainulf at my side, I think one we can defeat.'

'It is the emperor?' Drogo asked.

'Yes. False words have been placed in his ear. Lies have been told. I am sure when he sees the truth we will have nothing to fear.'

'You have sent an embassy?'

Pandulf looked at William and, if it was only his eyes that seemed to want to kill him, that was enough. 'Not yet.'

'Good,' William replied.

'What?'

William smiled at Pandulf's confused expression. 'Rainulf is of the opinion that Conrad should be approached jointly, that you and he should present yourselves to the emperor together.'

'To do what?'

'To set right what lies he has been told, to seek to deflect him from coming any further south.'

'What makes Rainulf think he will listen?'

'Sire, he will listen if you are penitent.' That was not an emotion pleasing to Pandulf, and try as he might he could not disguise it. 'Whatever rights you think you hold, sire, you must give up the lands of the Abbey of Montecassino.'

His reply was almost like a man with a wound. 'Give them up?'

'That must be what has made him act as he has. No

imperial host comes south of Rome without purpose.'

'Give them up?' he said again.

'As well as Abbot Theodore. I assume he is still alive?'

'I do not know.'

That was very like Pandulf: once someone was put in his dungeons, he had no interest in them at all.

'Then, sire, I would suggest we need to find out. I think also the Archbishop of Capua should be freed to return to his Episcopal Palace. You must do something to appease the wrath of the emperor, so he will listen, and that would also placate your citizenry.'

It took the Wolf a while, as being placatory was not in his nature, but eventually he acceded.

'Let us hope Abbot Theodore is up to a journey.' Pandulf was nodding, but that stopped as William added his next notion, making it sound as though it had just occurred. 'Perhaps Rainulf is wrong, perhaps it would be better if you accompanied the Abbot Theodore, took him to Conrad as a gesture of peace.'

William could almost see his mind working: there was no way Pandulf was going to put himself in the hands of Conrad, with Rainulf or the abbot at his side, given he knew what he had done and how it was perceived. He would be searching for an alternative, which was what William wanted.

'My mind is troubled, William.'

'How so, sire?'

The Wolf began to move around, his arms being used to emphasise his thinking as he posed a stream of rhetorical questions. 'Regarding what we do not know. Do we have knowledge of the lies Conrad has been fed? No. Do we know the size of his host? No. Do we have any notion of what he intends? No. Of what will satisfy him? No. These things need to be known before I can even think of an embassy. I'm sure Rainulf would say the same.'

'Would such knowledge alter what you will do, sire?' asked Drogo, William being grateful his brother had intervened; he was getting sick of doing all the asking.

'Oh, yes,' Pandulf said, his voice silky. 'If we knew how large was his army, we could plan how to confront it, Rainulf and I. If we knew Conrad's intentions, we would have some notion of how to deflect him. I think it would be better to know these things before Rainulf and I even think of discussing terms.'

'Terms?'

'Certain offers will have to be made.'

'You speak of things of which I know nothing, sire.'

'I have it,' cried Pandulf. 'Conrad, because of these falsehoods laid against me, would be a hard man to deal with directly. He must be brought to think on them first, to see that there are untruths. And, might I say, it would be to the advantage of Rainulf and me to be invited under truce to commune with him.

To just arrive, before he has had an opportunity to ponder, might see us seized and given no chance to plead for the justice we deserve.'

Pandulf turned to face them, beaming like a man from whom a great burden has been lifted.

'The solution is to send emissaries first, to find out that which we need to know and also to extract a safe conduct. And who could be better placed to undertake this than you?'

'What would I take?'

'Take?'

'Sire,' William said, with a glum expression. 'No emissary can just turn up with nothing.'

That wiped the smile off Pandulf's face. 'No.'

'There must be some kind of offer, one that Conrad will find so persuasive he will accede to your request.'

'The abbot?'

'A sick and undernourished man, as he must be, despite your care, may not impress the emperor or his advisors.'

Pandulf suddenly lost his temper. 'This is all that little swine Guaimar's doing, him and his whore of a sister. She's probably had Conrad inside her shift while she whispers lies about me in his ears. I should have strung the viper up, and once I was done with her, stuck her in a nunnery. Or maybe I should have just thrown her to my Normans...

With some effort he recovered himself; the brothers

could see him fighting to control his breathing and when he spoke, the reason for the sudden outburst was obvious.

'We must bribe Conrad to go away,' he said, in a voice now flat. He waited for a response, but neither William nor Drogo obliged. 'I have gold, let him have that and perhaps he will leave me in peace.'

'How much gold?' asked Drogo.

It was a telling indication of Pandulf's character and rapacity that he could answer the question without hesitation. 'I could give him three hundred pounds in weight.' He looked keenly at the brothers. 'For my title and my freedom.'

'A telling offer,' said Drogo; in fact it was a fortune.

The Wolf was looking at William. 'Will you agree to carry this offer to Conrad?'

'You will, of course, free your prisoners?' asked William.

'Of course,' the Wolf insisted, then obviously, the thought of handing over so much gold made him change his tack. 'But, you must not just make this offer of my gold unless you see it as necessary. Find out first what we need to know, see if we can contest with this imperial fool. Do not just say I will gift him my riches, and should you feel you must, add that there will a contribution from Rainulf too.'

That got them another suspicious look. 'I am sure Rainulf would not fail me and the revenues of Aversa are splendid, not to mention all that I have given him.'

'Never,' Drogo replied, with deep sincerity. 'He is your friend and you are his liege lord.'

'Good. When will you go?'

William said, 'As soon as our mounts are rested, but...'

Pandulf did not like that. 'But?'

'I fear we must have, sire, some token of your esteem, perhaps some part of what it is you are prepared to offer, to gift the emperor immediately, so that he will accept our bona fides. He does not know us and, besides that, he will be surrounded by his court. We may have to pay a bribe just to gain a hearing.'

Pandulf thought on that for some time, but it made sense: two strange knights just turning up with nothing would not be acceptable. 'I will arrange for you to take enough with you to impress both him and any others you need to bribe.'

'We must see to our own needs before we go,' Drogo insisted, 'and I think we should find out if the abbot is fit to travel, and the archbishop still of this world. The emperor is bound to ask after his welfare.'

'Do you need someone to escort you to the dungeons?'

'No, sire,' said Drogo, 'we know the way.'

* * *

The abbot was shrunk in his body, but he had the stoicism of his calling; the Archbishop of Capua had fared better, given the man attending the oubliettes was easily bribed by the local clergy, but he was weak. When William asked after Osmond de Vertin that got a raised eyebrow.

'Release him as well, and get a mendicant to look at him.'

They had to lift Osmond out, a stinking wreck soiled by his own filth, but a cot was arranged and when they left he was at least breathing in air that was less fetid than that to which he had been accustomed. Fed themselves, William and Drogo took possession of that gold crucifix and a heavy purse of Pandulf's gold, and back on their mounts, leading the old Abbot on a palfrey, to the good wishes of their confrères, they made their way out of the fortress and across the old Roman bridge that led north.

CHAPTER SEVENTEEN

Approaching the imperial encampment on the River Sacco brought back to William the experience they had had in the Vexin – that stench on the breeze of too many humans and horses in too small a space – only this host was greater than that assembled by Duke Robert. The hillsides were studded with pavilions, each with its own huge armorial banner – the imperial levies, both foot and mounted, encamped over miles of landscape, but again there was no doubt as to where the power lay. The massive imperial tent lay at the centre of what a Roman would have recognised as a triumphal way, surrounded by huge flags that bore the Salian device of a standing black griffin on a yellow background.

William and Drogo led the old Abbot towards the centre of the camp, soldiers standing to observe them as they passed. Odd, not one of them would know this elderly divine, bent with age, but somehow they saw in his person and his simple black Benedictine habit a man of holiness, and many crossed themselves, some even dropping on one knee. Others looked at the de Hauteville brothers, and judged them by a different standard.

William had talked with Theodore on the way, and had been impressed by the old man's concern, which was not for his own person – though he was glad to be at liberty – but for his monastery and the monks that had once inhabited the buildings and worked the farms, now scattered to the four winds and driven to living in penury by the depredations of Pandulf. William and Drogo had met a lot of monks and friars in their time, not all of them good men; this abbot was the exception.

Outside the great pavilion, the brothers helped the old man off his palfrey. By the time he was on the ground and steadied, a whole host of mailed men had emerged to observe this, including in the centre a striking-looking fellow of stocky build and greying hair, wearing a bright-yellow surcoat with a griffin device to match the fluttering ensigns. It was him William addressed.

'Sire, we bring you the Abbot of Montecassino.'

'Abbot Theodore,' said Conrad, coming forward to embrace the old man, 'I am glad to see you well.'

'Your Highness.'

The reply was weak, as was the speaker. Even although the imperial host, hogging the River Sacco as a source of water and supply, had moved closer to Capua, it had been a long journey; riding for hours was tiring for a fit man and it had exhausted him.

'Come inside and rest. You must eat, you must drink, and you must tell me what Pandulf has been up to and what I must do to put it right.'

Theodore waved a feeble hand towards the de Hauteville brothers. 'Then, sire, you need to talk with the men who brought me here, for what is needed is the stuff of conflict, and I am a man of peace.'

Conrad looked beyond the abbot to the brothers, standing, hands on their sword hilts, eyeing them up. Neither wore a helmet, so that their colouring could be seen, and that branded them as Normans, while their red and black surcoats identified them as mercenaries serving Rainulf Drengot.

'They come with good in their hearts.'

'That will be an unusual thing for a Norman,' Conrad said.

Drogo bridled, as he always did when he perceived an insult, but it was William who replied.

'To a Norman that sounds odd on Frankish lips, sire, given we have had scant reason to extend our trust to them.'

The way the men around Conrad stiffened, each no doubt a great lord in their own domain, implied danger, which had Drogo taking a firmer grip of the hilt of his sword. The emperor was indeed of that descent, from his sires as Dukes of Franconia, but it was an inheritance few referred to.

'However,' William continued, 'we did not come here to trade low opinions.'

'Why did you come?'

'To inform you of what progress Guaimar of Salerno made with the Lord of Aversa.'

'And where is Guaimar?'

'With his sister, staying as a guest of Rainulf.'

'Hostages?'

'I said guests, Highness,' William responded, in a sharp and disrespectful tone. 'If they were hostages I would have termed them so.'

'It does not do to show arrogance to my title.'

'Hear them,' the Abbot wheezed, 'I beg you. No more blood should be spilt.'

'Very well, Theodore, for you I will talk with them.' He made a peremptory gesture that had their horses taken from them. 'Leave your weapons outside.'

William nodded, Conrad being unarmed, and removed his sword and knife, Drogo doing likewise. The emperor spun on his heel, taking the abbot's bony arm to help him along and, removing a small sack off their horse, the brothers followed them into the tent, the courtiers at their heels regarding them with deep suspicion. On a great square table lay maps of the country surrounding Capua, and on another table stood a model of Pandulf's castle, the river and the bridge, made of wood.

'They are frantically repairing the walls,' William said, pointing at the model. 'This is more complete than the real article.'

'You came from Capua?'

'We stopped there to collect the Abbot Theodore.'

'Nothing else?'

William opened the sack and took out the gold crucifix, placing it on the map. 'Prince Pandulf bade us make you an offer to secure peace...'

'You will waste your breath in doing so,' Conrad interrupted, ignoring the object and looking once more at the old divine. 'His crimes are too great.'

'...of three hundred pounds of gold.'

It was telling how much that amounted to; every one of these noble magnates attending the emperor was bound to be rich, but to a man they gasped at the mention of such a sum. Even Conrad, who had more self-control, was clearly impressed. He picked up the crucifix and examined it.

'He has that much to offer me, a sum I would struggle to match?'

'It is what he says he has, and knowing him I would believe it.'

'What wrongs he must have afflicted on his fief to be so rich.'

'We also persuaded Pandulf to release the Archbishop of Capua,' Drogo said.

Conrad was looking at the old abbot, now seated and nodding, when he asked why.

'So he could not use him for the purposes of bargaining.'

'As if his gold is not enough,' Conrad replied, then seeing the questioning look on Drogo's face he added, 'and it is not.'

William spoke again. 'That is not the purpose of our coming here and we do not come as representatives of Pandulf or his money. If you take Capua you will take his gold. We come to offer you the support of the Lord of Aversa, on the terms agreed with Guaimar of Salerno.'

'Leave us,' Conrad said, abruptly, looking at his advisors. There was a certain amount of shuffling and confusion, not to mention affront, until they obeyed. Looking down at the abbot, he saw the old man had his head on his chest; he had fallen asleep. 'Guaimar proposed what we agreed?'

'He did.'

'So Rainulf will stand aside?'

'No, he will join with you.'

'I do not need him to do that. If his force is not in the field I can easily besiege Pandulf.'

'I know that, Conrad Augustus, but Rainulf will join you.'

'Why?'

'To have a say in any peace. Pandulf's men are Normans and they are our brothers. We would not see them suffer for their service.'

'They have taken Pandulf's gold, perhaps they should experience his fate.'

'What will that be?'

'To be skinned alive in a public place perhaps, or to have his heart torn from his living body. Maybe he will be placed in a sack with a cat and a snake, then thrown into the nearest deep water. Whatever his fate the world will be rid of him for good.'

'And your conscience will be clear.'

That brought forth a smile. 'I am the anointed Holy Roman Emperor. My conscience is always clear.'

Conrad moved over to the table and looked at the maps, pointing the top of the crucifix he was still holding at the city. 'It is always your way, you Normans. Whatever defeats others suffer you ride away. Perhaps it is time some of your kind learnt the harsh lesson of losing.'

'What purpose would that serve?' demanded Drogo.

'As a warning.'

'If you insist on such a lesson, Rainulf must oppose you. He will not stand by and see his confrères put to the sword.'

Drogo had to avoid looking at William; this was another gambit which had not been discussed with him, indeed he wondered if William had just made it up. But he could see where it led; the effect would be obvious. Conrad would be anticipating a siege of Capua, no easy prospect, while Pandulf was clearly, judging by the supplies he was garnering, preparing to hold out for a year.

He still thought he had the support of Rainulf, a force it would be wise to keep out in the field, one that could seriously disrupt the imperial host in both siege maintenance and, more importantly, in foraging. Every party sent out would have to be strong enough to face ambush from a Norman force that, challenged by superior numbers, would melt into the mountains and draw off men from Capua. That would extend the time it would take to subdue the place; could the emperor stay long enough to enforce his will?

Many a siege had been abandoned because it just went on too long. Those inside a fortress might be reduced to near starvation, but the men outside faced just as many difficulties, not least the threat of disease which always seemed to affect a host which stayed too long in one place. In any case, holding an army together was no easy task: tempers frayed, supporters became fractious and rationing became more and more troublesome.

But let Pandulf see Rainulf ride as a friend into

Conrad's camp and he would know his cause was lost. Without an external enemy the imperial army could forage far and wide, send away detachments to ease the supply and disease problems without fear that they would be attacked and decimated. And it was obvious that the emperor, thinking on the same subject, and studying that model of the formidable fortress he needed to take, would of necessity come to the same conclusions.

Conrad actually did that. He moved to stand by that wooden model, his finger tracing the various difficulties Capua represented. Pandulf had to be chastised, but how many men would expire to achieve such a need, and what of the possibility, one any sensible commander had to consider, of failure? If he could not show his power to chastise in Campania, the whole of the imperial domains in Italy could be affected; many a noble lord between Rome and the Brenner Pass would think he too could defy the emperor.

'And what happens to these men?'

'Many originally served with Rainulf. Let them do so again.'

'That is a bargain fraught with danger. Did you discuss this with Guaimar?'

'No.'

'Then let me speak for him, for I can tell you what he would say. He will be Duke of Salerno and Prince of Capua, but he would not be happy to have in his midst a host of Norman lances powerful enough to depose him any time they wish, which would be after I am no longer there to protect him.' He looked down at the still-slumbering abbot, and added. 'I doubt Theodore, saintly as he is, would welcome that either.'

The implications of that were obvious. Montecassino, given the wealth its lands produced, was a tempting objective for hundreds of idle men who had already tasted its riches.

'Rainulf expressly did not take part in the destruction of the monastery and he will not do so in future. You no doubt find the idea of a Norman and piety incompatible, but it is there nevertheless. Make Guaimar liege lord to Rainulf, confirm Rainulf as Count of Aversa, and I will guarantee he will serve him faithfully.'

'You?'

'Rainulf listens to William.'

The look Conrad gave Drogo showed how unconvincing he felt that to be.

'Rainulf,' William insisted, 'does not need me to tell him of his duty to a suzerain.'

'Is that the same duty he had exercised with Pandulf, to whom he has been loyal these past years? To this I cannot agree.'

'What if, after you were gone, there were no Normans in Aversa?' asked William.

Drogo actually growled then; he was getting

fed up with his brother doing things on the wing, strategies of which he knew nothing, so that he felt like a fool. What Conrad said next did, however, make him wonder if his brother had the mind of the Devil.

'If you're going to ask me for Pandulf's three hundred pounds of gold so that you can go home...'

'Not that,' William interrupted, an act plainly not welcome by the target, as well as a response which deeply disappointed his own brother. 'Rainulf has been sent an invitation by Constantinople to join the invasion of Sicily.'

'It surprises me he did not go, given that is your Norman profession, fighting for pay.'

When William did not respond, Conrad looked at him and, after a moment's thought, smiled, having deduced what fear had kept Rainulf in Aversa. Gone, Pandulf would have taken over his domains.

'Spare the garrison of Capua, let them join with Rainulf, and we will all go south to Calabria.'

'That will not last for ever.'

'It could last for years, long enough for Guaimar to consolidate his position, and who knows what might be had in a rich land like Sicily? Many of us may never return.'

William suspected Conrad was just prevaricating; he would know very well that the primary objective was Capua. Everything that followed from the capture of that and the Wolf would have to be dealt with as and when it needed to be. An added problem he must consider was the very fact that the defenders of the fortress would be Normans, and by reputation they were a race that did not give in lightly; much easier to let them march out and away.

'Rainulf undertakes to do what you say?'

'He does.'

Conrad had already decided what he was going to say, but his dignity demanded he appear to think on it for a while. 'Then return to him and say this. I will be under the walls of Capua in four days. It would be advantageous to our imperial purpose if he was to join me then.'

The journey back was one long whine from Drogo, who chose to harp on about Pandulf's gold, as though it had actually been offered, enough, he insisted, for their father to build a castle to rival the Duke of Normandy, never mind a stone tower. In reality he was just piqued at being kept in the dark; William had nurtured the plan he had espoused in the company of Rainulf, and Drogo had difficulty in accepting the need he had had to keep it to himself.

Their route took them to the lower reaches of the Volturno, where it ran through a huge flat plain before debouching into the sea. There it was possible to ford the river as long as it was not in spate.

* * *

From the outside, the fortress of Capua presented a formidable obstacle. Three sides of the castle bordered the Volturno, which acted like a superior moat, for here the river course narrowed, and fed as it was by the glaciers of the high Apennines, it flowed strong and fast for most of the year and was never low enough to make it easy to navigate. Crossing it by boat was not just hazardous, it was nearly impossible: with the river running in most places along the actual walls there was no ground on which to gather to mount an assault, which allowed the defenders to gather in strength at those few spots where any form of siege tactics could be employed long before the attackers could land there.

Sapping to undermine the walls was pointless: the river would soon flood any work of digging and, besides, it would be too close to the fortifications for safety; tunnellers liked to begin their sapping far away from danger, and be underground when close. Conrad had with him artisans and builders who were adept at constructing ballistae, mangonels and the like, but there was only one wall on which they could be usefully employed: the wide space that had once been, in Roman times, a sort of Campus Martius, and that was quite naturally the point at which the defence was strongest, the walls at their thickest, although they included a double gate. But that was sunk behind twin barbicans full of narrow embrasures, through which crossbowmen could rain bolts down on any attackers.

Pandulf had been in panic, but that had eased as he saw the work on the walls produce results, and as he listened to his Norman captains explain to him – for he was not gifted with a military mind – how formidable a place he occupied. The whole city and surrounding countryside had been stripped bare of anything that could be used to feed the garrison; the storerooms were full to bursting and the supply of water, that most vital element, could never be cut off.

If Capua had one fault, it was that forays by the defenders were as constrained by the natural defences as were those of the attacking force, therefore there was little use in keeping inside the walls all the horses the Normans usually required for battle, which in turn aided the defence, for the amount of forage required to feed them was much reduced, allowing for the storage of a greater amount of food.

The men he trusted assured him they could hold out, assured him that Rainulf Drengot, whom they knew well and under whom most had served, was a master of the kind of hit, run or ambush tactics that would make the task of feeding the imperial army near impossible. Half Conrad's men would never be available for the assault: they would have to guard against raids, escort supply wagons and man a perimeter outside Capua to ensure Rainulf did not make an assault on the town itself.

The gates were shut to Conrad Augustus and the citizenry of Capua well before the first imperial horsemen appeared on the concourse before the great gates. Conrad himself was not far behind, only holding back his entry till his advance guard had made sure no traps had been set and that the inhabitants of the ancient city would welcome him with gratitude. That they did, cheering him through the narrow streets to the echo, priests blessing him while those Pandulf had milked of their wealth prayed alongside that the Wolf would be cast into perdition.

There was the ritual to go through: a message must be sent to Pandulf, ordering him to surrender his castle to his suzerain, one which got a mocking reply.

'I demand to parley with the emperor,' Pandulf shouted from through one of the crenels atop the walls, joined, on either side, by most of the garrison, to show the enemy the numbers they faced. 'Under safe conduct.'

'And the emperor demands that you surrender your person to his mercy.'

'That I will not do.'

'Then by the laws of combat you must suffer pillage and death. May God be with you.'

As this was taking place, the imperial host was marching into position, thousands of lances and milites led by those mighty nobles, who fanned out to surround the fortress in a seeming flood of martial strength. Next, on the concourse, a mass was said, with a cardinal to take the Host for Conrad, and priests spread throughout the army to do the same for the soldiers. Pandulf and his Normans watched this in silence, each man having already confessed and been blessed by another set of priests within the walls.

Conrad could be seen, very obvious in his bright-yellow surcoat, and by his side stood Guaimar, while Berengara was also visible sitting on a dais outside a hastily erected pavilion; that Pandulf expected. What shocked him, when the imperial trumpets blew a fanfare, was to see Rainulf Drengot, with William de Hauteville by his side, riding slowly out from a narrow roadway that led to the esplanade, then to dismount and kneel before Conrad. If it affected him, and it did, the corollary for his Normans was even worse, setting up a cry of dismay.

The ceremony that followed Pandulf did not witness: he was too busy overseeing the loading of a boat in the water gate that led on to the river, with his wife, his children, his coffers and some hastily gathered clothing, urging his personal servants to hurry, alternately weeping and cursing at the perfidy of Rainulf Drengot and his own foolishness in not beheading Guaimar when he was still a boy.

That young man was kneeling before Conrad

Augustus, swearing fealty for the imperial possessions of Salerno and Capua, his heart nearly bursting with emotion, for he was now styled Prince Guaimar. Rainulf Drengot, in turn, swore fealty both to Salerno and the Holy Roman Emperor, as Conrad invested him with the proud gonfalon, hung from its crosspiece above his head as he took his oath, which was now his to display as the Imperial Count of Aversa.

When Rainulf rose, he made a point of embracing William, bringing him forward to kiss his gonfalon, which was, to those who knew the way of the world, an acknowledgement of his trust and his senior captain's future. He then led William to Guaimar, and bade him kneel to his immediate suzerain, and finally the heir of Tancred was presented to the Emperor Conrad Augustus in the same manner, which was as good as saying the words, 'This man will be my heir.'

William, full of pride and thoughts of a brilliant future, then mounted and rode to a point between the twin barbicans, to tell the Norman garrison that they were free to march out with their arms, their equipment and any dependants they might have, on condition that they took service with the newly enfeoffed Count of Aversa, and agreed either to leave Italy by returning to Normandy, or to join Rainulf and Byzantium in their attack on the Saracens of Sicily. Again a ritual had to be observed, as it had to appear as a proposal to be discussed instead of merely accepted.

But when you offer a man the choice of life as against certain death, it is no choice at all. Within the hour, the gates opened and Pandulf's Norman mercenaries, no longer wearing the blue and yellow surcoats of his colours, emerged, to march between two silent lines of imperial troops. There was noise: the jeering of the celebrating citizens of Capua.

At their heels came William de Hauteville, to cry out to Conrad, 'Your Imperial Highness, the fortress of Capua is yours.'

On the river, with his servants rowing furiously, Pandulf, the Wolf of the Abruzzi, was wondering where he could go to escape the wrath of those now occupying his castle.

CHAPTER EIGHTEEN

The Bay of Salerno was full of ships, the fleet that would transport the Norman mercenaries to Sicily, the galleys not only of Byzantium, but the ports of the east coast of Italy all the way up to Venice. It was some indication of the way affairs were conducted in Constantinople that the admiral of this armada was an ex-ship's caulker called Stephen Calaphates, a fellow of outstanding nautical ignorance who had achieved his present eminence because he had married the Emperor Michael's sister when her brother had been nothing but an obscure soldier, yet to catch the eye and fill the bed of the elderly Empress Zöe.

Guaimar exercised his right as suzerain over the number of Normans to be despatched: he was prepared to send foot soldiers he would recruit from the local populace, but was not prepared to trust the Italians left behind to protect him or his title. He insisted that the Count of Aversa stay in Campania with enough lances to ensure, should Pandulf reappear or rebellion break out, he had sufficient Normans to subdue any threat.

Thus, the command naturally devolved to William and, in truth, Rainulf was glad; his bones were getting too stiff for what his men were about to face, a campaign that could last years. There was another reason, too: having set aside Pandulf's niece as his wife – she had been sent to a nunnery – he had taken a new young mistress, and was busy, with hefty bribes, trying to get the Pope to annul his late union so that he could remarry.

Just as William and Drogo de Hauteville had once learnt to bear arms, then had been shown how to fight in everything from a skirmish to a real battle, now they were about to observe the difference between that and a campaign. The mere act of getting three hundred Norman lances, by sea, to where they would fight, was a monumental task, given they had to transport their horses – none would trust to be supplied in Sicily – mounts which had to be got on board ship and once on board, fed, watered and cared for.

Some went up the gently sloping gangplank without trouble, not distressed by its gentle swaying; most reared and bucked at that, as well as unfamiliar sights and smells, setting their forelegs and refusing to budge. Hooding, so they could not see, was the most common way to overcome their fears, but with many they were obliged to turn to mendicant monks and their concoctions of herbs.

A mix put in the animals' feed sedated the most troublesome and once on board each was placed in a narrow stall, fitted with sturdy straps so they did not suffer when losing their footing with the motion of the vessel. Kept occupied with quantities of hay, they fared better than the men who rode them, most of whom were green at the gills before the ships made deep water, which led to many a jest about their Viking heritage from the two de Hautevilles, too used to boats and an Atlantic swell to be affected.

With a fair wind and well-worked oars they made the Straits of Messina within two days and were gifted a sight of the ancient city they were about to help besiege, one that gave the channel its name. The straits might look like nothing, just over a league in width at their narrowest point, but it was a formidable piece of water with strong tidal flows, the legendary stretch of sea where the Greek hero Odysseus had faced the twin perils of Scylla and Charybdis. As they sailed down the coast, William, speculating on an opposed landing, was struck by the lack of beaches that were not overseen by high hills on a shore dotted with stone watchtowers. Sicily, for all its proximity to the mainland, would be no easy nut to crack without local help.

That the Byzantines had and the bulk of their army was already ashore, having landed in the territory of a Saracen emir who saw advantage in cooperation with his one-time enemies. Getting their mounts off their ships was no less hazardous than loading them, worse in many ways without a quay, which meant the ramp to the shore was much steeper, in need of constant sanding to provide a sound footing. Once they had got their horses onto land, William led his knights through a ravine between high surrounding hills, to a valley where the army was assembled. It was there William and Drogo met the man who would lead them.

It was rare for William de Hauteville to have to look up to anyone but, in the person of George Maniakes, he was in the presence of a real giant, a man near half as tall again as he. He had the frame of the biblical Goliath and a manner to match, being brusque in the extreme, with unfriendly eyes under a flat, wide brow and below that a nose which seemed to spread over half his face. Fresh from success in Syria, where he had achieved great victories in command of the eastern imperial armies, something he was keen these Normans should know from his own lips, he was cocksure of his ability. Neither de Hauteville brother was bothered by this display of conceit; they would judge him in battle, not in his pavilion.

Yet it was worrying that he clearly despised his admiral, quite happy to call him an idiot in the presence of strangers. Stephen had the task of sealing off Messina to seaward and it was clear Maniakes did not trust him to do so with any zeal, while the composition of the army did not inspire much faith either, being mainly made up of Bulgars and levies from the cities of Apulia, mostly Italians but including Lombards, both races who bitterly resented their service.

The cream of the force, the anvil on which Maniakes was sure he could crush the enemy, lay in the Emperor's five-hundred-strong Varangian Guard, the men of Kiev Rus. Huge and blond, with fearsome moustaches, they were fair of skin like their Norse cousins and bore huge axes as their fighting weapon. They were led by Harald Hardrada, a brother to the King of Norway, who could still claim to be a Viking and looked like one, a legendary fighter whose fame had spread far and wide throughout Christendom.

Hardrada had taken service with the guard on his way back from Jerusalem, and rose by sheer ability to the command. It was they who would lead the army to besiege Messina, the first objective, because it would provide, given its harbour and the proximity to the mainland, a secure base for supplies and reinforcements; Maniakes could safely advance from there on to the major emirates of Syracuse and Palermo.

'I would wager it is the Varangians and us who will do the work,' said Drogo, as he watched them pass, heading for Messina, their axes across their shoulders.

'I'm glad they are on our side,' William replied, and he meant it; these were the very same axemen who had defeated the last great Lombard revolt, including Rainulf and his brother, at Cannae.

As the last axeman passed, William fell in behind them, followed by the companies he now commanded.

It looked as if it would take a year to subdue Messina – it was a city of great strength which had been given much time to prepare – a siege of starvation more than relentless attack or enemy sortie. The sea was blocked to them, so few supplies could get through to the city, and that was a situation in which mounted Norman warriors, doing no more than foraging, were wasted, though it took William several months to persuade George Maniakes of this. He was a difficult man to like: a good general maybe, but a man of sudden temper, so convinced of his own superiority that he saw helpful suggestion as disagreement.

'Let me take my men and ravage the countryside.'

'To what purpose?'

William replied with an exasperated growl. 'We are of little use here if you are not going to try to breach the walls. Every day we hear rumours of forces being gathered to oppose us.'

'Rumours,' Maniakes trumpeted, looking down at William. 'As if these Saracens can ever agree to combine, they're worse than Lombards.'

William would have agreed they were little different when it came to tribal loyalty, but that did not obviate the possibility. 'Left alone they will.'

'You are paid, are you not?' Maniakes growled. 'Be content with that.'

'My men are fighters and they want more than just pay. If you keep them here they will grow feeble, and when you do need them, when we move from here and perhaps meet an army in the field, you will require them at their best.'

'I command here, de Hauteville.'

It annoyed William, the way Maniakes used his name; it annoyed Drogo even more, which was why he had been left out of this meeting. Big as Maniakes was, Drogo would still try to fell him. Yet he was right, he was the general in command, able to manage the endless trouble he had with his Apulian, Calbrian and Bulgar levies and keep his army tight as a fighting unit. William did not want to add to his difficulties, to seem insubordinate. He knew, even if he had never personally experienced it, that an army could quickly fall apart if the leadership was not stable.

'No one disputes that, George Maniakes, but I

command my men. You have your Varangians, who are
great fighters, and your Apulian and Bulgar sheep to
hold the lines. The garrison shows no sign of emerging
to take issue, but if they do, let the axemen deal with
them.'

'I will consider it.'

That having been said with reluctance, William
knew he had to press. 'What are the Messina garrison
praying for?'

'Divine intervention,' Maniakes hooted. 'They hope
their prophet will send a ball of fire to destroy us.'

'No. They hope to see you drawn off by the
combined force of the other Saracen emirs, Abdullah
in particular, and if you just sit here that might
happen. Let us Normans guarantee your back, George
Maniakes, and take away hope from the city we are
besieging. It is the only thing sustaining them.'

'I cannot do without good cavalry. Just because they
have not emerged to fight does not mean it will never
happen. You lack experience, de Hauteville, while I do
not. In my Syrian campaigns...'

Maniakes was off, listing his victories again, as well
as his genius for tactics and strategy, a litany that
William knew would brook no interruption. It was
like the high spring tides feeding the salt pans back
home on the Contentin coast: you just had to wait for
them to recede, but it did give the listener the lever he
needed. If this giant was so full of himself, it would be

better to feed his vanity than counter it.

'Then let us lead them out a company at a time, a hundred lances, and you, George Maniakes, who know so much more about fighting than I, will tell us where you want us to go.'

No great genius was required to fix the locations that needed to be subdued, the first being Rometta, sat on a high hill surrounded by mountains, the nearest fortress and littoral large enough to sustain a gathering army. Yet William knew he needed more than a hundred lances to attack such an obstacle, so instead he went for the next important target, the beach below Bàusu, a place where reinforcements could land from anywhere in Sicily or North Africa, and a location close enough to Messina to pose a threat from sudden raids.

Part of what he learnt on that journey was the suitability of the terrain for small-scale operations of the kind he was engaged in. The country was high hills and deep fertile valleys with few plains of any size to support a large mobile force, but it was well watered, so that and pasture were plentiful, which meant mounted men could move with speed and safety without having to carry too much in the way of fodder or food, the greatest constraint on cavalry mobility.

The local population, being Sicilian, had a jaundiced view of armed strangers; in their time they had seen too many invaders to care as long as they were left to till their fields and tend their vines, groves and orchards. Where he might have expected loyalty to a local overlord there was none; the Saracens had cleansed the land of the previous Greek/Byzantine nobility and, as long as they paid what was due in tribute, the new suzerains left the peasants in peace. The advantage of peasant indifference was that he could move without his opponents being forewarned, with the obvious connected fact that they, too, could do the same. The Sicilian peasant would no more warn him of approaching danger than a Saracen!

If the terrain, plus his determination to stay off the skyline, made the route to Bàusu torturous, imposing frequent halts along the way, it also meant that when they got close there was no risk of their mounts being blown by being pushed too far. William, without surcoat or mail, having set sentinels on the surrounding hills, went ahead on foot with a small bodyguard to reconnoitre the town.

He was careful to avoid being sighted and identified from the watchtower which covered the long open bay, getting close enough to see that the beach was full of small vessels and that from the west, a steady stream of supplies – grain, fruit and the like – was being brought in both by larger boats and, over the narrow roadway in the hills, by donkeys. Yet there was no sign of serious forces to oppose him: his enemies had either grown complacent or were encamped elsewhere.

'Some of that has to be for Messina.'

'The siege?'

William barely glanced at the man who had posed that question; no siege was watertight. Laziness, stupidity, indifference and ineptitude meant they leaked, but the greatest source of secret supply would be bribes. Some the ship's captains Stephen Calaphates had under his command would, for not very much money, turn a blind eye at night to local boats smuggling supplies into Messina. Such trickles of what would be seen as luxuries to a population on short commons helped to keep up the spirits of those who controlled the city. To deny them such, when hope was the weapon which sustained them, was worth a dozen battailes.

Yet it was also a place where a force could gather and be supplied, exactly the kind of thing about which he had spoken to George Maniakes, and some of those supplies would be for them. There was no doubt in William's mind that he could stop the present flow, but he did not have with him enough men to hold the place in the middle of hostile terrain. That such a thing might be needed in future had to be left to that; his task was to destroy what was here now, so the leaders of Messina would find this lifeline cut and the enemy soldiery likewise. He had another notion, but it was one which would have to wait until Bàusu had been destroyed.

Back in his encampment his men were eating dried strips of beef and fruit; no fires or cooking could be allowed and, once he had fed himself, William called together those in command of the various convoys to outline the tasks he had for each one. The first would depart by moon and starlight to cut the road to the west, the most likely route by which any relieving force could approach; others would, after he had begun his assault, block the two trails out of Bàusu he had identified to ensure no one escaped. William needed time to do what was required.

That night, they slept in their mail, swords close by, as they had done since leaving the siege works of Messina, under the stars, close to their snuffling and snorting mounts tied in lines. William did the rounds of the sentries himself to ensure they stayed awake and oversaw the first change. He slept little and was up before the first of his sleeping knights stirred. On a day in which they knew they would be fighting prayers were said first, the ritual each man followed of commending his soul to God, the first convoy mounting and departing long before the sun had touched the horizon.

They were tasked to ride quickly, so as to be astride the trail before the first traveller appeared. William led his remaining men more slowly forward on foot, horses softly plodding on the rein, seeking forest cover where it could be found, aware that if the men on the watchtowers were alert they would see, even in nothing but the prevailing gloom, that something substantial was disturbing the birds in the trees, yet without sight they would be unsure if it was a friend or a foe.

The point was reached where subterfuge no longer served, so William had his men mount, set themselves and their lances, and with a war cry that had struck fear into the hearts of half of Europe, kicked his horse into a fast trot on to what remained of a roadway, for the town which overlooked the beach. The folk lived by the sun and not the lamp, so most were still asleep, so he caught the whole town unawares. Certainly half-dressed men emerged to fight, but on foot, faced with lances and swords from men mounted, they were cut down in their doorways.

William wanted to control the beach, to ensure that no boat, not even the smallest used for fishing, got away, and that required they dismount. Shouting his commands, he formed his men up into an unbroken line, then began to march back up towards the line of buildings through which they had just charged. Like every tiny Sicilian town, Bàusu was a maze of narrow alleys into which he did not want to go, for in such constrained areas a mailed knight lost the value of his sword and became at the mercy of the knife.

The locals either slammed their doors in the hope of being ignored or fled in panic up the surrounding hills looking for safety, and some Saracens joined them. The latter ran into the Normans blocking the trails and if they were unarmed they were merely herded. The odd one, armed, was not and they, on the orders of William de Hauteville, were in receipt of no mercy. They suffered the same fate as any caught still in the town; he had too few men to think of leniency.

The remnants of the Saracens made for the mosque, the only substantial building they felt they could defend, and there they died either fighting or pleading for mercy as William and his men cut them down. That complete, the bodies were collected and placed inside before they fired the building. Remounted, men were sent to bring in the pack animals, a strong party to attack the watchtower – now with a flaming, smoking beacon on the crenellated roof – to take it if they could, to ensure no one got away if they could not.

Before the sun was fully up, the Normans had complete control and the destruction of the town could begin: houses, storerooms, the small warehouses. The only building not torched after being plundered was the Orthodox church in which the remaining Sicilians had taken refuge. Inside, William de Hauteville, in a halting combination of Latin and Greek, was questioning the locals as to what they knew of the surrounding countryside and how they carried out the smuggling into Messina, and he was not gentle, time being short.

He was not naïve enough to think that no enemy had got clear, nor that he would get back to Messina without incurring danger. News would spread that a Norman force held Bàusu, and the tocsin would sound to gather a force to retake it, but how far away would they be, how much time did he have?

Some of the men he questioned owned the boats on the beach and they were the ones who made their living smuggling. Faced with a sharp knife at their throats they were only too willing to tell him what he needed to know. When he felt he had exhausted the chances of more information, he could calculate what he had to do. First, every boat on the beach must be put to the torch. Next he must get his men and animals together, then fed and watered. That done they must be off on the shortest route back to the safety of the siege line.

The town was smouldering by the time they departed, each man leading a horse weighed down with any booty they could carry, everything else having been destroyed. At the top of every rise they could see beacons burning on the hillsides and they had to assume that the whole countryside was alerted. The temptation to push the mounts without mercy had to be avoided, given a blown animal was useless if they needed to fight.

They were walking through rows of vines when the first horsemen appeared, not enough to trouble them, a mere six riders, but it was worrying that on every hilltop over which they rode they stopped to wave the pennant on their lances; a bluff possibly, but also they might be signalling to a superior force heading for a place where they knew they could cut them off. Though the horses were far from rested, William had his men remount and set off at a trot to see what those trailing them would do and, when nothing changed, he began to look for a clear field in which to fight.

Tancred had always told him, 'If you can't avoid a fight, choose the ground on which to have it. Never let your enemy do that.' What he needed was an area in which he could properly deploy, one where he could stand and force the enemy to come to him, but at the same time he had to ensure that by doing so he was not allowing his opponents time to bring up overwhelming force.

It was a calculation with which William was comfortable, relying as it did on the same mental processes he had used at Bessancourt. Nothing in war is certain, that was another one of his father's doctrines. You had to make judgements based on what you knew and what you suspected, and William de Hauteville was working on two assumptions: the first that, given the time, only so much force could be gathered to range against him, the second being that they would be Saracens who had never faced Normans. They would not know what to expect.

'Tie up the packhorses,' he ordered as they emerged from an orchard into a broad valley of green fields left fallow, not very long, but bounded on both sides by quite steep hillsides. Then he dismounted himself, but hauled hard on his horse's head to stop him grazing. No horse works well on a full belly and the last thing he wanted was his mount thinking of pasture when he should be thinking of that for which he had been trained.

Whoever he was going to have to fight would now come to him, and since he intended to give battle straight away it would be their horses that would be fatigued. If the force was too numerous it would be necessary to break through them; let the Saracens have the booty. If the force was less or equal he would seek to destroy them. Having sent two men up each side of the valley as lookouts he addressed the rest, all of whom were making sure their horses' heads never got to the tempting grass at their hooves.

'It's about time these Saracens saw what Normans can do, and if they are better than we, then say goodbye to everything we have plundered today.'

That set up a growl; these men would fight doubly hard to keep their booty. William went to his own pack animal and rummaged in the pannier, pulling out the blue and white pennant his father had given him which, when opened, showed a chequer set across it.

'These are my family colours. Today, these are the ones you will follow.'

The shout from above made them all look up to a soldier with his arms spread wide, so lots of men were coming. He made a reins sign to tell William they were mounted and started to flash his five fingers four times. It could only be an estimate, but it seemed they were outnumbered two to one. Everyone had seen it, and it pleased William that none reacted.

'Check your girths.'

It was, in a sense, an unnecessary command: every man present knew to do that, and to ease the swords in their scabbards once or twice to ensure they would not stick from dried blood. Each would remove his helmet and dry his head before replacing it and tug at a friend's mail to make sure all was secure. These were habits, good ones.

'Mount up.'

That done, he led them out at a slow walk to the middle of the valley, which cut down the amount of room his opponents would have to gain momentum, their red and black pennants fluttering in a warm breeze. Each wing was elevated by the rising ground so he called them back to take station to the rear until they saw what their enemy intended.

And suddenly they were there, black-clad Saracen horsemen. Even at a distance William could admire the lines of their fine horses, but they were built for speed, not battle, which is why he would have been overtaken anyway. He felt vindicated by his halt, all the more so when he saw the sweat of the flanks of the enemy mounts; they had been pushed hard.

He tried to imagine what they were seeing: a line of men and horses, red and black shields, the tall lances and the fact that they were stationary, with one man out front, him. The man in command had also halted his horsemen and was riding back and forth on a spirited animal, the words of his exhortations floating across the grass, not clear, but obvious as encouragement.

William dipped his lance and the line began to move forward at a walk, each Norman making sure his thigh was near to touching that of his neighbours. The two men behind him opened a gap into which he fitted and the effect on the enemy leader was clear; seeing the Normans standing he had assumed they were waiting for him to attack, but their movement meant if he was going to control the action he must move now and, to William's satisfaction, he did, raising a round sword designed for slashing and pointing it forward, that followed by a high-pitched yell.

Immediately his men kicked their mounts into motion, and it was obvious that some reacted quicker than others. Already there were gaps in his line and that only increased as the pace of their charge did likewise. William knew he had no need even to canter; let them come to him, because their line was disorganised and his was not. On his flanks, the men who had taken station to the rear began to move back up the hillsides. They would not need to be told what to do.

His lance went down when they were a hundred paces distant in a gap that was closing at speed. His opponents were up on their stirrups, swords ready to swipe down and render useless those lance points, and while he knew what they were doing was foolish – based on the notion that in the face of such a furious charge the line must melt – he had to admire their courage. The problem they had was simple: they had never met Normans.

Their leader was the first to die on a lance point: thrown by the way as he slashed at the metal tip, it was quickly withdrawn then jammed forward again once his weapon was past the arc of being useful. The point took him in the chest and lifted him bodily off his saddle, his momentum driving it through to come out his back and lifting him bodily off a now rearing horse seeking to avoid a collision.

The forward motion of the Norman line was only what was needed, enough to ensure that when horse met horse, as they were bound to, their mounts could hold their ground, so many Saracens died as had their leader. Others sought to engage the men no longer holding lances, only to find that their opponents, in the main taller than they, could raise their swords higher and bring them down with terrible force on man and metal, might enough to cut through the mail they wore under their black garments.

Then the men on the Norman flanks began to press in from the sloping hillsides, so that many Saracens were now trying and failing to fight two foes. It could not last, for William's line was pressing forward, lances jabbing, swords swinging and in some cases knives slashing. The enemy broke, as they must, in ones and twos to begin with, then in greater numbers and, as they fled, had they looked over their shoulder, they would have seen the same firm line of shields they had charged against.

The near dead were despatched, any ambulant enemy taken prisoner; they would provide information and all the horses not so wounded they needed their throats cut gathered in as booty. William saw to his wounded – only four of his knights had perished, and they were set across their saddles to be taken back for a Christian burial. The enemy dead were left in the fields for the carrion to consume.

They rode back into the siege lines to cheers from men who were bored with their dull duty, many an eye drawn to the colours that still graced William's lance, and as he rode, he was thinking how proud his father would be to see that blue and white chequer aloft in such a setting.

CHAPTER NINETEEN

The next night, hogging the coast in a small boat with half a dozen armed companions, Drogo included, William sailed north towards the ships blockading the mouth of the port, at home in such a vessel; he and his brothers had fished often off the Normandy shore and had once sailed to the Norman Islands to chastise the pirates who raided the Contentin coastline. In the Messina Straits the current was a problem, impeding his passage, but he could see the ships strung out in a line, beating to and fro to hold their station, his destination being the vessel on the outer rim of the great hook which formed the eastern shore of Sicily.

He needed, he knew, to be near that shore, for those Sicilian boatmen he had questioned had told him so, and he also knew that it was the vessel closest inshore, a Ragusan galley of shallow draught, which controlled the section just above the outer siege work built south of the city by George Maniakes. The moon shone on the water, illuminating several vessels, which appeared like black shadows, but William steered for the one showing a red lantern and, once within range, shouted the Greek words he had been told to use.

It was obvious that those aboard were waiting for an approach, they were too alert for a time of day when even sailors slept, and as he came close the reply, also in Greek, was half whispered to him. Even although his knowledge of the language was limited, it was quite simply a demand to be told what he was carrying.

'Grain,' he replied, unsheathing his sword.

That had his companions doing likewise. As they bumped alongside, beneath a row of shaded lanterns, hands reached out in the gloom to pull them in. William grasped one using the security that provided to leap for the low bulwark. He got one leg over immediately, to be greeted by a surprised cry, but that turned to something else when the light from a lantern now unshaded showed, not a Sicilian fisherman on the deck, but a mailed Norman knight wielding a sword.

That surprise lasted long enough to get his companions on to the deck, by which time William was shouting his head off and cutting a swathe with his blade that had the sailors diving for anywhere that offered protection. Behind him he heard the splash as some went overboard, either because of their own fear or because his men had tossed them, it made no odds; all he wanted was what he was shouting for, the man who commanded the vessel.

They found him in a tiny cabin under the low poop, cowering on the deck, shaking like a leaf, pleading useless innocence. Below decks were the chained men who rowed this galley, bonded slaves to this cringing parasite. The rest of the small crew, at least those who had not gone overboard, had run for the forepeak, and were now seeking to ward off the point of Drogo's sword.

Daylight saw them ashore, the galley beached as near to the pavilion of George Maniakes as possible, William dragging the ship's owner in chains behind him, the rest of his freemen crew shuffling along with Norman blades beating their buttocks.

'We need to make an example of them,' William said, after he had explained to the general what he had discovered. 'I doubt this toad is the only one.'

He knew George Maniakes had a terrible temper; he also knew he was a man of uncommon strength, but he did not appreciate what happened, thinking it a waste of an opportunity to discourage other shipowners from allowing through smugglers. The general picked up the squirming owner in one hand, and literally squeezed the life out of him, blood eventually bursting from his tongue and his ears, and his eyes nearly popping from his head as he expired in agony.

The positive for William was he had proved his point. Not only had he destroyed a base for smuggling, he had fought and beaten the Saracens who rimmed the area and obviously constituted a threat. From now on the Normans would not be bogged down in the siege, they would be free to roam wherever William de Hauteville thought they could do the most damage to the enemy. It was a happy Drogo who led out the next hundred lances, the de Hauteville pennant now fluttering over his head.

It was hard to tell what impact the cutting of that lifeline had on the Messina garrison; their sudden offer to surrender surprised everyone, but they had probably pinned their hopes on Abdullah. The rumours of his gathering an army continued, but as yet no sign of it had come. George Maniakes took possession of the city, shipped off the fighting men to eastern slavery, then collected his army together to march on Rometta, the great fortress that controlled the road to the capital Palermo, a vital link if the whole island was to be subdued. Surprisingly, that too fell in only a month but not without heavy fighting that saw the Normans and the Varangians attacking a breach in the wall and only carrying the day by sheer tenacity.

Both William and Drogo had never fought so hard for so long, slipping on rubble and the blood from dead bodies, as well as the cadavers themselves. The Saracens fought like demons, selling their lives for every footstep, falling under axe and sword, only to be replaced by even more fanatical defenders who took their place and they had to be driven back into the city, then winkled out of alleys, buildings and even cellars.

Many of William's men died in that breach, as did those of Hardrada; no one came away from the assault without a wound and it was galling to find out, once the city had been taken, that their main opponent, the North African Emir Abdullah al Zirid, had got away with a sizeable force and still represented a threat.

George Maniakes now had open the road to Palermo, but he was well aware of the history of Sicily: going back to Phoenician times it had always been the case that the key to the holding of the island was the great port and city of Syracuse, on the south-eastern side. It was a hard lesson learnt by Athens, Carthage, the Romans, the Vandals and the Saracens themselves: leave it in another's hands and you were always at risk.

It also had a special significance for the Byzantines – when their greatest ever general, Belisarius, had evicted the Vandals from Sicily in 533 AD, Syracuse had been made their capital. It wounded them that the great cathedral they had built had been turned into a mosque; that inside the city there were hidden relics of saints and martyrs dear to Orthodox hearts. It was the general's decision, and he made it: the army marched for Syracuse and besieged it, while the dull Stephen brought his ships from Messina to blockade the great bight of a bay.

Syracuse was, by its very nature, a tougher challenge than either Messina or Rometta. The land access was constricted, the main part of the city located on the island of Ortygia, that part of a peninsula but with a wide channel separating it from the mainland. The defenders held stout defences on the landward side of that but could, at any time, retire behind the water barrier. The walls of the old city had first been constructed in ancient times, then added to, and were formidable, surrounding the whole island and making any attack across water fraught with peril.

The approach from the sea was to a wide bay full of fighting ships which would emerge from the fortified harbour, and on the seaward side a long coastline on an unpredictable stretch of sea made close blockade awkward. History abounded with sieges that had lasted for years: it took the Romans three years and they only succeeded because of treachery. Syracuse, unless betrayed, or some stroke of luck intervened, could only be starved into submission.

George Maniakes was not a patient man, and a dozen attacks were launched, none of which even dented the defences. He tried attacking across the bay only to find the vessels he was employing destroyed by fire ships, watching as they were consumed and the men who had manned them either frying in the flames or drowning in the sea as they leapt overboard from fear of a more painful death. He tried to attack at night, only to find his foes waiting for him with boiling oil and flaming balls of tarred hay, and while all this was happening, his shock troops, the Varangian Guard, stood idle.

Over six months the Normans ranged far and wide in the interior, in companies of a hundred lances, all the way up to the mountains which cut Syracuse off from the interior hinterland, yet that too was frustrating. No army of relief appeared, in fact no enemy fighters showed at all; it was as if they had decided that the ancient capital of Sicily must fend for itself. Just as exasperating was the way the Saracens had stripped the countryside of anything valuable. There was no need for Normans to destroy olive groves and vineyards, fields of sugar beet and wheat. That had been done for them.

Returning from another fruitless sortie, William joined up with the company led by Drogo and together they rode into the siege lines, sharing their irritation. That their men were dissatisfied they knew: pay was a thing which became the norm and was not inspiring; booty of the kind they had acquired from Messina and

Rometta was what elevated their spirits and there was none of that unless the city fell, and it was clear from far off that nothing much had changed since they last rode out.

Making their way to the general's pavilion to report, they could hear the raised voices from a hundred paces, or rather one, that of George Maniakes. Added to that, many of the senior commanders, including Harald Hardrada, were gathered outside with glum looks on their faces, and the brothers soon learnt the reason. If Syracuse was to be starved into submission then it was paramount the naval blockade was rigorous; nothing should get through. Still under the dense Admiral Stephen, it had failed: a convoy of grain ships had broken through his line of galleys to bring in relief supplies. What they were hearing was the verbal drubbing Stephen was getting from George Maniakes.

He was the son of a whore, his wife no better, which, unsaid, meant that Emperor Michael was from the same grubby stable. His fitness to do anything other than shovel shit from a pit was questioned, and it was clear that half the looks of worry on the faces of those around William and Drogo were caused by the fact that their general was going too far. Stephen might be an idiot, but he was the emperor's brother-in-law and in a hothouse court like Constantinople the words Maniakes was using, reported into those ears, would not be taken lightly.

'He needs to be stopped,' said William, 'for his own good.'

'Physically?' Harald Hardrada, who had posed the question, grinned and looked at the two de Hauteville brothers; he was as big and as broad as they, and a doughty fighter, yet he knew that George Maniakes was bigger and stronger. 'After you.'

'I think,' Drogo murmured, 'it might take all three of us.'

That was when they heard the gasping sound. Maniakes was still shouting but his words had become near incomprehensible, and it took no great foresight to deduce that the general had laid hands on the admiral. In William's mind was the way he had strangled that smuggling ship's captain. If he did that to his admiral the consequences would be incalculable.

All three leaders rushed into the pavilion to find Stephen, off his feet, held in the great mitt of Maniakes, and he was clearly in distress, already fighting just to breathe. William jumped on the giant's back, Drogo and Harald got hold of one upper arm each and struggled to get him to release his victim, all to no avail. It was only when William got his ear between his teeth and bit hard, threatening with his jerking head to tear it off, that Maniakes let go, and that was with a bellow.

It was William who was now in trouble, with Maniakes swinging his body to get at him, his only hope to stay glued to his back, while Harald and Drogo tried to subdue him from the front. Stephen had fled, screaming that he had been near to murdered. It was Drogo who solved the problem, because he burst out laughing. He was still trying to assist his brother, but the sight was too much for him, and soon Harald Hardrada was laughing too, which meant his efforts were rendered feeble.

'Stop giggling you two and help me.'

That only made things worse for Drogo. He was laughing so much he had to let go of Maniakes, still bellowing like a blinded Cyclops, and Hardrada was soon reduced to the same. It was the sight of that, two fierce warriors in fits, which stopped the general trying to dislodge William. He was breathing heavily from his exertions, but soon he was laughing too, his body heaving. William slid off his back and made sure he was out of arm's reach. All he could manage was a nervous smile because he could see the blood dripping from the general's ear.

'Here he comes again,' said Drogo as a fanfare of trumpets blew, words addressed to his brother and the Varangian commander, Harald Hardrada.

The city gates opened in what had become a daily ritual. The Emir of Syracuse, Rashid al Farza, would ride out in all his finery to goad the attackers, calling out to them in Greek his challenge to George Maniakes to come and fight him. It was a telling challenge for he was not far off the same size and everybody in the camp knew he had a fearsome reputation as a fighter. It was said he had personally killed over a hundred men in single combat and, while all took that with a pinch of salt, there was no doubt he was a formidable opponent.

Maniakes declined to accept, not from fear, but because a victory over this Saracen would not bring about the surrender of his city, while a defeat might severely damage the prospects of that, which was the only thing that mattered: the Byzantine host was here to subdue Sicily; personal insults its general-in-command could live with.

'He's beginning to annoy me,' William replied, shading his eyes from the low sun to take in the emir.

'Perhaps,' Hardrada suggested, 'I should take out my axe and chop off his arrogant head.'

Back and forth Rashid rode on a beautiful horse, just as beautifully caparisoned in fine-coloured silk. He wore a plumed helm and an old Roman cuirass designed to demonstrate that his chest beneath was just as muscled, greaves with fine silver decoration and the lance he carried had a long fluttering pennant. From time to time he would jam that into the ground as a challenge then haul out a great sword and wave it about his head, straight bladed instead of arced like the normal Saracen weapon, with one serrated edge which would cut through mail with ease.

The words that floated towards the siege lines left no insult unspoken, and eventually the soldiers would be goaded into yelling insults back at him, which he seemed to enjoy mightily as proof he was succeeding. After half a glass of this farrago he turned his horse, and since he had taught it to prance, it danced its way back into the defences, its tail stiff and high as if to apply equal denigration.

Both the de Hauteville brothers were itching for activity: it had become plain that with nothing to raid and no one to fight there was little use in their sorties, and they had been stuck in camp since the incident in which they had subdued Maniakes. The general laughingly jested that William owed him an ear, and one day he was going to collect his due. William did not laugh; he had seen too often the way the man lost control.

'What are you doing?' demanded Drogo the next morning, when he saw his elder brother mounted and mailed and bearing his lance and with it the de Hauteville blue and white pennant.

'When our friend comes out, Drogo, I am going to shut him up.'

'Are you mad?'

'He has made me mad. Yesterday he insulted our mother and father.'

'Yesterday he insulted everyone's mother and father.'

William glowered at Drogo, blazing blue eyes at either side of his nose guard in a fair representation of fury. In truth it was sheer inactivity which had made him want to take on the challenge, plus the feeling that the emir's behaviour was diminishing the spirits of those besieging Syracuse whilst bolstering those of his own side, and that was no aid to a speedy conclusion.

'You think I can't beat him.'

There was no chance of Drogo responding to that; his brother might have a more even temper than he, but you did not tell a Norman knight, even a blood relation, he was bound to lose in single combat unless you wanted to fight him yourself.

'I think, in our family, that I am the one who will not stand an insult.'

'You will just have to wait your turn.'

'Does Maniakes know about this?'

William looked towards the general's pavilion, to see the giant heading his way, trailed by Harald Hardrada. 'He does now.'

Drogo looked in the same direction. 'He might forbid it.'

'He does not have the right,' William replied as the usual morning fanfare blew out from the walls of Syracuse. 'If I fall, you take over the command.'

'God bless you, Gill.'

William nodded in response – only Drogo called him by the diminutive of his name in French – and then he spurred his horse. He was out in the open before Maniakes could stop him, and along the line the soldiers who manned the siege works rose to cheer, their yells of encouragement enough to drown out the emir's trumpets. If his general had wanted to forbid this he could hardly do so now: his whole army was involved.

Slowly he trotted into the centre of what would now be an arena, then hauled round to ride parallel with the city walls, attracting the jeers of the defenders. He had turned back again by the time Rashid appeared, gorgeous as ever, but more impatient, his horse dancing early as its rider communicated his excitement. Slowly William rode towards him and the Saracen responded, until they were abreast of each other and, as was normal prior to any exchange, both men were making assessments of arms and equipment.

William had already seen the great sword Rashid carried, even if that was still sheathed, but it was clear his lance was longer by at least a hand, and that was telling. The emir would have seen, before getting close, that difference in lance length and was looking at the Norman almond-shaped shield, so very different from his own round buckler, big enough to give protection to more of this potential opponent's body.

'Who offers me combat?' Rashid asked, looking down, his voice full of confidence.

'William de Hauteville, of Normandy.'

'I know of you, but I want George Maniakes.'

'He stands behind me, and through me you will have to go to get to him.'

'Very well,' Rashid replied, before hauling his mount round in its own length and letting out a great shout to his supporters, his lance once more raised in the air. 'Allah Akbar.'

Silently, William crossed himself as they responded with a great roar. It was a strange reaction from men, the majority of whom must be Sicilian and Christian, who surely could not love Saracen rule? Perhaps they loved their city too much to want to see it fall, perhaps they hated Byzantium even more. Rashid, who had ridden far enough, had brought his mount round again, which meant any such thoughts must be put aside. It was time to fight.

The mere nature of the emir's horse told William he would come at the same kind of fast gallop as the fellow he had killed on that expedition from Messina, while his would, as it always did, barely get above a hard canter, so if Rashid's slightly longer lance made contact it would be with greater force than his own. At all costs he must stay mounted: on foot in single combat against a horsed opponent he stood little chance. How to negate that advantage?

They were both moving now, the gap closing rapidly and, as always, the whole world narrowed to what lay at the end of his lance tip. William had to close his mind to the thundering approaching hooves of Rashid's animal, the flutter of his lance pennant and the rippling coloured waves of the silks that clothed both horse and rider. It had to narrow down to the slightest of gaps between the man's round shield and his lower body.

The trick Tancred had taught him when he was a mere fifteen-year-old boy was a hard one to pull off. It required a degree of physical strength which, if not pressed home properly, would work against him, because it required a fine balance between extension and power. Already both men were standing in the stirrups, and both had moved their shields to protect their trunk, for a lance point hitting either William's chain mailed chest or that leather breastplate of Rashid's would slice right through them.

They were only paces apart when William made his move, taking his couched lance and jabbing it forward so that it was extended, the shaft running under his outstretched arm, the only thing to hold it his clenched and mailed right hand. Rashid saw the move and tried to adjust his own weapon, which was an error, because in a fight you should never be caught in two minds. In acting his bulk worked against him; he might be near a giant but his movements were restricted by that very size. Had he stayed committed he would at least have got his lance point onto the centre of William's shield. As it was, doing something unfamiliar it wavered and as he felt the tip of his opponent's lance on his buckler he sought to shy away.

With full force William struck his buckler at the base, the force of his blow, a split second before he too was struck, bending back that shield just enough to get his lance point through, to strike Rashid at the place where his leather breastplate met his upper thigh. He was good, swift enough to jam his shield sideways so that the point failed to skewer him, as William intended, but ran along the outer side of his leg, hitting the high back of his saddle and shattering the shaft.

William took Rashid's lance on a high point of his shield, but in seeking to change his action that had lost a lot of force, although it still took and smashed the top half and spun William round so that he was nearly unhorsed by being flung sideways on to his saddle. Only the sheer strength of thighs moulded since childhood to stay aboard kept him on his mount until the two were past each other, the Norman already reaching for his sword, hauling on his reins to bring round his destrier and take Rashid before he could respond. Vaguely, in his ears, he could hear cheering from both sides, though he thought he could sense it greater from the trenches rather than the walls.

Rashid was too wise to make a quick turn to meet him. William had drawn blood and that required a quick assessment to see how it would affect his ability to fight, so he rode on until he was out of immediate danger, well away from William de Hauteville. The point of his opponent's lance was still embedded in his saddle, so he hauled it out and held it up to show the men on the walls of Syracuse, the implication being that it had missed him.

But he knew it had not, knew that he had torn mail and a long gash in his thigh which might hamper him if fighting on foot. There was no way to tell if that was the case until he needed to use the leg, so it was obvious to William that Rashid must at all costs avoid that kind of test. He now had his sword out, a blade already known to be of fearsome proportions, razor sharp on one side and serrated like a fine saw on the other.

William was approaching with no haste; if his man was bleeding let it flow and weaken him, and his sword was again a weapon shorter in length than Rashid's. But it was easier to use, as long as it was not left exposed to a blow which, combined with the great bulk and strength of the emir and the weight of his weapon, could break it in two.

There was no cheering now, there was silence as both sets of supporters watched a fight about to come to the point of decision. They saw the way William de Hauteville manoeuvred his mount with just his thighs, wending it left and right as he approached the emir, seeking an avenue in which to attack. They saw Rashid spur his mount to close quickly, and soon the air was filled with the sound of metal on metal as the swords were used to swing, thrust and parry, that mixed with loud, dull thuds as contact was made with shields.

What they could not see was the blood running into the silk on Rashid's horse, but both combatants knew it was there, the Saracen aware that the loss would weaken him, so he was trying to end this affair quickly, William de Hauteville knowing time was now on his side, that he must not seek a decision too hastily and expose himself to a blow that would equal the contest if not end it with his death.

'William is trying to tire him,' Drogo said.

'Are you sure?' asked Harald Hardrada.

Drogo indicated the line of Norman knights on either side, the men William led in to battle, every one of whom seemed to be with their leader in spirit, so intent was their concentration.

'Ask any one of them and they will tell you. His sword work is defensive.'

'He must win this,' growled George Maniakes. 'It will add months to their spirits if he does not.'

Out in the arena William was parrying more than attacking, but doing just enough of that to keep

Rashid guessing, moving his mount forward and back in a display of stunning horsemanship. The emir was pressing hard, wielding his great sword with an astonishing amount of ease, a testimony to his might, and more than once William had felt his own sword arm give under a blow. He had hoped that being so unwieldy Rashid would gift him opportunities, but so far that was not the case, and for all he was bleeding the emir showed no diminution in strength.

William was tiring and perhaps if this went on long enough it would be he who would be rendered defenceless. In all the fights he had engaged in none had seemed to require so much effort and, wondering how long it had already gone on, and how much longer it might, he could feel in his upper sword arm the beginnings of strain.

The move he employed, outright assault, standing in his stirrups and leaning right forward, surprised Rashid just enough to get his sword out of position and him off balance in his seating. There was no time to attempt a kill – to do so would render William vulnerable – but he did get his sword point under the emir's breastplate enough to push hard with both hands on his pommel, hoping for a result rather than expecting one.

It was that wounded thigh that did for Rashid: he could not hold his saddle and as pressure was applied to his stirrup foot it gave way and slipped free. His sword was in the air and as he tried to regain his balance he knew he was in maximum danger. Seeing William press forward again, sword angled across his body, ready to sweep at the point where his helmet met his neck, the emir did the only thing he could. He jabbed his other foot backwards, got it clear of the stirrup, and let himself slip on to the ground, his mount acting as a barrier to his opponent.

The emir tested his wounded leg, and it supported him, so Rashid used the flat of his sword blade to send his mount clear, and put a foot forward to swing at the forelegs of William's horse to bring him, too, down on the ground. It was horsemanship which defeated the aim, as William swung his mount sideways and clear, his sword in the air. It did not stay there, it swept down on his stationary opponent and took the emir on the crown of his plumed helmet with such force that it went right thought the metal and sliced the head in two.

There was a moment when the body stood stock-still, sword embedded, but then the huge frame of Emir Rashid al Farza keeled over into the dust, with William de Hauteville, gasping for air, lying over the withers of his sweating horse.

As he rode back into the lines, those on the walls of Syracuse were silent. The Normans, led by Drogo, were yelling '*Bras de Fer!*' And when that was translated for the Italians they too were happy to gild their champion with the title, Iron Arm.

CHAPTER TWENTY

It was only a patrol, twenty lances taken out by William and Drogo to alleviate their boredom, and because they had seen nothing to trouble them they followed the narrowing river that fed their siege lines and rode deeper into the hills than at any time previously. Many leagues from Syracuse, the country was high peaks, rolling mountains and deep valleys, so like very much of this island, but there was nothing to aim for. The nearest emirate of any size had declared itself neutral in the fight between what was essentially Abdullah-al-Zirid and George Maniakes.

The crossbow bolt missed Drogo's thigh by a whisker and embedded itself in the flesh of his horse. Surprised, he was still able to shout a warning to the rest and spin round the animal, even if it was screaming in pain, then kick it so he could close with his brother. William had not seen the bolt but he could hear Drogo yelling and that spelt only danger. In less time than it takes for ten grains of sand to pass through a glass the whole party was riding flat out to get to safety and they did not stop till they were sure that had been achieved.

'One man?' asked Drogo, as he sought to bind the wound to his horse. He had already been required to remove the crossbow bolt and that, because it was jagged, had torn a great deal of flesh and brought forth much blood.

'No one came after us,' William replied, looking back up the valley from which they had made such a hurried exit, one that narrowed to a pass between two high peaks. 'The crossbow worries me. It's a weapon for a trained man.'

'Maybe someone trained one of the peasants round here.'

'A single Sicilian peasant attacks twenty mounted lances?' William shook his head. 'Might as well tie a rope round his neck.'

'I think you've forgotten, brother, that we fled.'

William grinned. 'You did, we just followed you.'

Drogo patted his wounded horse, an animal whose head was very low. 'I can't ride this poor fellow. I'll have to go back to Syracuse on a packhorse.'

William, still examining the valley, was sure he saw something flash, a piece of metal which had caught sunlight. He nearly asked Drogo if he had seen it, but his brother was too taken with his mount. Looking round he saw the others were too busy with their own concerns to have noticed, and then, of course, doubt set in. The firing of one arrow did not make sense unless, William suddenly thought, it had been a mistake, an overzealous archer letting fly when he should not have done so. Were there more crossbowmen up ahead?

'It'll be dark in an hour, brother,' Drogo said, 'best be on our way.'

William turned and looked down the slope they were on, over the barren screed strewn with loose rocks and as far as to the point where the river bent to follow its course into an adjacent valley, obvious by the thick line of deep-green trees that edged it.

'Let's get to the other side of the river and stop there.'

'Why?' Drogo demanded, following his brother's gaze, 'we can do much better than that before dark.'

'I have a feeling we are being watched,' William said quietly. Drogo was too sensible to react; all he did was stiffen as he mentioned the head of the valley without ever looking up it. 'I saw something catch the sun.'

'There should be nothing out here.'

'That's right, Drogo, especially not crossbowmen.'

* * *

They set up camp on the far side of the river, at the very edge of the trees, and William set guards while Drogo arranged twine and twigs to give early warning of an approach on what might, given the cloud-filled sky, be a dark night; the horses would remain saddled and no one was to sleep. Then the brothers ate and drank before shedding their mail.

'We should not both go,' William insisted. 'Who will lead the men if we don't return?'

'They'll elect someone just as they elected us,' Drogo growled. 'Now let's get going.'

There was no arguing with his brother in that kind of mood, so as darkness fell they made their way along the riverbed to emerge from a line of bushes and stunted old trees that would get them to the bottom of that screed-covered slope without being observed. From then on it was boulder to boulder, always trying to keep out of sight of the point where the peaks narrowed to form a pass.

It took hours, moving slowly, testing each step to ensure they did not set off an avalanche of loose stones, and the point at which they first heard a voice had them sit still for an age until, speaking again, they could get some fix on its location. That meant a long route round a hillside in darkness, looking for foot- and handholds, solid rock or the odd piece of scrub. Close to the pass itself, they saw it was guarded, obviously by a strong, armed picket and moving even slower the brothers got themselves up above their camp so they could count their number. Fifty strong, they had small fires lit, ones that would not be seen from the riverbed and men were huddled around them cooking, eating and talking.

'Look at the clouds,' William whispered, touching his brother's arm.

It was faint, and again it would not have been seen from anywhere but at this elevation: the cloud base in the distance was tinged with the very faintest colour of orange.

'Fires,' Drogo responded.

'A lot of fires.'

'An army?'

'Has to be. Who else would be out here? It's a wilderness.'

'Abdullah?'

There was no need to answer that; the emir had got away from Rometta and there was no doubt he was determined. Here, behind this mountain barrier, was a perfect place to assemble his forces out of sight and since the Normans had really ceased to harry the littoral between here and the coast – for the very good reason there was nothing left to destroy – perhaps he could get his forces close enough to Syracuse to surprise George Maniakes. With his men engaged in a siege, he would be at a severe disadvantage, especially if the garrison of the city emerged to fight at the same time as Abdullah attacked.

'Do we need to see more?'

'No, Drogo, we need to warn the general.'

'You did not actually see this army, did you, all you saw was the reflection of the fires on the clouds?'

'No,' William replied, 'but why stand guard on the pass if there is nothing to hide behind it?'

George Maniakes moved forward to tower over William, then took one ear in his hand. 'If you are wrong about this, Iron Arm, I will have both of these.' William was terribly tempted to grab his balls and reply in kind; he disliked being threatened by anyone. 'You have seen the terrain, tell me how we can use it.'

What followed was a lesson in generalship: for all Maniakes's boasting he was good at commanding an army, his dispositions being made almost as William and Drogo spoke.

'We cannot fight Abdullah and besiege Syracuse, and we must fight any enemy we have in the field.' His finger traced the outline of the River Ánapo as it wended its way across the plain, his finger resting where it opened out and slowed in a flat patch of country. 'You say this is wooded all along its banks.'

'Yes,' William replied, 'deeply wooded.'

'Then that is where I want you and your cavalry. I will pull the army out of its siege works and take up a position here, but I will not let Abdullah see my full strength. If he comes, he must feel he can attack. We cannot leave the siege for too long or Syracuse will be as well supplied as ever it was. The Varangians I will hide behind my Italian and Bulgar levies. Once he does attack, you and your men will debouch from the tree cover and ride across his rear. Once you are formed up you are to bear down on his rear.'

'He will turn to face us with everything.'

'No, William, he will not. He will try to break through to Syracuse, try to beat his way past men he thinks poor fighters, but when he does so they will open their ranks and he will find himself attacking the Varangians. Your task will be to drive the Saracens onto their axes.'

'When do we move?'

'Not till the whole of his army is through that pass.'

Hidden by the trees, William stood relaxed, stroking his mount. He was too long in the fighting tooth now to be in the same nervous condition he had been at Bessancourt, and he knew that lined up alongside and behind him, the men he led were also experienced. To the west they could see the great cloud of dust sent up by the approaching host of Abdullah-al-Zirid who, it was hoped, had no idea of their presence, nor of that of George Maniakes.

The Byzantine giant had pulled his entire force out of the lines at Syracuse in a brilliant piece of organisation and had them in place without his enemy having the faintest idea of what he was about to face, and had done so at such speed that the Syracusans were left confused. Abdullah expected to surprise the Byzantine Army; instead it would be he that would get the shock.

He smiled as his brother approached, wondering what Drogo had in hands hidden behind his back, though there was a long wooden shaft extending above his head. 'I brought you a present.'

'What?'

Drogo produced his surprise like a conjuror, and as he unfurled it, William was stunned.

'A proper banner, brother, not a pennant, this time.' Large and rectangular, and made of silk, William fingered the blue and white banner, edged with the de Hauteville chequer, as Drogo added, 'For the glory of our family, Gill.'

William stepped forward and embraced him. On another occasion the men who observed this might have cheered; not now, they were too clever to let Abdullah know they were close. The time had come for prayer, and with no priests of the Latin rite with a Byzantine army, William led the devotions, kneeling under Drogo's banner, his heart swelling to think what his father would say to see this.

'God bless our arms and those of the men alongside whom we fight. Let the power of your Church smite that of Islam, and take into your merciful bosom any man who falls in your cause this day.'

With that he kissed his sword, then stood and, taking the edge of Drogo's banner, kissed that too.

The battle happened exactly as George Maniakes had predicted. Abdullah marched on, oblivious not only to the Norman presence, but equally to the fact that behind some low hills ahead of him the entire Byzantine force was drawn up to engage. As his leading files crested the rise and saw their enemy they halted in confusion, which was compounded when William Iron Arm led his Norman cavalry out to block the rear on perfect terrain for what they were the best at.

Abdullah was no fool: he stood his ground for some time and organised his forces to press home an attack towards Syracuse, ignoring the now stationary Normans lined up across the plain. Finally trumpets blew and Abdullah and his men charged off their hill towards the line of foot soldiers, this at the same time as William dipped his banner and began to move forward his convoys, lances half lowered.

They could not see, because of the hill before them, the way George Maniakes merely moved his unreliable levies right and left to form two horns of a trap, then brought forward the Varangians to fill the centre. They were in place by the time William crested the rise, but not yet engaged. That was when the Normans spurred their mounts into that deadly canter, driving before them the Saracen soldiers on to swinging axes that took off limbs and heads, and soaked the ground before the Varangian line in a deep pool of blood too great for the ground to absorb.

Those at the rear expired from Norman lances as well as swords and soon, as the horns closed in from left and right, it was an army utterly destroyed, a stunning and complete victory. There was no time to celebrate. Once the dead had been stripped and the baggage train plundered Maniakes was off at the head of his troops, to get them back to besieging Syracuse, the swiftest of them, the Normans, right on his heels.

Syracuse surrendered because the spirit of the Saracens was broken, not because of battle or starvation. The Sicilian inhabitants went wild when the gates were opened, as though they had not fought alongside their lords and masters, treating George Maniakes as a liberator rather than a conqueror, and from that stemmed all the trouble that followed, for he accepted the accolade of the mob as his due. The locals were less impressed when he immediately stripped out the religious relics they had kept hidden for decades, the bones of saints, and sent them off to Constantinople.

The general took over the palace of the emir, shipped all the remaining Saracens off to slavery, and then engaged in a raft of ceremonies which rededicated the churches of Syracuse back from being mosques to the Christian faith. The other thing he did was to bar from entry, into the city, his Norman and Varangian troops, yet he could not keep their leaders, who stood before him now in angry conclave.

'Recompense?'

'We have been denied our right to plunder,' said William.

The giant stood up and glared at him. 'You would treat Syracuse as a city like any other?'

'I would, and you should treat Syracuse as we treated Messina and Rometta.'

'They are not the same, you know that! This was once our capital, the churches our churches, this palace the home of the Sicilian Catapan.'

'No we do not,' insisted Harald Hardrada. 'You have decided that we must respect Syracuse, no one else.'

'And since I command,' Maniakes growled, 'respect it you will.'

'Then pay us some of the gold you found in the vaults.'

'That belongs to the emperor, not to me, not to you.'

'Then I am forced to ask what you expect us to do,' William snapped. 'Some of my men died to take this place...'

'Very few.'

That set Drogo off. 'You are generous with Norman blood.'

'I am generous with the blood of anyone my emperor employs. You are well paid, remember, and you got to plunder Abdullah's baggage.'

'General Maniakes,' William insisted. 'You must make a gesture to my men and the Varangians too.'

'Must, must!' Maniakes yelled coming close to tower over William, his spittle flying. 'Who in hell's name do you think you are addressing? No one tells me must.'

'Pay them some gold, keep them loyal.'

'No.'

Was it victory that had made him like this, William wondered, or the way the mob had kissed his feet and praised him as an angel sent from heaven to rescue them from the Infidel? It made no odds, Maniakes had changed, his head was swollen and instead of seeking advice he was denying the men who had won his prize what they were due.

'Then, I regret to tell you, general, that neither I or my men will continue to serve Byzantium.'

'There are other places,' Maniakes replied.

'Which you also may decide we cannot plunder. The Syracusans who so laud you fought you first. They stood on the wall while I engaged in single combat with Rashid and cheered him on to kill me. They were offered terms and refused, slamming their gates in your face, so they deserve everything which comes to a city that refuses terms from a conqueror. These are the laws of warfare and you choose to flout them for a few flower petals strewn in your path.'

George Maniakes just shrugged and went back to his chair, sitting down and staring on the papers before him. 'This discussion is closed. Tomorrow we will begin the march back to Rometta, then on to Palermo. Perhaps there you can fill your boots.'

'No!' That made the general look up sharply at William, his broad, flat nose twitching angrily and his flat forehead creased. 'We will not march to Rometta, but to Messina and take ship for Italy. I am obliged to remind you of your obligation to see us shipped back to the mainland and provisioned till we reach Salerno.'

Drogo was looking hard at his brother; was he bluffing?

'And I,' said Harald Hardrada, 'will take my men back to Constantinople.'

That made the giant's head jerk. 'You serve the emperor!'

'At the behest of the Prince of Kiev Rus. It is to him I owe my loyalty.'

The four men looked at each other in angry silence for half a minute, a long time in which no one even blinked. Finally Maniakes spoke, bowing his head to the work on his desk. 'So be it. Now that I have Syracuse, and the forces I can muster locally, I doubt I need either of you.'

* * *

William suspected George Maniakes was bluffing, and he also suspected the general thought he and Hardrada were doing the same, but neither got to find out; the way he had nearly throttled Admiral Stephen and the words he had used regarding the imperial house came back to bite him. A message arrived relieving him of command and ordering him to return to Constantinople. That news caught up with the Normans between Syracuse and Messina, and added to it was the name of the new commander, a eunuch none of them had ever heard of, though it was soon established his appointment came through court intrigue, not military skill; it seemed he had never fought a battle.

Naturally, as their leader, William put it to the men, but the air in Sicily had begun to stink of impending failure. Only the personal magnetism of George Maniakes had held tight a disparate army and that had been destroyed by his refusal to treat Syracuse as a conquered city. Few of the Apulian and Calabrian levies had fought with great will, neither had the Bulgars, and if they lacked a strong general would fight with even less, while Sicilian troops now being conscripted into the imperial army had not saved the Saracens.

They would achieve nothing without mercenaries and they would not fight for paltry rewards. It was time to return to that place from which they had come.

* * *

It was a weary force that rode into Rainulf Drengot's encampment a month later, to be greeted by women who had aged at the same pace as their bastards, some of whom, Drogo's included, had formed liaisons with the knights who had stayed behind, which promised much trouble. But there was recompense: they were greeted by three of their brothers, Humphrey, Geoffrey and Mauger. Matters had become more settled in the Contentin: a revolt by local barons had been crushed, so they were, at last, able to come south.

They brought news of home, of Tancred who had steered clear of that upheaval, fit and well, but still verbally embroiled with his more powerful neighbours in various disputes; of their cousin of Montbray, who had used his clever brain to become a power at the ducal court, which protected the family from interference more effectively than their father's squabbles. Other brothers had grown to manhood and fired with the tales of William and Drogo's exploits were also planning to join them.

And, of course, they had to report to their leader; meeting Rainulf Drengot was like meeting a stranger. He was sober, and none of the personal warmth he had shown William in the past was present. That which was present boded ill: an infant son on whom Rainulf clearly doted, and one he was quite open in crowing over as his heir; he even named the child as the future Count Richard of Aversa. If he noticed the stony face with which William responded to this it did not show, and it made no difference that his pleas to the Pope to annul his previous marriage had fallen on deaf ears.

'He's going to cheat you, Gill,' said Drogo, when they were alone again. 'He named you at Capua, and we were all there as witness. Challenge Rainulf, force him to keep to his word.'

'If I challenge him, I must force the men to decide between us and not all of them will follow us, you know that. We could end up fighting each other.'

'Are we to bow the knee to another bastard, as we would have had to do in Normandy?'

'I need to think.'

'There are five of us now,' Drogo insisted, 'and maybe more to come if our brothers speak true. When you are thinking, think on that.'

'Leave me in peace, Drogo,' William growled, 'go and take your resentments out on your woman.'

'What will you do?'

'The only thing I can right now. I will go and see Prince Guaimar.'

EPILOGUE

Guaimar had grown in stature, though he physically looked much the same – too young for his title, but he was now a man, and one at ease in his own station, which had not been the case previously. His sister was even more self-possessed, if that was possible, and certainly was now a fully mature woman of great beauty, though she still had about her an air of malice. Perhaps both impressions were underscored by the place in which William de Hauteville was given audience, the forbidding Castello de Arechi, which might be the princely home, but was a citadel that had an air of something disquieting in its ancient stones.

The Prince wanted to talk about Pandulf, imprisoned in Constantinople; of Montecassino, in peace and prosperity under a new abbot, Theodore having gone to meet his maker; this while he resolutely deflected any conversation of that which his visitor had come to discuss. Indeed, when William alluded to it directly, the Prince of Salerno abruptly changed the subject, demanding to be given chapter and verse of what had happened in Sicily.

'You will be pleased to hear,' Guaimar said, when he had finished, 'that George Maniakes has also paid a heavy price for his folly. As soon as his ship docked he was bound in chains and thrown into the deepest dungeon. Perhaps he is neighbour to the Wolf.'

'He was a good commander, and much respected, until he took Syracuse.'

'He betrayed you,' Berengara said, almost with pleasure.

William knew she was right, but he had no desire to give her the satisfaction of agreeing. 'I like to think he had a higher loyalty, one perhaps I did not understand.'

'It comes as no surprise that a Norman lacks understanding there!'

'He had, however,' Guaimar cut in, giving his sister a hard look, 'done us a service.'

'Which is?'

'The levies Maniakes took to Sicily did not go willingly and so he left behind a discontented province. Revolt broke out last year in Apulia, and if that has been dampened the countryside is, I am told, still afire with dreams of freedom, of throwing off the yoke of Constantinople completely.'

'Not a new idea, Prince Guaimar.'

'No,' responded Guaimar, his face alight with anticipation. 'But now that you have returned, we have at our disposal a potent force which might just make the difference. Arduin, who fought alongside you in Sicily, has been asked by the new Byzantine Catapan to take command of the fortress at Melfi.'

William knew Arduin well and esteemed him; a Lombard, he had been one of the few commanders to get anything approaching a fighting spirit out of Maniakes' conscripted Apulian levies.

'Unknown to the Catapan,' Guaimar continued, 'he is a Lombard first and holds any loyalty to Byzantium second, and has offered to hand it over to the forces of revolt. He who holds Melfi possesses a key that could unlock the whole of the Byzantine possessions. I can show you on a map...'

William shook his head, which stopped Guaimar from moving. He knew Melfi and had avoided it many times when previously raiding in that region. High in the Apennines it was near impregnable and commanded the route from Campania into Apulia. It would provide a base from which operations could be mounted, while also affording a safe haven into which to retire should too great an opposing force appear.

Had he been eager for the challenge, the prospect of possessing such a formidable stronghold and the advantages it provided would have excited him; the trouble was, he was not.

This prince had altered since their first meeting: before he had come across as honest but naïve, but there was now an undercurrent in his words, simply because they were formed of calculation. It did not, of course, take any great wit to follow his thoughts. The dream of kicking Byzantium out of South Italy had a long history, had been tried and been soundly beaten, even with the aid of a strong Norman contingent. Guaimar was raising that tempting spectre and dangling it before William as another way to avoid talking about the subject he had come to thrash out.

The two would naturally connect for Guaimar; he could divert these battle-hardened Normans to ferment revolt in Apulia, which would relieve him of their presence and might just bring in its wake, for little cost, great rewards in a part of the world where they could legitimately live off the land; in other words, plunder. And with this de Hauteville fully engaged, the question of the succession could be safely left in the air.

If he was annoyed, William knew Guaimar was merely acting as a prince should: looking to his own interests. Rainulf kept him in power, protected him from his own subjects, and was of an age at which going off on campaign would be a hardship. He had a bastard son who might or might not come into his title; it was an inheritance Guaimar could block with ease, indeed it would be he who would be ensuring that no papal dispensation came for annulment, so he could keep the old Norman leader in his purse.

The man before him was of a different stamp: in his prime, a hero hailed as Iron Arm by those he had led and perhaps a fellow harder to control as a vassal. Yet, if he did not commit himself Guaimar could just as easily dangle before William the prospect of that same succession for as long as Rainulf lived.

William was trying to work out what to do on the same basis; he was head of his family and they looked to him to make their way, that made even more pressing by the arrival of three more brothers. His father had been betrayed in Normandy and this prince, who had embraced William at Capua and had acceded in the impression that he should succeed to Rainulf's title, was very capable of doing the same.

Yet what he had said to Drogo was nothing but the plain truth. What made the Normans formidable was not just their military prowess but also their cohesion. To force a decision on the succession now would certainly fragment that, and it was possible that Guaimar would welcome such dissension; he might need his Normans, but he did not love them any more than his more forthright sister. William, just as much as Rainulf, lacked the means to force this prince to decide; all the advantage for Guaimar lay in the opposite!

If he led the Normans into Apulia and succeeded where previous invaders had failed, was he really prepared to hand it all over to Guaimar, who he suspected would do little to aid him? He might dream of a Lombard kingdom in South Italy ruled from Salerno, but if it was to come to pass it could only do so with Norman assistance.

Many strands of thought were running through William's mind at that moment but the paramount one was simple: from this moment on he must look to his own future and to that of his family, must look to take what would be his due, not wait to be gifted it by any other power. Never again would he leave himself or the de Hauteville name at the mercy of any prince or duke.

He would go to Melfi, take over the fortress, aid Arduin and nourish Guaimar's dreams. But like this prince, when the time came, he would look to his own interests and to those of his brothers. One day, he swore silently to God, just as he smiled at Guaimar in the way he had once smiled at Duke Robert of

Normandy, this Prince of Salerno would acknowledge the blue and white banner of his house. And that sister, Berengara, so arrogant and spiteful to his Norman blood? Perhaps one day she would be made to bow and scrape to please him.

AUTHOR'S NOTE

This novel, set around the time of El Cid and the Norman Conquest, is the first in a series that will chronicle the achievements of a remarkable family. Eventually seven of Tancred de Hauteville's twelve sons travelled to Italy to take service as mercenaries. What they achieved in that troubled land is simply astounding.

As a military leader, William of Normandy had all the wealth and resources of his extensive dukedom with which to conquer England: the sons of Tancred had nothing but their imposing presence, their swords, their lances, their horses, their martial prowess, plus their considerable intelligence and guile. They entered a land of rich fiefs and city-states that brought to Europe all the luxuries of the Levant, a territory, since the break-up of the Roman Empire, that had seen conquest, rebellion, tyranny and had suffered, for five hundred years, ruthless exploitation.

They challenged first the power of the Lombards, then the authority of the Pope, next the supremacy of both the Holy Roman and Byzantine Empires, and finally the Saracens to create a society more important for European civilisation than the Crusades. If the germ of the Italian Renaissance came from anywhere, it came from what they had created.

In telling this story, I am aware that it is one unfamiliar to most readers; few people even know of the exploits of the Normans in Italy and Sicily, and in the writing I have, quite deliberately, combined some of the real-life characters and the acts they performed, in order to keep the narrative exciting, while creating others.

I have made Guaimar a more central character than he was in reality, but he was heir to Salerno and it was he who persuaded the emperor to act against the true-life Pandulf of Capua; Berengara is an invention, but Rainulf is real, as is Conrad Augustus and the Abbot Theodore.

At the kernel is historical truth and the actual deeds of the brothers de Hauteville, heroes to those who served for and with them and deserving of a more recognised posterity.

IF YOU ENJOYED THIS, YOU MIGHT LIKE TO READ
JACK LUDLOW'S REPUBLIC SERIES.

READ ON TO FIND OUT MORE...

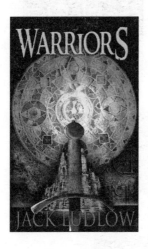